"I meant what I said about getting married."

For a moment Leah resisted Will's attempt to pull her toward him. But because she loved the tenderness with which he gathered her to his chest, she yielded.

She enjoyed the slight roughness of his throat and the way his cheek pressed against her hair. Maybe it wasn't such a bad thing that he'd be visiting their child.

Impulsively, she stole a kiss. As his mouth moved against hers, a kind of enchantment flowed through Leah.

It took all her reserve to pull away. "Bad idea," she said hoarsely.

"Not all that bad," Will murmured.

Her mystery man from Texas was in her house. He'd kissed her again. He'd asked her to marry him.

She wondered how on earth they were going to work this out. One thing she knew for sure—if she didn't land a new job in Seattle, she'd have to find one somewhere else.

Because she no longer trusted herself….

Dear Reader,

Nine-Month Surprise is the second of three books set in Downhome, Tennessee, a town that needs doctors and offers them a second chance—with dramatic and romantic results.

Many physicians today practice medicine in an environment worlds apart from the one in which my father served as a small-town doctor. He treated patients in rural Kentucky just prior to World War II, served in the army during the war and later became a physician in the small town of Menard, Texas. In later years he completed his residency in psychiatry and practiced in Nashville, Tennessee.

Today, medical treatment has become highly technological, subject to insurance restrictions and complicated by lawsuits. What I've created is an idealized situation, one that I believe many doctors would enjoy.

The story of Will and Leah involves a familiar theme—the unplanned baby—but to me it became fresh because these two strong characters made it their own. I hope you'll enjoy it!

The third book in the series will focus on the relationship between Karen Lowell and Dr. Chris McRay. Although she once loved him, his testimony sent her brother to prison for a crime he didn't commit.

If you enjoy this book, please e-mail me at jdiamondfriends@aol.com and visit my Web site at www.jacquelinediamond.com.

Happy reading!

Jacqueline Diamond

Jacqueline Diamond

Nine-Month Surprise

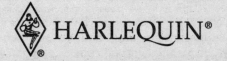

TORONTO • NEW YORK • LONDON
AMSTERDAM • PARIS • SYDNEY • HAMBURG
STOCKHOLM • ATHENS • TOKYO • MILAN • MADRID
PRAGUE • WARSAW • BUDAPEST • AUCKLAND

ISBN 0-373-75105-2

NINE-MONTH SURPRISE

In memory of Maurice Hyman, M.D.

Books by Jacqueline Diamond

HARLEQUIN AMERICAN ROMANCE

*Downhome Doctors

Chapter One

The moment the man with intense gray eyes walked into the country-western bar, Leah Morris sensed she was going to do something foolish.

Since arriving in Austin, Texas, two days earlier for job interviews, she felt like a different person from the shy teacher who'd spent most of her life in a small Tennessee town. She felt like the sort of woman who wasn't afraid to talk to a stranger or even offer to buy him a drink.

Not that she planned to do it. The man's confident air warned that he probably had either more ladies than he could handle or one special lady. Even so, when he scanned the noisy room, the pucker between his eyebrows made her long to soothe away his worries.

Leah twirled a strand of black hair around her finger and smiled. With an almost physical jolt, she noticed the man gazing in her direction.

His expression warmed as he studied her with new interest. His reaction gave Leah butterflies.

She tried to make an objective assessment. The fellow appeared to be in his mid-thirties, a few years older than she was. His dark-blond hair had probably once been thicker, and his intelligent, slightly creased face might have been boyish in his twenties. Now he was a man she wished she knew a whole lot better.

Embarrassed by her reaction, Leah sipped her margarita and pretended an interest in the bluegrass band sawing merrily away across the room. The whisper of a sophisticated male scent alerted her when the man approached.

He stopped close by. "Mind if I join you?" To counter the loud music, he leaned over and spoke in her ear.

Leah's skin prickled. "Please do."

She'd applied for teaching positions in Austin and Seattle because she wanted more out of life than Downhome, Tennessee, had to offer. This was her first real adventure, and she intended to enjoy it.

"I'm Will." The man extended his hand.

"Leah." When they shook, she felt the restrained strength in his arm. "Do you come here often?"

"To the Wayward Drummer? Not as often as I'd like. Great, isn't it?" Swinging into the seat, he ordered a scotch and soda. "How about you?"

"I'm new in town. A friend told me about it." The music rose to a crescendo, cutting off further comments.

Her companion rested his elbows behind him on the bar. No ring on his left hand, she observed, although that didn't prove anything.

The song ended. After the applause died, the bandleader announced the group was taking a short break. "Good," Leah said. "I mean, I was enjoying it, but I'd rather talk."

"So would I," the man replied. "But first I have a request."

"Oh?" Intrigued, she waited.

"Let's not pigeonhole each other." His gaze penetrated her defenses. "I don't care where you work or what your astrological sign is. I'd rather find out who you are as a person."

"Agreed!" Leah was glad to avoid being pegged as a small-town schoolteacher. "Now I have a question."

"Shoot." Although the bartender had set down his drink, Will ignored it and kept his eyes on Leah.

"Are you married?" A cheater wouldn't necessarily tell the truth, but she had to make the effort.

"Used to be. Not anymore." As if finally noticing the scotch, he picked up the glass and tossed down a quick swallow before adding, "That question says a lot about you."

"It does?" She hoped she didn't sound naive.

Will slanted her a teasing glance. "It tells me you're interested in me, which I like. And it goes straight to the point."

Leah waited a beat. He didn't continue, so she said, "How come you're not asking whether *I'm* married?"

He laughed, which made him look ten years younger. "Because it never occurred to me. You don't strike me as the kind of woman who plays around. Are you?"

"Of course not!"

When his hand cupped hers on the bar, Leah could scarcely swallow. She didn't understand why she was reacting so powerfully, except for the fact that she hadn't dated anyone seriously in the ten years since college. Or maybe because the guy had more mystery about him than anyone she'd ever met.

"Tell me your fantasy," he said in a low voice. "What kind of guy you want. The boy next door to settle down with?"

Being asked to put her longing into words was scary. "No. Someone exciting. Different. Someone who sets me free."

His mouth twisted. "That's a tall order."

"Think you can fill it?" She couldn't believe she'd said that.

The challenge seemed to amuse him. "Until I walked in here and saw your beautiful smile, I'd have had my doubts." Will gave an easy shrug. "I can be anything you want. It's your call."

Leah bit her lip. She hadn't told him the rest of the fantasy.

It involved a lingering seduction by a stranger. But she suspected he'd guessed that.

This flirtation was crazy—dangerous and irresponsible. She knew nothing about Will, not even his last name. On the other hand, he knew nothing about her, either. Like how boring and conventional most people considered her.

"I'll bet you could," she mused.

"Could what?"

She peered around to make sure no one else overheard. "Could be anything a woman wanted," she finished.

When his eyes widened, she imagined for an instant that she saw right inside him. She'd touched him in a way he hadn't expected, awakening something he hadn't felt in years.

Leah trusted her instincts. She had a knack for reading people.

"What are we going to do about this?" Will asked.

"You mean tonight?" But of course it had to be tonight. Leah was leaving tomorrow for a job interview in Seattle. While she would return if she got one of the jobs she'd applied for, there was no guarantee of that. And no guarantee that he'd be around if she did.

"Wait." He held up one hand. "I'm not trying to pressure you. Hey, we're both enjoying ourselves. Maybe it's enough that we're having this conversation. I don't mean to ruin it."

He'd noted her hesitation, Leah thought. She wasn't the only one good at reading people.

Another couple sat down two stools away, making her self-conscious about speaking up, and then the band filtered back from its break. Will appeared content to sit wordlessly as the musicians launched into another set.

She ought to be glad he respected her, Leah supposed. Instead, she struggled with disappointment and, at the same time, an aching awareness of him beside her. She drank in details: the muscles of his wrist beneath a thick silver watchband, a trace of roughness on his jaw that he'd missed while shaving.

She wished she dared ask the questions they'd skipped. What kind of work he did. How his marriage had ended.

When he shifted on the seat, his tight shoulders revealed tension. All along, without realizing it, she'd been detecting signs of restless energy and coiled need.

A need she realized she could release.

He turned sharply, his gaze boring into hers. A silent query disturbed the air as clearly as if he'd put it into words.

Was she as ready as he was?

Yes, she thought, her lips parting. *Oh, yes.*

On the far side of the room, a fiddler attacked his instrument with passion. Leah only half heard the notes wailing to the rafters. Her heart rate sped up and fire danced across her skin as Will stroked her hair. When he removed his hand, she felt a physical sense of loss.

She set down her glass, and he did the same. As they got up, he tossed some bills onto the counter and took her arm.

They made their way into a steamy July night. "I'm parked around back," she said. "You, too?"

He nodded. As they reached the lot, out of sight of other patrons, he caught Leah's arm.

She touched his shoulder and her face tilted upward. As he drank in the sight of her, his thumb traced her cheek and hairline. Then his mouth found hers.

Leah reveled in his eager kiss, in the caress trailing down her waist, in his spicy lime scent. When he cupped her bottom and brought her against his hardness, she thought she might melt.

Will lifted his head. "Are you sure about this?"

Leah rested her head on his shoulder. He was the perfect height, perhaps five inches taller, so she fit against him as if they'd been sculpted from the same block of marble. "Yes."

"I'll follow you," he said.

She gave him the name of her motel in case he got lost.

Alone in her rental car, navigating the glittering downtown streets, Leah knew she could still change her mind. Still do the sensible thing. Still back off from taking a ridiculous risk in all sorts of ways that didn't bear thinking about. And there were moral issues that she'd been raised to respect.

Just this once, why not take a chance?

She had no idea where her actions might lead, she acknowledged as she checked the rearview mirror and saw his headlights a car length behind. The funny part was that she didn't expect to get a lot out of the experience. What she wanted to do, most of all, was give.

She doubted Will had come into the Wayward Drummer to pick up a woman. Instead, she had the impression he'd been fighting his desire for her. This man was complicated.

She doubted she'd get a chance to figure him out. They might never meet again.

At thirty-two, Leah had stopped agonizing about finding Mr. Right. Since she wanted children, she planned to adopt a youngster who might otherwise languish in a series of foster homes or in an orphanage overseas. After she got settled in a new job, of course.

The decision not to worry about whether she ever married had freed her to take chances. Like inviting Will back to her room. Like coming to Austin in the first place.

Leah had chosen the Texas state capital for a lot of reasons: its large university, its bustling economy and a country-music industry that reminded her of Nashville, where she'd attended college. She'd also come because her cousin Josie had been urging her to visit.

Unfortunately, Josie had demonstrated the irresponsibility common to Leah's father's side of the family. She hadn't mentioned that her boyfriend had recently moved into her one-bedroom apartment, bringing along a large, shaggy dog. There wasn't even room for Leah to hang up her clothes, which in any case would be covered with dog hairs before she got to an interview. So she'd rented a room.

She'd arranged for two job interviews: at a public and a private school. After having dinner with her cousin last night, Leah had squeezed in a visit to the State Capitol and the LBJ Library and Museum and bought a large poster to show her students this fall. Unless a new job came through faster than expected, she'd still be teaching at her familiar classroom in Downhome.

Tonight, she'd decided to check out a bar her best friend had recommended—a tip from someone Karen had met recently. *What a lucky break,* Leah thought.

The rearview mirror showed Will in place behind her as she caught an east-west artery toward the airport area. Leah recalled a conversation she'd had a few months earlier with Jenni Vine, who'd recently moved to Downhome from L.A. In dire need of doctors, the town had advertised widely and Jenni, a family practitioner, had been the first hired. She'd also become a friend.

Jenni had offered to prescribe contraception before Leah left on her trip, but she'd declined. After drifting apart from her college boyfriend ten years ago, she'd been celibate, and certainly hadn't expected to go to bed with anyone soon.

Contraception. What was she going to do about that? she wondered. She'd have to use something.

As she neared the motel, Leah watched in vain for a pharmacy. Still debating what to do, she turned into the lot and parked outside her room.

Will eased his dark, late-model sedan into a space some distance away. Leah wondered whether he'd chosen it so she wouldn't see decals that might indicate where he worked. Since they'd agreed not to pigeonhole each other, he had a right to his privacy.

She enjoyed the way he strolled toward her with quiet confidence, neither arrogant nor uncertain. "Problem?" he asked when he saw her expression.

"I'm not on the Pill." That ought to be blunt enough. "I didn't see a drugstore."

"It's taken care of." Catching her hand, he added, "Not that I do this sort of thing often. I just believe in being prepared."

Leah refused to worry about why he considered it necessary to be prepared. She hadn't taken him for a hermit, had she?

When she opened the door, she noticed at once how impersonal the room looked. The only signs that it belonged to her were her book on the nightstand and the robe tossed over a chair. It even smelled impersonal.

Will closed the door and, standing behind her, slipped his hands around Leah's waist. Feeling his body press into her back as he stroked upward through her blouse, she relaxed, trusting him. When he cupped her breasts, she gasped with pleasure.

Their contact felt so intimate. And powerfully stimulating as his thumbs aroused her nipples and his mouth soothed the sensitive curve of her neck. Then Leah turned, and Will kissed her on the mouth.

His fingers made short work of her blouse and bra. Soon, his palms began caressing her bare breasts, filling her with hot longing.

He didn't speak. He seemed utterly caught up in what they were doing, and so was she.

Leah didn't recognize this woman who yearned to excite a stranger. She couldn't explain why she felt no shyness as she traced her tongue along his throat, down to the pulse point.

When he tossed off his jacket she reached for his belt, but it defied her efforts. "I guess you don't make a habit of this sort of thing, either," Will murmured as he guided her hands to his bulge. Together, they undid the belt and zipper.

Leah didn't care to admit her relative inexperience. He probably wouldn't stop, but it might make him careful. And she preferred to strip away his inhibitions the way he'd removed hers. She wanted to dissolve whatever had made him frown when he'd come into the bar. She wanted to make him happy.

Being with Will was fun—helping him remove her skirt, kicking off her shoes, finding herself half lifted and half tossed onto the bed. He poised over her, pants sliding down as Leah removed her pantyhose. Will shifted her panties out of the way and pressed against her, bare flesh to bare flesh. Surprised as he parted her, she caught her breath.

"Sorry," Will said. "I can't wait, honey."

"It's all right. More than all right."

He was inside her, big and fierce and gentle. Curving over her, sucking her nipples as he moved in and out. Ecstasy radiated through her.

Abruptly, she remembered. "Will! The protection!"

He stopped. "Oh. Damn." A cool emptiness replaced him, and then he was back. Leah felt his movements as he unrolled the condom.

She liked observing him from below as he sheathed his erection. His dark-blond hair sprang every which way, and his eyes had an unfocused air, as if he'd lost track of time and place.

He glanced up and smiled. The worry lines had vanished. "I can't tell you how fabulous you look."

"Not half as fabulous as I feel," she admitted.

Leah had always been awkward around men. First, she'd been a tomboy with buckteeth, and then, transformed into what passed for a swan in her small town, she'd intimidated her classmates. Since college, she hadn't met a man who stirred more than a flicker of interest.

Until now.

How right she felt with Will amazed her. Completely natural, as if they were partners in this venture. When his palm stroked her soft mound, she opened to him without hesitation.

He moved inside her slowly, but after a few thrusts, control escaped him. Pushing harder and harder, he drove into her until Leah thought she might burst with desire. She wanted to savor this rainbow of sensations, but there was no time. Instead, she clutched Will's shoulders, anchoring herself as she lost track of everything except the joy of dissolving into him and the ragged moan of satisfaction tearing from his throat.

His breathing echoed against her, mingling with her own. Off came the rest of their clothing as he pulled the covers over them and kissed her for a long time.

Leah loved this moment of closeness. She liked everything about Will—his abandon, his tenderness, the frankness with which he regarded her.

When he got up, she wanted to call him back. A minute later, he returned, and she realized he'd gone for more protection.

"Now let's do this the right way," he said.

Leah hadn't imagined her body capable of responding again so quickly. Will proved her wrong. This time, he tantalized her until she begged for more and then he filled her. They rocked together, completely in tune.

It was much more than she'd fantasized. More than she'd believed possible.

The intensity built gradually, floating them onto a higher plane. Leah could have stayed there forever, or so she thought, until without warning she soared even higher as rapture seized them both.

The embers lingered long after the flames faded. *They'd been meant for this,* she thought as she curled blissfully against Will.

And he felt the same way. "That was wonderful." He spoke as if he could hardly trust his own perception.

"Wonderful," she repeated, and drifted into sleep.

WHEN LEAH AWOKE in the morning, he was gone. She thought he might be taking a shower, but she found the bathroom empty.

Wrapped in her robe, she pushed aside the front curtains and peered across the lot. The space where Will had parked sat empty.

Perhaps he'd gone to work, although it was Saturday. She searched all over the room for a note. Nothing.

Stunned, Leah sank onto the edge of the bed, trying to make sense of what had happened. Surely, she hadn't mistaken the depth of passion between them. That hadn't been merely a one-night stand. It had meant something.

To her, anyway.

It dawned on her that she had no idea how Will actually felt. He might do this kind of thing all the time. He'd known exactly the right words to lead her along and, as he'd said, he'd been prepared.

Oh, come on, she argued silently. *You're jumping to conclusions.*

Feeling uneasy, Leah went to shower. Maybe Will expected to run into her tonight at the same bar. But if so, why hadn't he made arrangements?

Probably because he wasn't going to be there.

With a rush of shame, she registered that she'd invented a relationship that existed only in her mind. She'd given something special, and by leaving without a word, the man had thrown it in her face.

He hadn't lied—at least, as far as she knew. But she had. She'd lied to herself, Leah scolded as she scrubbed every inch of her skin. She'd thought it would be fine if she never heard from him again. Now, too late, she saw the truth.

She was a rube who believed in fairy tales. Last night, she'd tasted paradise—a fool's paradise. She'd expected happily-ever-after from a man who never wanted to see her again.

Leah wrapped her arms around her chest and held on tight, trying to subdue the pain. She couldn't comprehend why he'd left that way, when they'd shared so much, but it hurt.

She should have known better. Should have listened to her better judgment, should have realized what an easy target she'd been. Will had played her every step of the way, and she couldn't even blame him. This disappointment was her own fault.

Thank goodness for the water splashing over her. It washed away the tears, though not the sense of loss. Because at last—not the first time she'd made love, back in college, but only now—she had lost her innocence.

LEAH GAVE THE ROOM a final inspection to ensure she'd left nothing behind, other than her pride and her delusions. Except for the rumpled sheets and the maid's tip on the nightstand, no trace remained of her visit.

She probably wouldn't take a job in Austin even if one were offered. Too many bad associations. She never wanted to risk running into that louse again.

There was still Seattle, though, where she planned to stay with a college friend who ran a day care center. Thinking about the future, Leah squared her shoulders. She didn't intend to quit seeking adventure just because her first one had turned out miserably.

From now on, however, the journey wasn't going to involve

men. Or acting stupid. Thank goodness no one but her would ever know about this.

Remembering the clerk's instructions about checkout, Leah set her key on the nightstand before fetching her suitcase, carry-on bag and purse. With everything safely outside, she shut the door and heard the lock click.

In the room, the phone rang.

She glared at the door. Great timing. But her friends and relatives all had her cell number. The only one who might call would be the clerk to remind her of the deadline for departure.

It certainly wouldn't be Will. She refused to delude herself. In any case, she had no way to get in.

The phone rang three more times and stopped. By then, Leah had finished loading her car.

She drove away with a sense of relief at putting the whole incident behind her.

Chapter Two

Will snapped his cell phone shut. He felt relieved that she hadn't answered, because he didn't know what he could have offered. An apology, at best.

His edginess had started building earlier in the week, when his ex-wife had accused him in an e-mail of being a rigid workaholic. Then yesterday, when he drove the twins to his parents' ranch for a visit, emotions had rushed back from a boyhood spent feeling like the odd man out among his three rough-hewn brothers.

When he'd returned to Austin, Will had been seized by a restless longing for something he couldn't name. Leah had showed him what it was. Flirting with her in the bar had made him feel like a man again, and the sex had been mind-blowing.

But he'd taken stupid risks. Forgetting the condom at first, for one thing. Getting involved with a transient, for another. A woman living in a motel was likely to be desperately seeking someone to latch on to. And Will had no illusions about what a superficially attractive package he offered, if she'd gotten close enough to see the MD decal on his car.

Two other doctors came into the lounge. In no mood for chitchat, he turned away to pour a cup of coffee from the decanter. He would require more than a few cups this morning to make up for the lack of sleep.

The delivery room had paged him at 3:00 a.m. He'd been grateful the beeper hadn't woken Leah.

After dressing, he'd stood by the bed, admiring the way her dark hair spilled across the pillow. Remembering the glow in her blue eyes, Will had been tempted to rouse her and explain why he had to leave. With uncharacteristic impulsiveness, he'd considered confessing who he was and giving her his phone number.

Then what? He remembered all too well the experience of a colleague who'd had an ill-considered affair with a waitress. Of course, the man had been cheating on his wife, so he'd had even more to lose, but the subsequent stalking and suicide threats had lasted over a year, and the whole incident had wrecked his marriage.

Leah hadn't seemed unstable. If Will had met her under other circumstances, he would have considered her delightfully sweet. But innocent women didn't go around picking up men in bars. She had to be playing some game.

He'd already made the mistake of marrying the wrong woman. Allison hadn't been a nutcase, but in his book, she came close. No matter how frustrated a woman might be, that didn't justify dumping her husband and children for a rich playboy. The husband, maybe, but definitely not the kids.

A smile touched Will's face at the thought of his six-year-olds, outgoing Diane and reserved India. They deserved a dad who shared his spare evenings with them, not a strange woman. And one who cut back his schedule so he could enjoy more time with them before they grew up. For heaven's sake, they were already about to start first grade.

That was why he'd decided to relocate to a town that offered them all a second chance. His announcement that they were moving out of state had ticked off Allison, but since she'd visited the twins only sporadically in the two years since she'd run off with a guy who didn't like children, she had to accept it.

Due to his commitments in Austin, they were moving less than a week before school started. Luckily, Will's housekeeper had agreed to accompany them. Eileen McNulty was the answer to a single father's prayer.

As his pager went off again, Will set down the cup and looked at the number. The delivery room. He had two patients in labor, so the summons didn't surprise him.

His new position required working occasional evenings and weekends, but judging by his earlier visit, things were a lot quieter in Downhome, Tennessee. Moreover, Will's office would lie only blocks from home.

True, the town lacked a hospital, so he'd have to perform surgery in a facility about twelve miles off. And he understood some candidates for the position had balked at the requirement that they handle occasional on-call duties for nonobstetric cases. Will figured he'd enjoy getting to know a range of townspeople, and he liked the idea of practicing old-fashioned community-based medicine.

No doubt about it, he mused as he left the doctors' lounge. He was going to be much happier away from the stresses and temptations of Austin.

ALTHOUGH THE VISIT to Seattle proved a soothing relief after her experience in Texas, Leah returned without a firm job offer. She'd been impressed by the Rosewell Center, a private school for children with mild handicaps, special talents and emotional problems that made it hard for them to fit into regular classes. Given a nurturing environment and challenges tailored to their temperaments and abilities, the kids flourished.

"The staff at Rosewell said they might have an opening next semester," she explained to her principal, Olivia Rockwell, who'd stopped by to catch up on the news. Eager to post the pictures and maps she'd gathered on her trip, Leah showed up six days before school started to work in the classroom.

"Can I be selfish and hope they don't?" After finding a thumbtack, Olivia fixed a loose upper corner of a poster. The African-American woman was tall, with a commanding presence. In her mid-forties, Olivia had embraced maturity by letting her hair go dramatically white-on-black. "It does sound exciting, Leah, but we'd certainly miss you."

"I have mixed feelings," she admitted. A warm welcome home from her friends, including a swim party at the community center, had gone a long way toward reviving Leah's spirits since her return three weeks earlier.

"How can you bear to leave all this excitement?" Olivia, who also served as principal of the adjacent high school, gave her a teasing grin. "They say our football team might beat Mill Valley's for a change."

"We're known for our intellectual depth, not our brawn," Leah replied, although she doubted most citizens, who placed great store in football victories, shared her opinion.

"Intellectual depth? Well, I do my best." Olivia was being modest. Since moving here from Memphis fifteen years earlier, she'd made a tremendous difference in the town, as had her husband, Archie Rockwell, who owned the hardware and feed stores and currently served as mayor.

In addition to other civic activities, Olivia had organized a search committee—along with the police chief, Ethan Forrest, and Leah's friend, Karen Lowell—to recruit physicians after the town's two doctors, a married couple, had retired. Their first pick had been Jenni, who'd not only fit in beautifully but had fallen in love with Ethan.

"Have you been to Pepe's Diner?" Olivia asked. "I heard they unveiled his new murals last night, but I haven't had time to look." The Italian restaurant had shed its old decor for the creations of a talented local artist.

"Oh! That reminds me. I'm meeting Karen there for lunch—" Leah glanced at her watch "—in ten minutes!"

"Better get a move on." The principal stepped back to survey the room. "Those other cities do look beautiful, but remember, there's no place like home."

"I plan to come back for visits." Leah would never give up her friends, or her aunt and cousin, who lived in town. Still, she had no siblings and her mother had died of cancer eight years earlier. Her father, who had remarried, lived in Denver.

"It won't be the same. But I'm an old married lady with two kids. You couldn't pry me loose from my roots for all the excitement in the world," Olivia said. "Now you'd better ske-daddle or you might have trouble finding a table. The place will be crowded."

"I don't want to keep Karen waiting," Leah agreed.

"Have fun!"

After collecting her purse, she hurried out, barely noticing the familiar August heat and humidity. The K-8 elementary school stood on a street with the funny name of Grandpa Johnson Way, after the town's founder. Turning left, she passed the Snip 'N' Curl salon, owned and operated by her aunt, Rosie O'Bannon. The windows featured blown-up photographs of town residents in stylish hairdos, which Leah preferred to the usual images of models.

On her right lay the old Johnson House, presently occupied by quarrelsome Beau Johnson, a member of the city council and the owner of the Tulip Tree Market. He'd never married, and had practically disowned his only relative in town, Yvonne Johnson, a nurse at the clinic who'd had a baby out of wedlock.

Farther down the street, Leah passed the weekly *Gazette*—
edited and published by Karen's brother, Barry—and the Café
Montreal. She cut diagonally across The Green, a square park
where the café's owner, Gwen Martin, sponsored a monthly
farmers' market and craft fair.

On Tulip Tree Avenue, the town's main thoroughfare, she
blinked at the unusual sight of half a dozen people standing
in line in front of Pepe's Diner. That *never* happened.

"Is this because of the murals?" she asked her cousin Mark,
a police lieutenant, who was waiting with Captain Ben
Follows. Ben moonlighted as pastor of the Downhome Community Church.

Mark nodded. "Pepe won't let anyone in to see the paintings unless they order lunch."

"We're in line for takeout," Ben added. "I think Karen's got
a table for you."

"Oh, good. Thanks!" It was a hot day to stand outside.
Besides, Leah's stomach had been bothering her all morning.

Slipping through the door, she found the interior cooled
by ceiling fans, although noisier than usual from the capacity
crowd. Scents of garlic and olive oil swirled around her,
along with the unwelcome smell of fresh paint. The odors
made Leah so dizzy she had to catch the back of a chair for
balance.

As she adjusted, she scanned the murals that had replaced
faded images of grapes and wine jugs. The artist, a talented
young man named Arturo Mendez, had covered one wall with
vibrantly colored images of proprietor Pepe Otero and his
three grown children wearing baggy peasant-style clothes
and picking grapes. On the opposite wall, the family was
making wine in a vat while Pepe's ex-wife, Connie, peered
in through a painted window, her face a study in envy.

Pepe bustled over. "Karen is in the back," he informed her

with a trace of an accent from his native Argentina. "So, how do you like my pictures?"

"I love them," Leah said. "You're the talk of the town."

"Not for long." The compactly built, dark-haired man went on to explain. "Gwen is having the artist paint the walls of her café. The project is under wraps, just like mine was—you know Arturo's artistic temperament."

"I hope you're not mad at her for stealing your thunder." Pepe's and Gwen's establishments maintained a friendly rivalry.

"No, actually, we're…going out." He gave her a contented smile.

"Oh." Leah hadn't paid attention to town gossip this summer. Although pleased for the two restaurateurs, she felt sorry for her aunt Rosie, who had a longtime crush on Pepe. "Good for you."

"Excuse me." He hurried off to assist a waitress with an overburdened tray.

Leah's stomach was nagging again, probably from hunger, so she was relieved to see breadsticks on Karen's table in a back corner. "I hope I'm not late." In addition to the bread, small bottles of vinegar and oil topped the red-and-white tablecloth, Leah noticed as she sat down.

Her friend regarded her over her menu. "I got here early." Karen, who managed the Tulip Tree Nursing Home, had a passion for punctuality. Two years younger than Leah, she had a forthright manner and strong opinions.

"Can you believe this crowd?"

"It may get worse. Barry's running shots of the murals in today's *Gazette,* so if anybody didn't know about the unveiling, they soon will." The newspaper came out on Tuesdays.

"I'll stay away for a few days till things quiet down." Leah studied her menu. "What are you having?"

"I'm strongly tempted by the scampi. What do you think?"

A reddish-brown curl fell across Karen's cheek. She pushed it behind her ear.

Usually, Leah relished scampi, but today the prospect of garlic butter put her off. "I'm more in the mood for spaghetti Bolognese."

"I thought you didn't like that much meat." In Pepe's sauce, the ground beef nearly overwhelmed the tomato base.

"Can't a girl change her mind?" A waitress brought ice water, which Leah sipped gratefully, then Karen and Leah both ordered.

She didn't mention her indigestion to Karen. Leah had a natural reticence about discussing intimate matters, even with someone she'd been close to since grade school. She'd kept quiet about her plans to leave Downhome until shortly before her trip, and she hadn't mentioned her insane one-night stand to anyone. Nor did she plan to.

Besides, they had other things to talk about, including Jenni and Ethan's wedding in two weeks. After they'd exchanged a few tidbits about that, Karen gave an update on the physician-search committee.

They'd chosen an obstetrician from Texas named Dr. Rankin, who was due to arrive later this week. Leah recalled that he was the one who'd recommended the Wayward Drummer when Karen had asked on her behalf.

She hoped the subject never came up, because she found her memories both painful and confusing. What she needed to do was chalk the experience up to a life lesson and move on.

She returned her attention to her companion. Karen was describing a pediatrician who'd applied for the second opening at the clinic.

"Beryl's from St. Louis, a single mom. She has a thirteen-year-old son that she wants to remove from bad influences." Karen selected a breadstick from the basket. "I am *so* glad she applied."

The previous candidates all fell short. A pediatrician from Wichita had barely retained his medical license after an arrest for smoking marijuana. Another applicant had turned out to be in questionable health.

That left Dr. Chris McRay. Unlike his competitors, he'd grown up in Downhome, where he wanted to return to be near his grandmother. Leah had liked Chris in high school, but she would never mention it to Karen.

Her friend couldn't forgive Chris for testifying against her brother, Barry, in a manslaughter case when both men were eighteen. His word had sent Barry to prison for five years for a crime he swore he hadn't committed, and for which he believed Chris had framed him.

It was a nasty business. Better by far to hire the lady from St. Louis.

Karen had used up most of her lunch hour by the time they had finished eating. Although she ran the nursing home more or less independently for distant corporate owners, she rarely cut herself any slack, not even to linger at lunch. In addition to putting in a full week, she escorted residents on outings during her free time. Several had become good friends, including Chris's grandmother, Mae Anne.

"I guess we can't have lunch again next week, can we?" Karen said. "You've got school starting Tuesday."

Leah took out her personal organizer. "How about a week from Saturday?"

"Good! We can eat at the farmers' market." The monthly event was always fun.

They set a time and place to meet, and split the bill. The lunch crowd was thinning by the time Karen departed.

Still at the table, Leah glanced at her organizer. She kept getting the sense that she'd overlooked some key date in her preoccupation with traveling, preparing for school and arranging much-needed repairs to her roof. But she couldn't imagine what it was.

As she scanned the dates, it hit her. She'd missed her period.

That couldn't be right. Her periods had always been regular, and she kept track of them. Leah got a disoriented feeling, as in one of those dreams where she overslept an exam or paraded naked in public.

She remembered being glad that her period had started in early July, before she left for Austin, because it meant she didn't have to worry about it while traveling. Checking her digitized calendar, she noted that the next one had been due nearly three weeks ago, the same day the roofers arrived. That must be why she'd forgotten.

She was three weeks late. Leah went cold.

Grateful that she sat in the rear of the restaurant, shielded from most diners, she reviewed what had happened that night at the motel. Although Will had used condoms both times they made love, he'd begun without one.

Still, it seemed unlikely she'd become pregnant from a single encounter. Leah had heard that most women tried for months before conceiving. Besides, traveling would throw a woman's system out of whack.

She ought to ignore the whole thing. In a few days—perhaps a week, on its regular schedule—her period would show up.

A breadstick shredded in her hands. Annoyed at the evidence of her agitation, she dropped it on her plate.

Then she thought of an even scarier possibility.

Her mother had died of ovarian cancer, which often produced vague symptoms. Since not even regular checkups guaranteed an early diagnosis, Leah had vowed to seek help at the slightest sign of abdominal distress or general exhaustion. The first she definitely had, and she'd been sleeping more than usual, which she'd attributed to jet lag.

She didn't dare put this off. For privacy's sake, perhaps she should contact a doctor in Mill Valley, but she'd started seeing Jenni as a patient and liked her. Also, the new doctor could be trusted to keep confidences.

Suddenly, Leah couldn't bear to wait another day. If Jenni wasn't completely booked, maybe she could work in another patient this afternoon.

One way or another, Leah had to learn the truth.

The Home Boulevard Medical Clinic was a few blocks away. The one-story brick building had always seemed inviting, but today she had to force herself up the steps.

In the waiting room, she said hello to one of her former students and the boy's mother. "You aren't sick, I hope?" the woman said.

"No, no. Just a routine…visit." She could hardly claim to have a checkup when she lacked an appointment, Leah realized.

She felt more and more uncomfortable. Maybe she ought to leave and call a doctor in Mill Valley after all. Otherwise, she risked becoming the subject of speculation.

Before she could retreat, the young receptionist spotted her. "Hi, Miss Morris!" Patsy Fellows said brightly. "Did you want Dr. Vine to work you in? She's in the lunchroom, but she might have some time later."

Leah gestured toward the waiting patients. "She's obviously busy."

"Oh, no, they're here to see my mother." Estelle Fellows, Ben's wife and Patsy's mom, worked as a nurse practitioner as well as the clinic's business manager. "Hold on. Here's Yvonne."

Yvonne Johnson, Jenni's nurse, regarded Leah questioningly. Despite her exotic looks—long silver hair and violet eyes—she had a no-nonsense quality that Leah liked.

"I'm, uh, if Jenni has a few minutes she could spare…" Remembering the inquisitive woman behind her, Leah finished lamely. "I have a couple of questions."

"Let me ask," Yvonne responded, and bustled off.

Lingering at the counter, Leah realized she didn't want to sit down and risk engaging in further conversation. Nor could she take an interest in any of the magazines. Especially not— she couldn't help noticing—the large number that featured babies on the covers.

Yvonne reappeared a minute later. "She said to show you into her office. She'll be right with you."

The nurse led the way into the clinic's interior. As Leah inhaled the medicinal odor that pervaded the facility, her stomach went into a tizzy, which reminded her all over again of her concern.

Probably just nerves, she thought sternly. Or the meat in the spaghetti sauce.

Yvonne ushered her into Jenni's corner office. Since the doctor had only arrived at the beginning of June, it remained rather bare except for a couple of framed degrees, a scattering of reference books and a large painting of a woodland scene.

Jenni entered a moment later. The blond doctor, whom Ethan had dismissed as a California surfer-girl type before he got to know her, greeted Leah warmly. She pulled her chair from behind the desk so they could sit face-to-face.

"I knew this had to be important or you'd have waited for an appointment," she said. "Unless it's a social visit?"

Leah shook her head. "No. I…" She hesitated, trying to figure out a discreet way to broach the subject.

"Spit it out," Jenni suggested. "It's easier that way."

Gratefully, Leah let the words fly. "I might be pregnant. Otherwise, I was afraid it could be even more serious—you know my family history. I figured I should come right in."

"What are your symptoms?" Jenni listened to a recounting of her late period and upset stomach, and, as an after-thought, sore breasts. Her comment was, "I assume you have reason to think you could be expecting."

"Unfortunately, yes. I realize how stupid that makes me look, when you urged me to use contraception. Well, we did…mostly." Without going into detail, Leah explained how they'd forgotten the condom at first. "But he put it on before…climaxing."

Unaccustomed to discussing such intimate matters, she stumbled over the term. Thank goodness Jenni didn't ask about the circumstances.

"There *can* be semen present before ejaculation." Her calm, professional demeanor never wavered. "It's possible you're unusually fertile. Since there's an easy test, let's rule out pregnancy before we consider any other possibility."

Unusually fertile. That would be just her luck. "Does Yvonne have to know?" Leah's cheeks burned at the prospect of her situation becoming common knowledge.

Jenni tilted her head. "Yes, but don't forget, she's been through a similar situation."

Remembering how the nurse had held her head high during her pregnancy—and refused to this day to disclose the name of the father—Leah conceded the point. Besides, she had to trust someone.

Following Jenni's instructions, she went off to give a urine specimen for testing. Then Leah changed into a hospital gown and underwent a physical exam.

The results came back just as Jenni was finishing. "The result is positive," she reported. "That confirms my observation that your body's showing the kinds of changes we expect during early pregnancy."

Stunned, Leah hugged her knees as she sat on the examining table. She was going to have a baby. Will's baby.

Chapter Three

This altered everything about Leah's life and plans. Will, on the other hand, would never find out about it. She had no way to reach him even if she wanted to.

Nevertheless, in spite of the difficulties ahead, she felt a spurt of excitement as she sat on the examining table, trying to absorb the news. What she'd regretted most about staying single was that it meant never giving birth to a child. Part of her longed for that experience, though she would never have attempted it on purpose.

Now she'd have a tiny baby with fingers that would curl around hers. A little boy or girl toddling on chubby legs. An eager, freshly washed face like the ones she saw in her classroom each morning.

"I have no idea what to do next," she admitted. "I mean, I'm happy in a way. I've always wanted children, but I figured I'd adopt."

Holding her clipboard, Jenni leaned against the washstand. She'd had a difficult early life, shuffled from one relative to another because of neglectful parents, Leah recalled. The experience had given her a depth of understanding beyond her years, and it showed.

"Let's talk about the father," the doctor said gently. Her

obvious concern and lack of judgmentalism dispelled the last of Leah's hesitation.

"He's someone I met in Austin," she said. "We got carried away." That seemed simpler than relating the whole ugly story, and less embarrassing.

"Are you planning to tell him?"

"I don't know where to find him." To cut off further inquiries, Leah said, "I really really really doubt he wants to be involved."

Jenni accepted her statement. "It's too bad your child won't know his or her genetic heritage, not to mention having a father to help raise him, but apparently, it can't be helped."

"Thank you." More than ever, Leah was struck by how much she could have used her mother's support. Despite all her connections, she felt basically alone.

"As your physician, I'm concerned about your emotional as well as your physical health, so let's talk about how you'll deal with gossip," Jenni said. "If you want to, of course."

"Sure." Leah shuddered. "In my position, things could get nasty." She hadn't forgotten Beau Johnson's harsh reaction to Yvonne, or the unpleasant comments some of the students' mothers had made within her hearing.

"You won't be able to hide your condition for long," her friend pointed out.

"I could leave town. It's no secret that I've applied to other schools." No sooner had she uttered the suggestion than Leah rejected it. "That's all I need. I'd have no job, no friends and no place to live."

"You're more familiar with Downhome than I am." Jenni frowned. "Is there any chance you could lose your job on moral grounds?"

"Not while Olivia's the principal, but I hate putting her in a tough position." An idea hit Leah. Much as she disliked lying, it might soften the criticism, and it would deflect questions about the baby's paternity. "I could say that I had artificial insemination while I was in Seattle. I've mentioned plenty of times that I planned to adopt, so it wouldn't seem totally strange. I'll tell Karen the truth, but as far as anyone else is concerned, my private life is none of their business."

She braced for objections. Jenni reflected briefly.

"Under the circumstances, I don't see what harm it can do, unless the father shows up, demanding his rights," she said.

"He has no idea where to find me." For the first time, Leah considered that a good thing.

"Normally, we'd include a report from the Seattle clinic in your medical records. Obviously, we can't do that. However, I can truthfully put down that the father is unknown and that you state that you were inseminated at an unidentified facility in Seattle. You *are* stating that, right?" she added teasingly.

"You just heard me." Despite her anxiety, Leah appreciated the conspiratorial humor.

Jenni made a note on her clipboard. "Folks will be curious. Even though our staff is sworn to protect patient privacy, your condition will become unmistakable within a few months. You ought to develop a more complete story, such as how you planned it and why."

"I'll say I did it on the spur of the moment," Leah replied. "I mean, it could happen that way, right?"

"Clinics usually do a lot of screening," the doctor replied. "However, this unidentified facility might have lax rules. Perhaps you used a private physician that you heard about from your friend?"

"Sure." Leah had never realized lying could be so complicated. And she hated involving Jenni in the deception. But how fair was it that *she* faced all sorts of repercussions, while Will faced none at all?

The doctor went on to explain about proper health care during pregnancy, and provided several brochures, along with a prescription for neonatal vitamins. "Our new obstetrician is arriving day after tomorrow. It isn't necessary to return for a few weeks unless you're having problems, but when you do, perhaps you should visit him instead of me."

Leah didn't care to share her most delicate feelings with a stranger, especially a man. "I'm staying with you."

Jenni looked pleased. "I have to admit, I like treating mothers-to-be. Of course, if complications develop, we'd need Dr. Rankin's help, but there's no reason to expect any problems. He should probably handle the delivery, though. He'll have staff privileges at Mill Valley Medical Center." The clinic had an arrangement with the hospital twelve miles away.

"We'll deal with that in due time," Leah said. "Right now, I'm trying to figure out how to settle my stomach. Any suggestions?"

Jenni had several, including eating frequent, small meals. "I seem to recall hearing that you provide snacks for your class, so that should help. Which reminds me—I've been meaning to talk to you about Nick."

Nick Forrest, soon to be Jenni's stepson, would be in Leah's class this year. "That's right. He's diabetic, isn't he? Tell me about his special needs."

Jenni explained that, thanks to the boy's insulin pump, he didn't require shots, but had to eat regular meals and avoid excessive sweets, as well as monitor his blood sugar levels by pricking his finger and testing the blood droplet. She and Ethan would drop by to make sure all went well, she promised.

"Good," Leah said. "I'd love to have you educate the kids about his condition. That should allay any teasing."

"Great idea!" They set a date. When they were done, Jenni said, "Go ahead and get dressed. By the way, congratulations."

"Thanks." Accepting best wishes under the circumstance felt odd. Yet having a baby *was* cause for joy, Leah thought.

"Don't forget to stop by the front desk," Jenni added from the doorway. "You'll need another appointment. Also, Yvonne will give you vitamin samples to get you started."

"Thanks." As soon as the door closed, Leah took several deep breaths. Pregnant. How exhilarating and how terrifying.

She'd often watched students' mothers as their waistlines expanded. She'd been both curious and envious that a child grew inside. And despite their discomforts, the moms had mostly beamed with contentment.

Still, they had almost always had husbands or at least boyfriends to help out. Helen Rios, the manicurist at Aunt Rosie's salon, was moving to Knoxville soon with her fiancé, the artist who'd painted Pepe's murals, to start a new life. It would shortly include their baby.

Leah, on the other hand, faced going through the entire experience alone.

Her aunt and Mark would help, she felt certain. So would Karen and Jenni, of course. But it wasn't the same.

Lots of women managed, and so would she, Leah decided firmly.

When she pulled on her slacks, they strained over her midsection. Karen hadn't noticed the problem this morning, so no doubt her heavy lunch had contributed, but already her body was changing.

It reminded her that she would need a new wardrobe. Other things, as well: clothes, baby furniture and a car seat.

So many changes. So much to consider.

After she finished dressing, she went to the reception desk, where Yvonne discreetly slipped her the vitamins. The nurse frowned at Patsy, who was sorting through a cardboard box.

"That girl is out of her mind," the nurse confided. "The new ob-gyn sent some books and stuff ahead for his office, and she's mooning over his picture."

"I heard that!" The receptionist skewered her with a mock glare. "He's cute, that's all. And he's divorced."

"Terrific! An obstetrician she can flirt with," Yvonne grumbled. "This is a medical office, not a dating service. I don't know where they're to find a nurse for him—they've been advertising for weeks—but I hope they do, because I've got my hands full as it is. Plus, I prefer a female doctor any day."

"Me, too," Leah agreed.

"You should see Dr. Rankin. With him around, work is going to be way more interesting." Patsy retrieved a framed photo from the box and thrust it toward her. "Look!"

Leah took the picture. Stunned, she stared, barely managing to keep her disbelief from showing.

It was Will, kneeling on a lawn, a breeze ruffling his hair as he favored the camera with a heart-stopping smile. He had his arms looped around two little blond girls, one on each side.

Dr. William Rankin, she thought numbly. In a crazy way, it made sense. Karen must have asked him to recommend a country-music bar in Austin, and he'd cited the Wayward Drummer.

Now he was moving to Downhome. Her situation had just become a whole lot more awkward.

The obstetrician who might be expected to deliver her baby was its father. Yet he'd made it clear he wanted nothing to do with her. Presumably, with her child, as well.

Still, unless she fled, they couldn't avoid meeting again. Besides, seeing the joy he showed for his two daughters gave Leah pause.

"Well?" Patsy said. "What do you think?"

"Cute girls," Leah responded, and handed the picture back. She went out the door, too flummoxed to make any further attempt at chitchat.

Two shocks in one day. Knowing she couldn't carry on a coherent conversation with anyone, she hurried to her car and drove home.

One fact stood out in her mind. She wasn't going to let that man chase her from this town or her friends.

Beyond that, Leah had no idea how she was going to handle this.

IN THE BACK OF THE CAR, Diane squirmed. "Daddy, can I stay with you today?"

"You don't want to go to school?" The girls had been atwitter all weekend, partly about settling into a new home but mostly about preparing for class. They'd even set up a pretend classroom for their dolls. Now, however, it sounded like Diane had a case of cold feet.

Will had to admit that he shared a touch of her nerves. Their first day of school didn't seem nearly as casual as escorting his kids to kindergarten had been. He was much more aware of starting them on a path that would eventually lead to— heaven help them all—adolescence.

"I want to be a nurse," Diane replied. "Let me work with you."

"Me, too," India said.

"They don't let kids work at medical offices," Will informed them as he drove.

He wished he had a clearer view of the girls than his small mirror provided. Safety required strapping them into the rear seat, something his ex-wife hadn't always bothered to do, despite his warnings.

He refused to think about Allison or how she ought to be here. In many ways, the three of them were better off without her.

"Tell people we're midgets," Diane commanded.

"We could sit very still on your couch," India countered.

"Won't work," Will said, "but thanks for the suggestions."

Last Thursday, the twins had accompanied him to the clinic, where they'd been thrilled to spot themselves in the photo on his desk. The receptionist had fussed over them, providing sugar-free lollipops and paying them compliments.

The rest of the staff had acted a bit more reserved. Will figured they'd all relax once he settled in.

"Anyway, you have to study," he told his daughters. "I studied for years and years to become a doctor."

"I don't want to be a doctor," Diane said.

"Why not?"

"I told you! Because I don't want to go to school!"

"You liked it when you saw the place," he said over his shoulder. He'd taken the girls to the elementary school on Thursday to register them.

The principal had assured him that the first-grade teacher, Miss Morris, was warm and nurturing, as well as an excellent educator. Too bad she hadn't been around. He'd have liked to talk to her about the difficult transition the girls were making.

"What if we get lost?" Diane demanded, which surprised him, because usually she was the braver of the pair. "What if Mrs. McNulty can't find us?"

"Then I'll come get you in person," he responded promptly. "Listen, I'll make sure Miss Morris has my phone number, okay? If Mrs. McNulty isn't there, ask your teacher to call me."

"She might not have a phone," Diane protested.

In the mirror, he saw India reach across and take her sister's hand. "It'll be okay," she said quietly. "I'll stay with you."

His heart swelled with love for his two little sweethearts. They made everything else worthwhile.

Will realized he should have left the car at the clinic a couple of blocks away, when he pulled into the lot and found it filled. He'd noticed the high school next door but hadn't realized until now that the two shared parking facilities.

Trying not to let the girls see his irritation, he backed out and located a free space on the street. By now, the twins had pasted their noses to the windows as they stared at the passing children.

What a lot of kids there were for such a small town, Will noted as he emerged. From kindergarteners to adolescents, they skipped, strolled or slouched toward the campus, some accompanied by parents and others with friends.

Most had a shiny, well-groomed appearance, although here and there he saw a child who might be neglected. When he'd visited the town last month, the police chief had explained that he and Dr. Vine were conducting an outreach program to help some of the needier youngsters.

Diane wriggled out of her booster seat unaided, while India waited patiently for him to release her. Both girls caught his hands, staying close as they crossed the street.

Diane made no further mention of her fears, although perhaps she was putting on a bold face in front of fellow students. Thank goodness Will didn't have to deal with a screaming temper tantrum like the one a little red-haired girl was throwing on the sidewalk.

"First-grader?" he asked as they came alongside.

"Yes." Her mother, a harassed-looking woman with a round face and ultrashort hair, sighed in resignation. "She'll be all right as soon as we get into the classroom. I've got two older ones, and they adored Miss Morris."

That sounded promising.

In front of the building, Will spotted a familiar face. Chief Ethan Forrest accompanied a self-assured little boy, who glad-handed a group of other kids as if preparing for a junior career in politics.

"Gotta watch *that* kid," Will joked as he approached. "He'll be running for mayor before you know it."

"Good to see you." Ethan started to shake hands, then noticed that Will didn't have one free. "This is Nick."

Will introduced the girls.

"They'll be in the same class," the police chief said. "Make them feel at home, will you, Nick?"

The kids made funny faces at one another. India giggled.

"Best chums already," Will noted.

They joined the swarm going through the double doors, by-passing a father so intent on videotaping his little boy that he didn't notice what a roadblock he created. Inside, the cheery corridor featured student drawings and paintings.

Will had forgotten to ask the number of the classroom, but with Ethan as his guide, they proceeded down the hall and around a corner. Children's shrill voices bounced off the walls and feet clattered on the linoleum.

He flashed back to his first day at school. He'd been one of the ranchers' kids, marked by loose-fitting jeans and a T-shirt, in contrast to the town youngsters, with their brand-name outfits. Although most parents had escorted their young-sters, his father merely idled the pickup while his elder brothers, Burt and Mike, exited with Will.

He'd clutched his lunch bag, scared to death of the unfa-miliar commotion. Mike had walked him to the classroom, smacked him on the shoulder and offered, as a parting bit of advice, "Don't pick your nose."

That day had marked the start of a long journey that had

increasingly isolated Will both from his peers and from his family. He didn't regret deciding to focus on his education and prove the naysayers wrong, however.

Thank goodness India and Diane wouldn't have to struggle to prove themselves. He intended to be there for them at every step.

Will followed Ethan into a classroom arrayed with desks and chairs scaled for Lilliputians. The walls blazed with alphabet and number charts, illustrations from books and a couple of travel posters. One featured Seattle's Space Needle, and another showed the familiar sight of the Texas Capitol. He wondered fleetingly if the teacher had put them up to welcome the new kids in town.

Then he saw her.

Crouched in front of a teary little boy, she was talking earnestly. Her long black hair fell tantalizingly across her shoulders and her blue eyes went wide as she uttered what appeared to be words of sympathy. After a moment, the child stopped crying and hugged her.

Will got a tight feeling.

Leah. Downhome. Miss Morris. Impossible.

He couldn't be mistaken about that cover-girl face or the gently sculpted lines of her body. A body he hadn't been able to stop thinking about for the past month. Exquisite. As sweet as his dreams. But good heavens, what kind of mess had he created? Yet here the woman was.

He struggled to sort out how such a coincidence could have occurred. He recalled mentioning the Wayward Drummer to Karen Lowell, a member of the physician-search committee, who'd mentioned a friend planning to visit Austin. This must be the friend.

A knot formed in Will's gut. That night at the motel, he'd made some huge mistakes. Jumping into bed with a stranger was the most egregious. Leaving without a word hadn't exactly put him in a defensible position, either.

That left the question of what he was going to do with his children. Could he trust her with them?

When he caught Leah's eye, a flicker of something he couldn't read crossed her face, quickly replaced by bland welcome. She'd been expecting him. Sometime since her return, she must have figured out who he was.

"Hi, Leah! I mean, Miss Morris!" Nick bounced across the room. "Want to see me prick my finger?"

Ethan made a choking noise. Leah kept a straight face. "You know what? We're going to talk about diabetes on Wednesday, so everyone understands. Dr. Vine's agreed to make a presentation, and I would really appreciate if you'd help."

"You bet!" Satisfied, the little boy headed over to talk to a friend. After the chief said a good-natured farewell, Leah turned toward Will.

Just as in Austin, her smile lit up the room. Combined with her open, unaffected manner, her striking appearance made it hard for him to think straight.

Fortunately, she directed her comments to his daughters. "I'm excited to have twins in my class, but I'm sure you're two very different individuals."

"I'm Diane. I like pink and India likes blue." The little girl indicated their jumpers, which were identical, except for the colors. Will wondered how much Eileen had influenced their choice of the same style, and made a mental note to take them shopping himself next time.

"Even though I'm the teacher, you'll need to teach me about yourselves," Leah went on in her musical voice. "Do you want to sit together or would you like to sit separately?"

The girls exchanged looks. "Together," Diane said.

India's head bobbed.

"That's fine," their teacher said gravely. "Later in the year, when you feel more comfortable, you can switch if you want to."

"You need to get our dad's phone number," Diane told her. "In case Mrs. McNulty can't find us."

"I'll do that. You're a very responsible young lady," Leah told her.

India took Diane's hand. "Come on," she said in an urgent half whisper. "Let's go sit by Nick." The little girls scampered off.

With only the slightest hesitation, Leah shifted her attention to Will. "I guess I'll have that phone number now, Doctor." She didn't bother to disguise a touch of irony.

He could have sworn his face grew warm, but he hadn't blushed in years. "Certainly, Miss Morris." Since he hadn't had business cards printed yet, Will took out a prescription pad. Unable to find a pen, he borrowed a watercolor marker from her desk.

As he scrawled the number, he grew more and more uncomfortable. He had to let her teach his kids, since she appeared to be the only first-grade teacher in town. Besides, yanking them now would upset the girls and raise far too many questions. All the same, there was no way he and Leah Morris could ignore what had happened.

"We have to talk." He kept his voice low.

She gave a friendly nod to a new arrival, the woman whose daughter had thrown a tantrum. Sounding politely impersonal, Leah said, "When would you suggest, Dr. Rankin?"

His housekeeper retired to her quarters—in this case, a separate guesthouse, much to Will's satisfaction—by 7:00 p.m. Adding his address to the note, he said. "How about seven-thirty tonight at my place?"

She quirked an eyebrow but, to his relief, didn't refuse. However, she added, "Let's make it eight."

"Eight will be fine." He suspected the hour mattered less than her power to control the terms.

She tucked the note into her skirt pocket and, after one last assessing look, moved on to the short-haired woman, who caught her arm eagerly. "Leah, I hope you'll let me serve as the class mom! Nobody's beaten me to it, have they?"

"A few people dropped hints, but nobody's signed up. That would be wonderful, Minnie," she said. "I can't believe Sybill's old enough for school!"

On his way out, Will lengthened his stride. The curious thing was, he realized as he scooted down the front steps, that he felt almost as off center as he had on his own first day of school.

By eight o'clock tonight, he would regain his usual iron self-control. And they would figure out how to put the whole embarrassing incident behind them.

Chapter Four

By the time the last child hurried out that afternoon, Leah's back and shoulders ached. Even so, she trudged around the room straightening desks and picking up dropped papers. Surely, she didn't feel this exhausted every year on the first day of school, did she?

At naptime, when she'd expected to have a few minutes for reflection, she'd put her head on the desk and promptly fallen asleep. In nine years of teaching that that had hardly ever happened.

Jenni had warned of requiring more sleep than usual. Leah had figured that meant going to bed half an hour early. Well, live and learn.

On the short drive home, she finally allowed her thoughts to stray to Will. Thank heaven she'd learned of his identity in advance and discovered the two Rankin girls' names on her class list, because the sight of his intense gaze and expressive mouth had hit her hard.

She was proud of maintaining her poise during their encounter. The fact that it has taken place on her turf had helped. The prospect of meeting him at his place tonight didn't thrill her, but they must get this over with.

The question remained: how much did she intend to tell

him? He clearly wanted to deal with the issue of their affair. She'd rather save the matter of her pregnancy for later, but that might not be wise. Given his occupation, he was sure to find out, and he might be angry if it appeared she'd tried to keep it secret.

At the two-bedroom cottage her parents had bequeathed her, Leah fixed a salad. She carried it to the country-style table at one end of the living room.

Usually the décor lifted her spirits with its mix of conventional furnishings and quirky accents, including a carved red chest and a Japanese-style print silk scarf framed on the wall. Tonight, however, she was too busy wrestling with her decision.

So far, no one except Jenni and Yvonne knew about the pregnancy. She hadn't had occasion to use the artificial insemination story, so it didn't present a stumbling block to whatever she and Will decided.

If she admitted the truth to him before anyone else found out, they could concoct a story together. They might say they'd dated for a whirlwind few days and fallen in love. Eyebrows would be raised no matter how they put it, but if he decided to stand by her...

Leah glared across the room at her reflection in the glass of the built-in cabinets. She had no business indulging in infantile fantasies. The man who had walked out on her without a word was not going to fall on his knees and ask her to marry him.

Nor did she want him to. In fact, she wouldn't marry Will Rankin if he begged her—and not only because he'd betrayed her trust.

After college, she'd longed to see the world. She'd begun looking into teaching English at a foreign school or joining the Peace Corps, but there'd been no question of that after her mom fell ill.

By the time her mom had died a year later, Leah had taken

on a job in Downhome. A short time later, her father had announced his plans to marry an old friend in Denver. Perhaps as a way to cushion the blow of his rapid defection, he'd given Leah the family house, saying her mother would have wanted her to have it.

A bolder person might have rented it out and pursued her old dreams. However, losing her mother—and, in some ways, her always-distant father—had left Leah feeling insecure.

Clinging to the comfort of old friends and routine, she'd persuaded herself that traveling during the summers ought to be enough. Three-week jaunts to Europe, Asia and South America had proved educational and exciting.

She hadn't realized how quickly life was slipping past, although she'd begun to feel restless on her thirtieth birthday. The defining moment had come a year later, as the result of an offhanded remark from her cousin.

Mark, four years Leah's junior, had told her at her thirty-first birthday dinner, "I'm glad you don't feel you have to chase after something new all the time."

Aware that a longtime girlfriend had dumped him because she considered him stuffy, Leah had tempered her response. "I like to try different things, Mark. I'm just quiet about it."

He'd dismissed the comment. "You've worn your hair long and straight for as long as I've known you. You'll probably wear it the same way when you're eighty. And that's great, because it suits you."

She'd had a sudden vision of herself as an aging, stereotypical old maid, still dwelling in the house where she grew up. Even if she married, it would be to some boring guy who lived down the block.

Leah had made up her mind to leave Downhome. This summer, she'd put her plan into action.

Now Will Rankin lived down the block, or almost. The

mysterious man who'd stirred her in Austin had metamor-
phosed into a respected obstetrician with two children.
Although she could never call him boring, he hadn't turned
out to be a daredevil, either.

Leah had made up her mind to leave town, and she meant
to do it. If the job in Seattle didn't materialize, she'd move
somewhere else. Hawaii. Alaska. Las Vegas. Anywhere but
here. A child didn't have to tie her to one place.

A man was a different story. He'd restrict her in all sorts
of ways.

Okay, so she'd settled that. Even if Will threw himself at
her, she'd still say no. Leah smiled at the unlikelihood of such
a development.

All the same, she planned to inform him of the pregnancy.
For the child's sake, she hoped he would want some involvement.

But not too much. He'd already blown his chances for that.

Will insisted on doing the dishes so Mrs. McNulty could
retire early. Although he didn't expect Leah until eight, he
meant to put the girls to bed well before then, to recuperate
from a busy day.

They'd greeted him after work with crayon pictures that
included their names. Since the twins had learned many of the
basics in kindergarten, they'd been encouraged to add any
words they wanted.

Diane had written "Dog cat horse."

India had scrawled the name "Nick."

His little girl had her first crush. If that boy broke her heart,
Will would make sure the police chief gave him a spanking.

Guiltily, he remembered what he'd done to Leah. Although
she'd shown no sign of suffering a broken heart, he owed her
an apology.

Eileen supervised the girls' baths. Procedures that frustrated Will, like settling squabbles over who went first and shampooing hair without creating hopeless tangles, came easily to the experienced housekeeper.

She'd joined the family two years ago, after Allison left. Previously, she'd raised two generations of children in other families, along with a daughter of her own.

At seventy, Mrs. McNulty could have retired, but what would she do all day? she'd responded when Will had asked. Divorced, she'd always worked, first as a maid and later as a housekeeper. She might have considered moving to Florida to be near her daughter's family, she'd said, but they led their own lives.

She'd been thrilled to have two young charges again. Desperately seeking a solution to recurrent child-care problems, Will had been overjoyed to find her. The move to Tennessee hadn't fazed her, thank goodness.

He'd finished loading the dishwasher when the housekeeper's substantial frame filled the kitchen doorway. "The girls are ready for their night-night story," she told him. "There's a coffee cake in the fridge, and I could make a pot of decaf for your guest if you like."

Will nearly dropped the box of dishwasher detergent. "I'm sorry?" He hadn't mentioned inviting anyone.

Mrs. McNulty favored him with a knowing glance. "Dr. Rankin, what's the first thing you do when you get home?"

"Hug the girls," he said.

"After that."

"Change my clothes." He saw her point. Tonight, instead of throwing on jeans and a polo shirt, he'd merely removed his jacket and tie.

The housekeeper sniffed the air.

Okay, so he'd shaved and applied lotion. After a hard day's work, he didn't want to appear slovenly.

"I knew it wouldn't take long for the females in this town to discover you," Eileen continued. "All the same, she must be pretty special for you to invite her home this fast." He hadn't even thought about dating any of his acquaintances in Austin.

However, the last thing Will needed was for word to spread about his private connection with Leah. Not that Eileen gossiped, but he preferred to keep certain matters private. "It's a professional meeting," he said without elaborating. "She's doing me a favor by dropping by."

"I see." Eileen's nose wrinkled ever so slightly. *He shouldn't have put on so much aftershave,* Will thought. *It was a dead giveaway.* "We'll leave it at that, then. I'll be on my way."

"Sleep well," he said.

"Oh, I plan to."

After she let herself out the back door, Will cast an assessing glance over the room. Mrs. McNulty had done a terrific job of setting up the household in only a few days, considering what little she'd had to work with.

The one-story house, which the physician-search committee had found for him to rent, lacked personality, and the modern furniture Allison had left for her family seemed more functional than aesthetic. One of these days, Will was going to buy his own place and hire a decorator with good taste. No hurry, though.

He went in to see the girls, who'd chosen to share a bedroom. They and their dolls crowded around when he sat on a bed, but instead of their usual story time, tonight they wanted to tell the tale of their first day of class.

"Go ahead," Will told them. "I can't wait to hear it."

The girls spilled out their anecdotes. Miss Morris had told a funny story, Diane said, and recounted it. Miss Morris had visited Austin last summer. Could he believe that? added India. Miss Morris served healthy snacks and taught them about nutrition, Diane said. They both wanted to grow their hair longer so it could swing like Miss Morris's.

Will stifled a groan. This was going to be a tough year, filled with stories of the one person in town he didn't want to hear about. He only hoped the girls wouldn't detect Miss Morris's voice in the living room later or they'd come pelting out, and no doubt, tell the entire class about it tomorrow.

When they'd finished and he'd kissed them both, he said, "I have a colleague arriving in a while to discuss some business. I'm going to close the bedroom door and the hall door so we won't disturb you, okay?"

The little girls nodded uncertainly.

"No fair interrupting," he said. "You both need your sleep. If you stay up late, I might have to keep you home from school tomorrow."

Horror showed on India's face. Diane wrung her hands dramatically. "Oh, no, Daddy!"

He hadn't expected his threat to cause such alarm. "Go to sleep. You'll be fine in the morning."

They dove under the covers. After stepping out, Will stood in the hallway listening and was amazed to hear none of the usual chortling and whispering. He wondered how many kids were afraid of being kept home. Only ones who loved their teachers, or who loved learning, as he had.

In the living room, he took out a stack of medical journals. The field of obstetrics changed rapidly.

When the bell rang at eight, Will gave a start. He hadn't read a single word of the article in front of him. He'd been too busy rehearsing what to say to Leah.

The effort was a waste of time. As he hurried to answer, he discovered he'd forgotten every word he'd planned.

When he opened the door, Will simply stood for a moment, enjoying the sight of long, shiny black hair and velvet-smooth skin. He got a physical buzz even stronger than he'd experienced at the bar, because now he knew how delicious Leah's lips would feel beneath his and how her body could tantalize him.

He took a tight grip on his musings, and got the impression she was doing the same. "Miss Morris," he said. "How punctual."

"We both want to get this over with, I presume," she replied coolly.

Will ushered her into the living room. The hard contours of the room softened around her. "Care for a drink?"

"No, thanks." Leah wore a light-blue dress, belted at the waist and covered with cornflowers that seemed to emit a delicate fragrance. "I brought you something. Are the girls around?" She reached for her handbag.

"They're in bed. I told them I was expecting a colleague." He nearly touched her waist to guide her toward a chair but stopped in time.

"Good. I don't want them involved in…whatever we have to discuss. But I'm sure they'll enjoy these."

From her purse, she produced two photographs. One showed India and Nick proudly carrying trays of snacks to their classmates. In the other was Diane pushing the red-haired girl in a swing.

She'd captured both children in moments of uninhibited animation. From his own frustrating attempts with a camera, Will knew how much sensitivity that required.

"I take shots of all the children on their first day," Leah said. "Usually, I give them out at parent conferences, but I printed yours early."

"I'll treasure these." No exaggeration required. "I should have brought a camera with me this morning."

After Eileen had started to work for him, she'd rescued the girls' photos and drawings from assorted boxes and drawers and assembled them into a family scrapbook. Will planned to add to it regularly.

"It's more important to experience life than to record it." Leah remained standing, shaking her head when Will gestured toward the couch. "Some parents are so busy viewing everything through a lens that they become emotionally isolated."

Will remembered the father with the video camera, but didn't bother to mention him. Instead, hoping to break the ice, he said, "My housekeeper left a coffee cake in the fridge. Would you care for some?"

"No, thanks."

"At least, sit down," he blurted.

"We're not going to pretend this is a social call, are we?" Leah regarded him skeptically. "We both know why I'm here."

"So we can put this behind us."

She folded her arms. "Yes, that would be nice, wouldn't it?"

The sarcasm raised Will's guard. "Nice? I should think it's essential."

"Convenient, in any case," Leah muttered.

Irritably, he realized she didn't intend to simply shake hands on an agreement to keep silent. Then he remembered that he hadn't yet apologized. "You have a right to be angry. I acted like a jerk."

"Yes, you did." Her taut stance eased by a fraction. For heaven's sake, how had he transformed the welcoming, delightful lady from the Wayward Drummer into this tightly wound challenger?

"I'm sorry. I tend to be self-protective," Will conceded. "A man in my position…"

"Which, as I recall, was with your pants around your ankles," Leah quipped tartly.

Amusing as it was, the remark stung. "That's true. However, knowing practically nothing about you, I had reason to be cautious. Under the circumstances, I believed you might turn out to be unstable."

A wing of dark hair fell across her temple, partially obscuring her face. "Don't insult me. You summed up your conduct just fine a moment ago." She was evidently referring to the comment about acting like a jerk.

"We both screwed up." Will considered. "May I be blunt?"

"Certainly." The air in the living room crackled with renewed tension.

Will wished they could sit down and talk, but Leah still showed no inclination to get comfortable, so he forged ahead. "I moved here for a fresh start."

"That's why I went to Austin. Ironic, isn't it?"

He nodded. "My divorce became final this summer and believe me, that marriage was a huge mistake, except for my little girls. I'm not ready for another relationship and I know it. Okay, I acted selfishly. I took what I needed, and you gave it. You have my thanks for that, but you made your own choice for what I presume are your own reasons. You have no right to hold me responsible."

Her chin lifted. Will wished he weren't tempted to cup it with one hand and soothe away the tiny distress lines crinkling her eyes.

For a moment, he thought he glimpsed something else in those depths. Disappointment, perhaps. And resolve. He got the sense that he'd missed some subtext to the conversation, but then, he'd never been particularly good at reading people.

"So that's the bottom line?" Leah said. "You can't be held responsible for anything, and you don't want me intruding on your privacy?"

He didn't like the way that sounded. Maybe he ought to suggest a compromise—perhaps that was what she'd hoped for—but if he backtracked, he was likely to be drawn into an involvement for which neither he nor the girls were prepared.

For heaven's sake, Will was only human. He'd love to get close to this woman again. But the repercussions could be devastating, especially in such a small town.

"That about sums it up," he said, and felt like a heel. The worst part was that he liked her more than ever.

"I'll hold you to that." Despite the strain in her voice, Leah seemed relieved. What *was* going on with her?

Her willingness to withdraw so readily bothered him, for practical as well as intuitive reasons. Although accustomed to being an outsider, Will hoped things would be different in Downhome, for his daughters' sake. He certainly didn't mean to alienate their teacher. "As for India and Diane…"

"What's between us has nothing to do with them," she answered sharply. "They're wonderful children. I enjoy having them in my class, and I'm glad to see that they're already forming friendships."

Will was pleased, because he didn't relish the prospect of trying to find another school, possibly many miles away. And he knew he wouldn't find a better teacher. "That's fine. They love being in your class."

Leah glanced around edgily. She'd shown courage in coming here, Will reflected. This meeting must be, at least, as hard on her as on him.

He reached out and touched her hand. When she didn't object, he took it in his, noting how small and firm it was.

Will had a sudden, inexplicable urge to protect this woman, but against what? Or, more likely, whom, if not himself? "I'm sorry it came to this," he said. "You seem like a decent person. I guess we both acted uncharacteristically."

When she faced him, moisture glinted in her eyes. "Yes, well, it's a real mess, isn't it?"

"Not necessarily." He didn't see the problem, as long as both of them remained discreet and kept their emotions under guard.

She pulled away without making a fuss. "It's important that we go our own ways and that nobody hears a breath about this. Not your housekeeper. Not anyone."

"Okay." Although he shared her viewpoint, he didn't understand the urgency. The woman definitely had other matters on her mind, but they concerned her personal history. "Wait!"

She glanced at him inquisitively.

From an end table, Will fetched the marking pen he'd discovered in one of his pockets. "I borrowed this from your desk and forgot to put it back."

Leah took it with a wry smile. "Always relieved to get one of these back. I buy writing utensils by the boxcar. Usually, it's the kids who swipe them, though, not the parents."

"A bad habit of mine, I'm afraid." One of Will's former colleagues had threatened to chain a pen around his neck so he'd stop taking hers.

Leah opened the front door. "Don't show the photos to anyone for a while, including the girls. They might ask how you came by them."

"Right." He made a mental note to store them in his desk drawer. Mrs. McNulty took care not to poke around his home office in case he brought home confidential information.

Leah peered outside. "Looks like the coast's clear. Good night, Dr. Rankin."

"Good night, Miss Morris." He watched her hurry down the walkway. Apparently, she'd parked around the corner, because she strode off until the darkness closed around her. A wise precaution, given the risk of gossip.

The men in this town must have cotton in their heads, Will mused as he went inside. A woman that appealing and intelligent should have her pick of boyfriends. Instead, for reasons he still didn't comprehend, she'd gone to Texas and tried to capture something—love or excitement, maybe—with a stranger.

Too bad, she'd picked the wrong one.

For a painful beat, he wondered if he'd made a mistake. He'd always dreamed of marrying a soul mate, of sharing his life with someone who understood him in ways no one else did.

But if that kind of relationship existed, he doubted he'd ever find it. Nor, he supposed, did he really want to try. The fallout from his marriage had been too bitter.

Will paced through the house to look in on his girls. Wearing angelic expressions in sleep, each daughter curled to face her twin across the gap between their beds. Diane cradled her favorite doll, while India had piled so many stuffed animals on her bed that it was a wonder she found room to move.

As always, the sight of the twins restored his spirits. With them, as with no one else, he'd made a deeply human connection. It was all he needed.

Yet they couldn't stay babies forever. Stealing another peek at the new photos, Will noticed that Leah had caught the twins at the very beginning stage of making new friends. One step at a time, they were separating from each other and, he supposed, from him.

A little disconcerted that it was Leah Morris who'd awakened him to this transition, Will went to put the photos in a safe place.

Chapter Five

Leah had decided to walk the half dozen blocks to Will's house because she needed exercise, although she'd worried that she might be tired heading home. Instead, powered by fury, she practically burned a track down the sidewalk, scarcely noticing the cooking smells wafting from the tidy frame houses on either side.

So Dr. Stiffneck didn't want to be held responsible for anything. Well, fine by her! She'd intended to set aside her pain and tell him about the pregnancy before anyone else learned of it, but after that little speech, absolutely not!

It was questionable whether he'd buy the artificial insemination story when it came out. But why shouldn't he when it obviously suited his mind-set? True, he'd apologized, but it had been more of an I'm-sorry-I-got-caught response than one expressing real regret.

And that crack about her being unstable! If she were that volatile, she'd have responded by slapping him. He'd certainly deserved it.

Leah's pace slowed as she considered how his cheek might have felt beneath her palm. He'd shaved after work, she could tell, and put on aftershave lotion. But what had that business been about offering her coffee cake, as if they were Lucy and Ethel?

Or two people who might become friends.

Friends! Impossible, yet she supposed she'd have to pretend something in front of others. He *was* Jenni's coworker and the father of two of her students.

The ticklishness of the situation struck Leah afresh as she rounded the corner onto her street, Bennington Lane. Fortunately, Jenni and Ethan were taking only a brief honeymoon, so she wouldn't have to rely on Will for treatment, but if she suffered any complications, bypassing him for a doctor in Mill Valley would be tricky.

No sense borrowing trouble that might never happen. As for the delivery, there had to be a way to arrange for another doctor to handle it.

Peering ahead through the dusk, Leah saw that she'd neglected to switch on her houselights. In the dimness, the cottage looked lonesome and a bit shabby, tucked between a two-story home and a vacant lot where her neighbor, Eunice, grew vegetables. With the best part of the season over, the aging cornstalks and sprawling tomato plants gave the yard an unkempt air.

Leah had no trouble unlocking the front door in the dark. Having lived in this house since she was eight, she could put her hand on the keyhole by instinct.

Inside, she switched on a lamp. Its glow bathed the oak floor, the arch of an interior doorway and the cut flowers in a glass vase.

What the place lacked in elegance, it made up for in coziness. By contrast, Will's house lacked loving detail, as if waiting for someone to care about it.

He had a wistful quality that, despite her resistance, had touched Leah. For all his crustiness, the man seemed lonely. Several times, she'd had the impression he wanted to reach out but kept fighting himself.

He'd said his divorce only become final that summer. No wonder he wasn't ready to form new bonds.

And she *had* made her own choice that night in Austin, Leah reflected. No one had pressured her.

If she wasn't careful, she might forgive him. When he'd taken her hand a little while ago, she'd ached to hear him call her "honey" again. His wounded quality had stirred the same cherishing instinct that had led her astray in Austin.

She needed to guard her heart. And to boot him out of her mind.

Leah sank into the couch, kicked off her shoes and propped her feet on a cushion. The one thing she had to concede about Will was that he made a terrific father, she reflected as she leaned back. It was obvious he doted on those girls.

Her baby, on the other hand, wouldn't have a father. Tears slid down her cheeks. She wished the world were a perfect place.

But it wasn't. At least she knew where she stood with Will. Absolutely nowhere.

In the long run, she'd be safer and happier going it alone. No emotional roller-coaster rides. No false hopes and devastating letdowns.

Sternly, Leah brushed the tears aside. As soon as her feet stopped aching, she got up and went to make a cup of tea.

WILL SPENT THE REST of the week treating patients and observing the clinic's operation. Despite its small size, he quickly discovered, the medical facility didn't lack for strong personalities.

He liked Dr. Vine, a well-trained clinician with a down-to-earth attitude and steel in her spine. Right now, however, she spent every spare minute preparing for her wedding, so he couldn't expect any help from her in navigating the prickly forest of support staff.

The most trying issue was his lack of a nurse. Yvonne Johnson, who made no secret of her resentment at performing double duty, avoided Will's gaze whenever possible and addressed him with icy formality as she prepped his patients.

The physician-search committee had advertised in vain for help. Taking matters into his own hands, Will got on the phone to several nursing registries and solicited applications. With luck, he hoped to bring someone on board in the next few weeks.

He also encountered a distinctly guarded welcome from the fortyish Estelle Fellows, who juggled roles as business manager and nurse practitioner. Her heart was in patient care, an area she made it clear she had no intention of relinquishing. Nor did he want her to.

Will wished she would take him at his word that he considered a nurse practitioner an essential part of an obstetric service. She had the education, patience and personal experience as a mother of four to complement his more high-tech skills.

He was prepared to explain the exact nature of those skills on Friday when Barry Lowell, the editor and reporter for the weekly *Downhome Gazette,* came by for an interview. Talking to the press wasn't Will's idea of fun, but the townspeople must be curious about their new doctor. Besides, the man's sister had been part of the committee that had selected Will.

The only time he could spare was during his lunch break, so he hastily downed a pastrami sandwich from the Café Montreal. Barry Lowell turned out to be a dark-haired fellow with a scar slashing his forehead and an attitude that Will couldn't quite read. Inquisitive, of course, but also watchful and a bit wary.

After shaking hands in the reception area, the two men adjourned to Will's office. Barry set up a tape recorder and took a seat on the couch.

Apparently mistrustful of the mechanical device, he also

flipped open a notepad. "I'm sure you have a tight schedule, so let's get started."

"Great." Despite the temptation to retreat behind his desk, Will chose a seat in the open. He didn't want to come across as one of those doctors who believed they were gods on Mount Olympus.

Leaning forward, the reporter said, "Let's start with why a city boy wants to move to a place like Downhome."

Will didn't feel like discussing his divorce and need for a change, so he tried a humorous approach. "Actually, I grew up on a ranch. Smelling cow manure makes me feel right at home." The green fields around Downhome supported numerous dairy farms, a fact confirmed whenever the winds picked up.

The reporter gave him a crooked grin. "Then you ought to love it here." He consulted a paper, presumably containing a list of questions. "I know obstetricians deliver babies, but so do family doctors and midwives. What makes you special?"

If there was a hint of challenge in the phrasing, Will let it pass. "Although I love bringing babies into the world, I spend much of my time monitoring complicated pregnancies and performing surgery for a variety of conditions. Also, I'll be doing initial fertility workups for any patient who needs them." He would refer tough cases to facilities in Nashville. Modern fertility procedures required extensive labs and highly specialized personnel.

"Does that mean we can expect a baby boom around here?" the reporter joked.

"Judging by the number of patients I've already met, I'd say we're in the middle of one," Will responded. "I gather this town draws from a large surrounding population."

"Lots of farmers live closer to us than to Mill Valley." Barry stretched his shoulders. "Speaking of a growing population, let's try a political hot potato."

That didn't sound good. "I'm not a politician and I'm certainly no expert on local issues," Will protested.

Barry ignored the disclaimer. "There's a proposal coming before the city council to build a shopping center outside town. It would include a supermarket, restaurants and movie theaters, along with housing. If we receive an influx of new residents, some people think Downhome ought to build its own hospital."

This was the first Will had heard of it. "Sounds like a major undertaking."

"In your professional opinion, are the facilities here adequate for a significant increase in population?" His pen poised over the pad.

Will knew he'd better choose his words carefully. "As far as I can tell, this town is well served in the short term. If the area does grow, that will be the appropriate time to assess our changing needs."

Barry wrote down the comment. "If you wield a scalpel as skillfully as you field my questions, Doc, your patients are in good hands."

"Thanks." It crossed Will's mind as he watched the reporter that Mill Valley might have a plastic surgeon who could at least minimize Barry's dramatic scar.

He didn't intend to mention it, but Barry must have noticed his attention. "How do you like it?"

"It makes a fashion statement," Will replied.

His comment surprised a smile from the man. "Let me explain about it before you hear the talk." Despite an attempt to sound casual, bitterness crept into Barry's tone. "I got this in prison. I served five years for manslaughter. I suppose I should protest my innocence, but nobody believed me then, and I don't see why they would now."

Will wasn't sure of the proper response—perhaps none

existed. Instead of searching for one, he said, "Sometimes it feels good to wear a scar on the outside to represent the one on the inside. That way, you don't have to keep up a pretense."

The reporter shot him a startled look. "You hit that nail on the head, Doc." After a moment, he added, "To have that kind of insight, you must carry a few scars of your own."

The comment struck a little too close to home. "Since this is a newspaper interview, I'll note that I'm thirty-six years old and divorced, and leave it at that," Will responded.

Appreciation colored Barry's expression. "Man, you're quick."

"But I'm not the one controlling what gets into print," he pointed out.

"Don't worry. I only skewer people I don't like."

Will chuckled. "I'll make sure to stay on your good side."

After switching off the recorder, the journalist stood up. "My sister already wishes she could clone you to fill our other vacancy. You don't happen to have a brother who's a pediatrician, do you?"

"I've got three brothers," Will told him. "One's in the marines, one's a charter pilot and the youngest is a rancher."

"Where did you go wrong?" the reporter kidded.

"I'm still trying to figure that out."

He escorted Barry to the front desk with a sense of having navigated alligator-infested waters and escaped more or less unscathed. After the man left, Patsy beckoned him to a corner.

"There's a woman here to see you." The receptionist kept her voice low. "She doesn't have an appointment and she won't explain what she wants."

Will hadn't seen anyone he recognized among the waiting patients. "What's her name?"

"Winifred Waters."

That rang a bell. "She applied to be my nurse." With a sinking feeling, he remembered scheduling an interview for today's lunch hour and not writing it down. "Damn. This is my fault. I should have seen her half an hour ago." Will did some fast calculating. "Have I got a lot of patients lined up?"

"I'm afraid so." Patsy made a helpless gesture. "We're completely booked this afternoon."

Will hated to make his patients wait. On the other hand, he desperately needed a nurse, and it wasn't fair to ask Ms. Waters to reschedule.

Before he could decide what to do, the door beside the reception desk swung open and a formidable-looking black woman in a light-blue pantsuit marched in. "Are you Dr. William Rankin?"

The woman's fierce expression gave him a sudden urge to deny it. Instead, Will said, "Yes, I am. Ms. Waters?"

"That would be Mrs. Waters." She extended a hand, which he shook. The woman had a strength to match his own. "It appears your office is running late."

"I'm afraid so." He was about to apologize and confess his mistake, but she went right on talking.

"You can rely on me to get things on track. You've read over my credentials—" she'd mailed him papers documenting her return to college for a nursing degree, followed by two years' experience with a Knoxville obstetrician "—so let's not waste any time." To Patsy, Winifred said, "Why don't you call Dr. Rankin's next patient? I'll prep her."

Patsy's jaw dropped. Yvonne, passing by, seized her chance. "I'll show you where we keep the charts."

"Just let me wash my hands," said Mrs. Waters. "I insist on proper hygiene at all times. I'm sure you agree, don't you, Dr. Rankin?"

"Absolutely." Although Will felt as if he'd been buffeted

by Hurricane Winifred, why not give the lady a chance? "Go ahead, Patsy."

"If you say so." She hurried to the front.

The rest of the afternoon sped by. The receptionist hadn't exaggerated the tight scheduling, but despite the need to learn her way around, Winifred kept things moving smartly.

Yvonne took to her at once. Patsy appeared uncertain, while Estelle watched the newcomer with a critical eye.

Will didn't realize the extent to which the two were staking out their turf until the end of the day. Estelle, who showed signs of a frayed temper understandable on a Friday afternoon, rebuked Will for walking off with her third pen in a row. He was about to apologize when Mrs. Waters stalked into the records room.

She planted herself in front of the nurse practitioner. "If there is a problem with Dr. Rankin, his nurse will take care of it," she said crisply. "I will be happy to make sure he has pens. In fact, I will stop by the store on my way home and buy him an entire package of pens."

Will smothered a laugh at her endearing outrage. The last thing he wanted was to offend Estelle. "That won't be necessary, but thank you," he said.

"I wasn't aware that you'd been hired," Mrs. Fellows told the newcomer coldly.

For once, Winifred hesitated. Will took pity on her. Besides, he'd fallen in love with this woman, professionally speaking. "I'm sorry. I meant to mention it. Mrs. Waters will be joining us full-time beginning…?" He turned to her.

"Monday will do fine." She favored him with the most melting glance he'd ever seen.

"And I apologize about the pen." He fished in his pocket and, to his embarrassment, found all three, which he handed to Estelle. "I really have to stop doing that."

"I meant what I said about the pens," his nurse told him. "I'll keep them at my station—when you need one, you just stick your hand out, palm up. Unless we're in surgery, of course. Then you'll get a scalpel."

With a snort of frustration, Estelle swept out. Will supposed he'd slid backward in his attempt to make friends with her, but it couldn't be helped.

"I want to thank you, Doctor." Although Winifred stood a head shorter than Will, she had considerably more heft. It suited the strength of her personality, he decided.

"I'm the one who should thank you," he admitted. "You've been a lifesaver." Since he hadn't had a chance to interview her, he added, "Tell me why you want to move here from Knoxville."

"My daughter's no-good husband up and left her with my two grandbabies, so I had to come back. This is my hometown," she explained.

"Good timing." Will was profoundly grateful to have solved his most pressing problem. "I'd appreciate it if you'd go easy on Mrs. Fellows, though."

The nurse shrugged. "If you say so. Her daughter's nice enough, but that woman makes my mouth pucker. I stand up for my doctor."

"So I noticed." He grinned. "Thanks. I'm afraid you'll have to see Estelle one more time today, though, to get your personnel paperwork."

"Yvonne already gave it to me," Winifred said.

He understood Yvonne's urge to sign her up. "I'm afraid I've placed an unfair burden on her. She's been unhappy since I arrived."

"Well, she's happy now," Mrs. Waters said.

"I imagine so." Will would have hugged her, but it didn't seem dignified. "Welcome aboard."

"Yes, sir!"

A burden lifted from his shoulders. Walking past the business office a few minutes later, however, he observed Estelle scowling at her computer and decided he'd better mend fences.

Will stuck his head in. "I really am sorry about the pens. I'll buy you a pack myself."

She waved away the offer. "Don't bother. I got irritated and took it out on you. There're plenty of bigger headaches around here than a few missing pens." Hitting a key to close a file, she added, "We pay a company in Mill Valley to process our bookkeeping and billing, but every year, we get more forms to fill out. I can't believe how bad it is."

Will had heard the same complaint in Austin. "It's the insurance companies."

"Yes, and the school district switched to a new one this year," she grumbled. "You wouldn't believe how much information they expect. But Leah Morris ought to be pleased they expanded the maternity coverage."

He couldn't figure out what maternity coverage had to do with Leah. Feeling woolly-headed, Will said, "I don't think I quite followed that."

"Oh, that's right, she's teaching your girls, isn't she?" Estelle clicked open another file. "I suppose I shouldn't have said anything, but you *are* likely to end up treating her. Well, I'd better not complain about women's morals, not with Yvonne working here, but I'm kind of old-fashioned. Anyway, the whole town's going to find out as soon as she starts to show, aren't they?"

"That's usually how it works." That he managed to say anything sensible at all amazed Will. He'd better depart before she noticed his stunned reaction. "I'll see you later."

"You're on call from noon to 8:00 p.m. tomorrow, don't forget." She went back to glaring at the computer screen.

Will hurried to his office and closed the door.

Leah was pregnant.

Was it his? For Pete's sake, why hadn't she said anything?

She'd dropped a comment that went right past him the other night, about what a mess they'd made. He hadn't understood why she'd said that, until now.

Counting backward, he estimated the right amount of time had elapsed since they had spent the night together for her to have missed a period. And if Estelle was only now filling out the insurance form, Leah must have learned of her condition recently.

Will debated whether it would be improper to access her file and learn who she'd listed as the father. Probably, and, in any case, he decided against it. No matter what he might learn, he had to discuss this with her face-to-face.

Gulping in a series of breaths, he leaned against the desk and tried to grasp what the pregnancy would mean if he *was* the father. A huge nasty scandal, that's for sure. One that might hurt his girls.

He felt betrayed, more by fate than by Leah. He'd done his best to provide contraception. Sure, he'd forgotten the condom at first, but…

A baby. A child with Leah's dark hair and dazzling smile. Diane and India would be thrilled, but of course they wouldn't understand the possible repercussions. Right now, Will couldn't fully grasp them, either.

He was reaching for his phone when he realized he didn't have Leah's number. It must be in the computer somewhere, but now that he thought about it, he ought to sleep on the matter before confronting her.

Tomorrow, though, they were going to hash this out.

Chapter Six

"Take a good look in the mirror and tell me you're absolutely sure you want to do this," Rosie O'Bannon warned as she fastened one of the Snip 'N' Curl's cosmetic capes around her niece's neck. She herself wore a smock, a new addition to the salon's standard pink uniforms.

Against the light-green walls, the rosy color—chosen in honor of the proprietor's name—gave the place the air of a candy store. Otherwise, only a few blown-up photographs of clients softened the expanse of mirrors and bright lights.

"Aunt Rosie, I'm sure." Above a counter bristling with brushes and gels, Leah stared at the same old face she saw every morning, except for a slight flush that might derive either from pregnancy or from her decision to change her appearance.

It was eight-thirty on Saturday morning, half an hour before the beauty shop officially opened. Even so, the smell of dyes, nail polish and other witches' brews struck Leah more sharply than usual, thanks to her hormones.

She appreciated her aunt's willingness to come in early on a day so busy she'd been unable to book an appointment. For the moment, they had the place to themselves.

Jolene Ark, the other hair-cutter, would no doubt breeze in

at the last minute as usual. Helen Rios, the pregnant manicurist, opened her station at ten.

"You've worn it this way since you were a little girl," her aunt reminded her, fluffing the freshly washed dark hair that fell past her shoulders.

"Mark said the same thing!" Leah blurted. "I feel like I'm stuck in a time warp."

"My son would love for everybody to be stuck in a time warp," Rosie said ruefully. "I swear, that boy's as conservative as an old man!"

"And more conservative than some old women." Leah pictured the retired school principal, eighty-year-old Mae Anne McRay, who served on the city council and tutored underprivileged students.

"What he needs is a girlfriend." As she talked, Rosie eyed the magazine photo that displayed the style Leah had picked. "There's Amy Arroyo. If she ever did anything with her hair other than sticking it on top of her head, Mark might notice her."

"If she ever took her nose out of a book, she might notice *him*." Tall, angular Amy, the police chief's secretary, seemed perpetually out of sync with the world.

"Now let me concentrate," her aunt said. "If I'm busy chatting, I'll cut your ear off!"

Although accustomed to Rosie's exaggerations, Leah fell silent as the scissors scythed through her hair. Watching dark tresses drop to the floor, she told herself the hair would grow back. Of course, she might not want it to.

The chin-length style she'd chosen ought to be both practical and flattering. Most of all, it would mark a new stage in her life. Motherhood. Hopefully, a new job. And perhaps, a bit of delayed adolescent rebellion tossed into the mix.

In the mirror, she studied her hard-working aunt. With her hair dyed almost the same shade as Leah's, Rosie seemed ageless to her fond niece. Still, lines around the eyes and mouth testified to the hard work she'd put in during the ten years since a traffic accident had killed her husband, Mark Sr.

"Your hair's getting thicker," Rosie commented. "If I didn't know better, hon, I'd guess you were having a baby."

Leah hadn't realized her pregnancy would become evident this early. Perhaps she ought to confide in her aunt. If anyone had a right to the truth, it was her family.

And Will, an inner voice warned. Leah almost wished she'd told him about her pregnancy on Tuesday. But he'd been so infuriating!

"Well?" Rosie said. "I can take off more, if you want."

She'd stopped snipping. Staring at her reflection, Leah saw the transformation that had taken place.

Damp hair curved around her face like a bell. Although the style lacked the fullness she could expect once the hair dried, the shape gave her face a more sophisticated air.

"I love it!" she announced. "It looks great, and it'll be so much more practical after I have the—"

She stopped. She supposed she ought to ad-lib an end to that sentence to cover her slip. Her brain, however, refused to work fast enough. Besides, she had grown tired of pretending.

"After I have the baby," she concluded.

"You don't mean you're adopting, do you?" her aunt asked cautiously.

"You were right about the hair," Leah admitted.

Rose set aside the clippers. "I don't believe this. You, Leah?"

"You're the first person I've told," she admitted. "Please don't spread it around."

"Of course not." Rosie sank into the adjacent swivel seat. "Hon, I'm shocked. Don't take this the wrong way, but you've always been…"

"A Goody Two-Shoes?" Leah decided to forestall the

obvious question by breaking in her cover story. "While I was in Seattle, my friend told me about this doctor who does artificial insemination without a lot of red tape. My maternal instincts kicked in, I guess."

Her aunt blinked. "You mean, you—I mean—it's a test-tube baby?"

"Not exactly." Leah hadn't considered that she might have to explain the mechanics of the process. She'd need to look the procedure up on the Internet. "It wasn't grown in a lab, exactly. But, well, there you go."

Rosie shook her head. "Wow! I'm floored." She toyed with the edge of her smock. "Won't it be hard raising a kid alone? Of course, you can count on me to help! But the fact is—well, I wasn't sure I ought to tell you, but…"

Chimes tinkled as the front door opened. Gwen Martin, the café owner and organizer of the craft fair, poked her head inside. The steely gray bun she always wore made it obvious she didn't spend much time here as a client.

"I realize you're not open yet, but I broke my nail and I can't find a file anywhere," she said. "Do you think Helen would mind if I borrowed one of her implements for a teensy second?"

Her aunt's plump body tensed and her mouth formed a hard line, which startled Leah. Nothing in Gwen's manner indicated animosity, and Leah hadn't heard of any conflict between them. Still, given her aunt's soft spot for Pepe, his romance with Gwen must grate.

Her aunt recovered her aplomb. "I'll lend you my personal file." Briskly, she scooped her purse from a drawer. "If you use something of Helen's, she'll have to sterilize it."

"Oh, that's right. Thank you!"

While Gwen rasped away at the nail, Rosie activated the hair dryer, cutting off further discussion and attacking Leah's hair with uncharacteristic ferocity.

What had she been about to mention when they were interrupted? her niece wondered. It was difficult to imagine the usually outgoing woman harboring secrets.

By the time the dryer shut off, Gwen had called her thanks and departed, crossing paths with Jolene. Right behind her came two customers: school secretary Ellie Sanchez and Amelia Cornish. Amelia's husband owned Antiques Anew, a furniture-manufacturing company on the outskirts of town.

"Your hair!" Ellie cried, rushing over to Leah. "Gosh, it looks great, but everyone's going to be shocked."

In the glass, Leah's gaze met her aunt's. She guessed they shared the same reaction: that she had bigger shocks in store than a new hairstyle.

"Out with the old, in with the new," she told Ellie.

"Everybody loves you the way you are," the secretary responded. "We don't want you to change. Still, it's flattering."

"Thanks. You can give all the credit to Rosie." Arising, Leah removed the apron and insisted on paying, despite her aunt's halfhearted protest. "You did me enough of a favor by working me into your schedule."

"I was kind of hoping we could talk." Rosie patted her hand. "Never mind."

"I'll call you tonight."

"Oh, don't bother. We'll see each other soon enough."

Making a mental note to call her aunt anyway, Leah went out onto Grandpa Johnson Way. Vehicles packed the curb, and, from the end of the street, she heard the hubbub on The Green. People traveled as far as twenty miles to shop at the farmer's market.

To her annoyance, she spotted a produce truck double-parked in front of her car. The driver must be delivering goods, because he'd left the cab empty. There were no keys inside, either.

No use summoning a tow truck. The only one in town belonged to the Corner Garage, and by the time the owner took a break from his repair work and trundled over here, the offender would be long gone.

On the other hand, a quarter of an hour or more could pass before the truck liberated her car. Remembering her vow to exercise more, Leah decided to walk home, a distance of about a mile. She'd phone Karen, who lived nearby, to pick her up for their lunch engagement.

At least she wouldn't have to worry about finding a parking space near The Green at the busy noon hour, Leah decided, and set out for home.

She cut through the Café Montreal's jammed lot and crossed Home Boulevard midblock. While taking a shortcut between the fire department and the medical clinic, she noticed a maroon sedan parked behind the building, a type of low-key luxury car uncommon in Downhome.

With a start, Leah realized from the MD sticker and the Texas plates that the vehicle belonged to Will. The clinic opened for a half-day on Saturday, so she assumed he was working, although Jenni's car also filled its reserved spot.

She sped up her pace, hoping to clear the lot without attracting attention. Leah hadn't quite reached the far side when she heard the rear door open.

She couldn't help glancing back. A light breeze tousled Will's dark-blond hair as he emerged.

"Leah! I spotted you from my office." So his arrival wasn't by chance. "Where are you off to?"

"Home." She couldn't imagine why he'd bolted out. Surely, they'd said everything they had to say Tuesday.

"I'll give you a ride." The statement rang out like a command.

"Don't you have patients?" Leah grumbled. For heaven's sake, she ought to be able to walk home if she wanted to.

"I just stopped by to do some paperwork. I'm not on call

until noon." He beeped his car open. "I was heading for your house, anyway. Hop in."

"You were going to *my* house?" She felt stupid, repeating his words, but they'd caught her by surprise. Still, since the man obviously didn't intend to take no for an answer and the day was hotter than Leah had expected, she slid inside.

Thick, inviting cushions. A world-class sound system. The guy sure knew how to live. Leah had never cared much for fancy cars, but she appreciated the quiet elegance.

The motor hummed so softly Leah could scarcely hear it as Will threw one arm over the seat and, checking behind, eased into reverse. He'd dressed casually today, in slacks and a short-sleeved shirt that clung to his chest.

She inhaled his pleasing scent of lime and laundry soap. Being in his car and under his protection felt good.

Who was she kidding? Leah demanded silently. He wasn't protecting her. He was seizing control—an entirely different matter.

The car pulled onto Tulip Tree Avenue. "Why were you going to my house?" she asked.

"You did something with your hair." He had a disconcerting way of avoiding her inquiries.

"I cut it off."

He cast another look at her. "It's pretty. Why'd you do it?"

"Because I'm tired of being the same boring person I've been for thirty-two years." Usually, Leah expressed herself in a less-assertive manner, but around Will, she refused to soft-pedal her attitude. "I'm changing my life. I went to Austin to interview for jobs and I did the same in Seattle. It's time to move on. It's time for a new look, too."

They passed the Corner Garage. Judging by the clutter of vehicles awaiting repairs, Leah had guessed right about how long it would have taken to summon the tow truck.

"You're leaving Downhome?" Will frowned.

"As soon as I land a job." With no risk of running into him there, Leah supposed that she should feel free to accept one in Austin, but she'd fallen in love with the Rosewell Center.

"This business of seeking changes," he said. "Was I part of that?"

Through the windshield, the sun glinted off the silver watchband encircling his wrist as he gripped the steering wheel. Leah remembered how it had caught her eye at the bar, when he'd struck her as exotic and enticing.

Now she was driving through her hometown beside the man. Who could have foreseen it?

"Call it an experiment," she said. "One that blew up in my face. But don't worry. I can handle it."

"You sound ready to write me off." From his tone, she gathered he wasn't accustomed to being dismissed.

"I'm not the one who did the writing off. Or, rather, the riding into the sunset." She wasn't sure where this stubborn mood had come from. It certainly wasn't typical of the low-key Miss Morris.

"You're right. I have no claims on you." A more naive woman might have interpreted Will's tone as regretful. Not Leah. "But there's something you haven't told me that concerns me very much, whether you like it or not."

His words hung in the air, heavy with implications. *Oh, damn,* she thought. *He found out about the pregnancy.*

She supposed she should have expected as much, considering where he worked, but she resented the intrusion. "You read my file."

"Actually, no." Will swung onto Jackson Street. "Care to tell me where to turn next? Your street's somewhere around here…."

"Two blocks down on the right."

"Okay." He proceeded past a small neighborhood park, where lush green trees overhung meandering paths. "Estelle let it slip that she was filling out your insurance forms for maternity care."

After he turned, Leah pointed. "That's my house. As for the baby, don't worry about it. If you'd read the file, you'd be aware I was artificially inseminated at a clinic in Seattle."

Already having spoken the lie once this morning to Rosie, she supposed she ought to be used to it. It still felt wrong.

"You wouldn't object to a DNA test, then?" he asked.

Rats. She'd pegged Will for a take-charge guy, but she hadn't expected him to be this aggressive. "Why would you bother?"

"Let's go inside." He parked at the curb.

Leah didn't wait for him to help her out before hurrying to the porch. However, to her intense frustration, she couldn't get the key into the lock. Surely, she wasn't that nervous!

Will lifted the ring, isolated a different key and opened the door. She'd been using the one for her classroom.

Okay, so she was a little tense.

He studied the living room. "I like your decor. It's cheerful and straightforward. Like you."

"Thanks." Leah quashed the impulse to indicate a couple of special purchases she'd made on her travels. She hadn't invited him here to chitchat. Actually, she hadn't invited him at all. "You have something to say, so talk."

He strolled across the floor to admire a Persian-style carpet beneath the sofa. "It's eclectic, but it works."

"Will!"

He swung toward her. "The woman who made love to me in Austin was not cold-bloodedly planning to be inseminated. You can't expect me to buy that."

Since he'd threatened a DNA test, Leah decided against putting up a fight. "Okay, I invented that. It sounds better for public relations purposes and I figured you'd prefer being let off the hook."

As Will stood motionless, she imagined she could see his thoughts smashing against one another. Unfortunately, she couldn't read them.

"You put in your medical chart that you were artificially inseminated?" he asked at last.

Leah nodded. "That leaves you a free man. You can forget the whole thing, if you like. In fact, I *want* you to forget the whole thing."

His hands clenched. "Until what?"

She failed to grasp his meaning. "I don't understand."

"Leah, circumstances change, and so do people's minds. They misread their own emotions. One of these days, you might decide… Wait." Will raised his hands in a stop gesture, like a traffic cop. "I skipped the most important part. The baby."

Unbidden, her hand flew to her abdomen. She saw his gaze follow. "We'll be fine," she said. "I plan to move out of state. You won't even have to see him or her. Or me."

In a flash, Will crossed the room and gripped her shoulders just firmly enough to hold her in place. "Leah, I'm a father. I won't let my child to grow up without me. If this baby really is mine…"

"I thought we'd established that!" He had a lot of nerve.

Will released her. "We've established that you believe it's mine. If you're in the habit of picking up men in bars…"

Leah had never met anyone so infuriating. "If you're in the habit of picking up women in bars, you ought to be used to unplanned babies by now!"

Unwillingly, his mouth curved. "You sure are a spitfire."

Spitfire? Her? If she wasn't so angry, she might feel flattered. "I haven't slept with a man in ten years, okay? So there's no doubt. But if you'd prefer a DNA test, just steer me in the right direction."

He ducked his head. "Point taken." Will indicated the couch. "Let's sit down and do this the civilized way."

"Claw at each other until we both bleed?" Leah demanded.

He chuckled. "For some reason, you have a reputation as an angel come to earth. I can't understand it."

"You bring out my dark side." She sank into a chair. "Congratulations."

Will straddled the arm of the sofa. "Leah, I'll admit, you've thrown me for a loop. But there's a child's future at stake."

"I was having an adventure, and it's not over yet," Leah said. "Being pregnant doesn't make me a different person than I was before. And it doesn't make you different, either."

His gray eyes snapped with impatience. "We both know we ought to get married."

"You're kidding!" Leah had never heard of such a cold-blooded way of suggesting that a man and woman spend their lives together. If she'd fantasized about a loving proposal, he'd have shattered her dreams right there.

The truth was, it hurt. Just a little. Deep down, where she hadn't yet stopped being vulnerable to him.

"Look at it logically," Will persisted. "We're having a baby. My daughters adore you. We both have our reputations to protect. Plenty of people get married for worse reasons."

"How romantic!" Leah declared. "You talk about marriage as if it were a campaign tactic we should adopt to fool the voters. Well, I'm not running for office, and you're not my campaign manager, thank you!"

Will blinked, clearly disconcerted. "I didn't mean it that way."

His apology failed to soothe her outrage. The fact that she'd craved Will from the start and that in a way she still ached for his touch, only made her angrier.

"Let's set the record straight," Leah said. "I don't want to go on living in Downhome. I don't want to be Mrs. Dr. Rankin, and much as I like your little girls, I don't want to be their cookie-cutter stepmom."

If she could have bottled the emotions fleeting across his face, she could have sold them to Hollywood for a million bucks.

"What *do* you want?" he asked cautiously.

"Starts with an *A*," she prompted, just as she might prompt a child to spell *apple.*

He smacked one fist against his thigh. "I can't believe you're making light of this."

"I want wild, flaming, other-side-of-the-country adventure!" Leah snapped. "There's nothing frivolous about it. That's who I am. You took me for a pushover once. Well, I'm not."

His mouth clamped shut. He seemed to struggle for self-control before he said, "What about our child?"

Although tempted to declare that her child didn't need him, she knew that wasn't fair to the little one. "Once I get established in another city, you can visit," she conceded.

After launching himself to his feet, Will began to pace. "I don't accept that my relationship with our child will be subject to your whims."

"What are you going to do, sue me?" Leah refused to be intimidated.

"No." Will cleared his throat. "But I think we should negotiate terms."

"With a pair of lawyers?" she demanded.

Stiffly, he resumed his seat. "We can do it ourselves. But I'd like us to agree on specific terms in writing."

Although tempted to refuse, Leah could see the man wasn't going to retreat. In a way, she admired his determination to stay involved with their child.

Besides, he must have undergone a similar process with the twins and their mother. That meant he had some experience.

"Exactly how do you propose to do this?" she asked cautiously.

Will appeared to take her question as consent. "Let's keep it informal. We can both bring up whatever issues come to mind and I'll write down what we agree on."

"I suppose it can't hurt." At least this way, Leah supposed, the man would have no excuse to continually throw roadblocks in her path.

He produced a prescription pad and patted his pockets. "Sorry, I don't seem to have a pen."

Leah handed him one from her purse.

"You realize you may never get this back?" He gave her a shadow of a smile.

Responding to his pleasantry, she said, "I'll hunt you down."

"If you try it, I advise you to watch out for my nurse," he warned. "I hired one who moonlights as a bodyguard." After scratching on the pad to start the ink flowing, Will returned to the subject at hand. "I'll pay support, of course. We can work out the amount later."

Leah hadn't considered the financial angle. "All right."

"Also, I expect my name on the birth certificate as the baby's father."

"I can't agree to that!" She might as well arrange an ad in the newspaper announcing his paternity.

"It's not negotiable," Will told her. "This child didn't come from a sperm donor."

They could argue the point for hours. Suddenly, Leah felt exhausted. "Wait. I've got a lunch engagement with Karen and I need to rest. Can we finish this some other time?"

Will hesitated. Then, folding away the pad, he took out his personal organizer. "My housekeeper's leaving for Nashville tonight and returns on Monday, so the girls and I will have the house to ourselves. Why don't you join us for dinner tomorrow. I'll barbecue."

"We can't talk about this in front of them," Leah protested.

"Of course not. We can talk after they go to bed."

It sounded dangerously cozy. She eyed the man with suspicion, but if he was planning to try to change her mind about marriage, she detected no hint of it.

"I suppose so," she conceded. "I'm not crazy about the girls seeing us together, but if you're going to be involved with the baby, it's inevitable."

"Six o'clock, then." After tapping in the data, he added, "Leah, I have one request."

She cocked her head. "Yes?"

"Don't tell anyone the artificial insemination story, at least not until we've resolved these issues." He studied the pen and then, as if remembering where it came from, returned it to her.

It galled Leah to have to consider his wishes regarding her pregnancy, considering that Will had reentered the picture by chance. Still, he was behaving reasonably, she supposed.

"I won't spread it around, but I already mentioned it to my aunt," she said.

"Your aunt?"

"Rosie O'Bannon. She runs the Snip 'N' Curl," she explained. "My cousin Mark is on the police force. They're the only relatives I have around here."

"This cousin of yours doesn't have a hot temper to go with his gun, does he?" Will might have been teasing, but she wasn't sure.

"Not that I'm aware of." Leah walked him to the door. "Anyway, Rosie agreed not to mention my pregnancy to anyone, so Mark's temper shouldn't be a problem."

"Good." At the threshold, Will reached out for her. "I wish

we didn't have to be at odds over this. I meant what I said about getting married."

For a moment, Leah resisted his attempt to pull her toward him. But he felt so solid, and she loved the tenderness with which he gathered her to his chest.

She enjoyed the slight roughness of his throat and the way his cheek pressed against her hair. Oh, she did want to be near this man. Maybe it wasn't such a bad thing that he'd be visiting their child.

Impulsively, she stole a kiss. As his mouth moved against hers, a kind of enchantment flowed through Leah.

To pull away took all her resolve. "Bad idea," she said hoarsely.

"Not that bad," Will murmured. Yielding to the inevitable, he added, "I'll leave you to rest. But if you'll give your consent, I'd like to read your medical file. I want to make sure nothing is overlooked."

She supposed refusing the help of an expert would be foolish. "As long as Jenni doesn't mind. Remember, I haven't told her you're the father."

"She'll probably approve," he told her. "Well, I'll see you tomorrow night."

"Six o'clock." Leah didn't understand why she hated to let him go. After she closed the door, she leaned against it, missing him.

Her mystery man from Texas had been in her house. He'd kissed her again. He'd asked her to marry him.

She wondered how on earth they were going to work this out. One thing she knew for sure: if she didn't land the job in Seattle, she'd have to find one somewhere else.

Because she no longer trusted her own heart.

Chapter Seven

Will drove the five blocks to his house in a fog. He could still taste Leah's kiss on his lips, and he wanted more. Which was exactly how they'd landed in this situation in the first place.

A baby! She'd admitted it belonged to him. He'd scarcely had time to register the importance of that fact, but now memories flooded over him.

He recalled the nights of changing diapers, warming bottles and soothing crying infants. Despite his exhaustion, he'd found the experience exhilarating.

When he'd first gazed into his daughters' eyes, he connected with them in a way he'd never before experienced. He loved them more than his own life.

The one blessing that had sustained him through his miserable divorce had been Allison's willingness to give up the girls. By contrast, Leah clearly intended to keep him outside their child's—and her own—inner circle as much as possible.

Will didn't want a protracted legal fight. Nobody won in those cases except the lawyers. Moreover, he knew his actions that night in Austin might make it possible for her to portray him in court as little better than a sperm donor.

He intended to negotiate the best arrangement he could. Even if it fell short of ideal, things might change as the child grew and expressed a need for a father. Leah seemed both reasonable and caring, which made him hope she would put the little one's best interest above her negative feelings toward Will.

That she carried his baby made her all the more desirable. He pictured Leah's house again. With its bright colors and fresh mix of styles, it was so much like her. Had she agreed to marry him, she would have enlivened his home the same way.

For a while, perhaps. Then her dissatisfaction would have turned every conversation into an argument. He'd discovered how corrosive resentment could be, and he never wanted to go through such a situation again. She'd made her choice, and perhaps it was best for both of them.

And for the girls. Those two little scamps deserved his undivided attention, since in essence they had only one parent.

Will went inside, leaving his car in the driveway in case he had to go on call. No one was there, so he exited via the back and crossed the yard to Mrs. McNulty's small house.

Through the open door, he saw India and Diane playing dolls in the living room. Visible directly beyond them in the bedroom, the housekeeper was folding clothes into a suitcase on the bed.

"Dr. Rankin! Come in," she invited.

Each doll, he noticed as he entered, had its own valise. India was storing tiny clothes neatly inside, while Diane struggled to shut her case around the stuff she'd crammed in.

"I wish I had one of those jackets with sparkly stuff on it," the housekeeper called from the back. "I don't know who is going to be on this *Grand Ole Opry* tour. You suppose they'll dress up?"

"I have no idea." Will had never had the time or money to travel for pleasure. "By the way, how are you getting to Nashville?"

"I'll catch a bus from town," she responded. "It connects with the tour terminal."

"Sounds perfect." That his housekeeper had found an outing to her liking pleased Will. He wanted her to enjoy their new surroundings. "Where are you staying?"

She gave him the name of the hotel. "I'm sharing a room with another lady, a complete stranger. I hope she doesn't snore!"

"Bring earplugs," he advised. "You want me to find some for you?"

"No need. I've got a set somewhere. Thanks, Doctor!" She mostly stuck to his formal title, although he'd assured her it wasn't necessary.

Will eased onto the floor between the girls. "I'm on call until bedtime, but we'll have all day tomorrow together."

"Can we go to Nick's house?" India asked.

"I'd rather visit Sybill!" Diane piped up.

Will still hadn't mastered the art of balancing the pixies' social lives. "Mrs. McNulty's the expert at figuring out how to schedule these things. But maybe we'll see them both in church in the morning, okay?" They nodded. "Also, I've invited a guest for dinner tonight."

"Who's cooking?" Diane went right to the important part—in her view, anyway.

"I am," Will said. "Something wrong with that?"

"Steak, corn and baked potatoes?" his daughter demanded.

He gave an exaggerated sigh. "That's all I can cook. I was hoping you wouldn't notice."

"You can make spaghetti," India pointed out.

"I already told Miss Morris we were going to barbecue," he said.

Two pairs of gray-blue eyes lit with excitement. Their whoops brought the housekeeper to the front. When she heard the cause of the uproar, she cast a wise smile in Will's direction and retreated again.

He doubted she'd figured out who his guest was last Tuesday. Still, she must have encountered Leah when she'd picked up the girls at school, and Miss Morris obviously met with her approval.

There was no way he and Leah were going to be able to keep their—what was it? "friendship?"—a secret for long. In any event, the girls would have found out at dinner, and they couldn't be expected to withhold that kind of information from their caregiver.

He did hope to prevent them from spreading the news all over school. What an uproar that would create!

"Will Miss Morris read us a bedtime story?" India asked.

"I'm sure she'd be happy to," Will said. "Now I have a request for you two."

They regarded him curiously.

"I'm sure you'll want to tell all your friends how Miss Morris came for dinner," he said, "but they might not think it's fair. If she has to go to everybody else's house for dinner, she won't have time to come here again."

He supposed that wasn't a very straightforward approach. But trying to explain the value of discretion so six-year-olds could understand—while, at the same time, not giving Eileen any more ideas than she already had—surpassed Will's creative ability.

"We can't tell our friends?" India asked, clearly disappointed.

"Not right now." Okay, maybe he did owe them more of an explanation. Will tried again. "Listen, we're living in a small town. It's not like Austin. Here, everybody knows everybody, and they talk a lot."

"I like to talk!" Diane said. "So does Sybill. Her dad's the city manager!"

"Really? Well, it's okay to discuss most things, but everyone's entitled to privacy." Receiving no reaction, he said, "You wouldn't want the whole town to find out how long you spend in the bathtub, would you?"

India looked indignant.

"Or that you have kitty cats on your underwear, right?"

Diane made a face.

"Well, Miss Morris should be able to visit us without making her other students feel that she's ignoring them," he said. "She has a right to spend her free time any way she chooses."

"I like privacy," India agreed. "I don't want people to talk about me."

"Has anyone been talking about you?" Will had learned that conversational hints often provided insight into the girls' lives.

"No," India said.

"Yes, because you have a boyfriend!" her twin retorted.

"I do not!"

Apparently, India's friendship with Nick had drawn teasing. "You're too young to have a boyfriend," he told her. "But it's okay to have a boy who's a friend."

"That's right." India narrowed her eyes at her sister.

"Well?" Will interjected. "What do you say? Can we keep Miss Morris's visit to ourselves?"

Both girls agreed. "I can keep a secret," Diane added for emphasis. "Sybill tells me secrets all the time."

Mrs. McNulty poked her head in. "I can keep things under my hat, too. Which reminds me. Maybe I'll buy a cowboy hat while I'm in Nashville." With a wink, she returned to her packing.

"Daddy, your face looks red," India told him.

"He's blushing," her sister said.

That made his cheeks grow even hotter. "Men don't blush," Will told them. "It must be the light."

"Uh-huh!" Diane struck a skeptical attitude like one of her favorite characters on a sitcom.

Since he hadn't started dating again in Austin, Will hadn't had to deal with these matters before. He supposed he should have anticipated a bit of awkwardness around his daughters and housekeeper. The problem, to paraphrase Leah, started with a *B*.

For baby.

In his pocket, the phone rang. Expecting to hear the service that handled off-hours calls for the clinic, Will was less than pleased when his ex-wife's voice rang in his ear, and she barely greeted him before demanding to speak to the children.

Allison's carping tone still had the power to irk him. Striving to rein his temper, he allowed her to talk to the girls, who, mercifully, stuck to such topics as their new friends and school. No mention of a visit from their teacher tomorrow night.

When they were done, Will took the phone across the yard into the main house. He had no desire for his children to hear the rest of the call, if it proved typical.

He'd met Allison eight years earlier when he'd interned at the hospital where she worked as a nurse. She'd become his girlfriend and his mainstay during that difficult year, helping with advice and massages. He'd clung to her support as he put in long hours and struggled to pay the massive student loans hanging over his head.

At the end of the year, Allison had given him an ultimatum: marriage or a breakup. Unable to imagine life without her, he'd agreed, but their dating experience hadn't prepared him for marriage.

Illogically, Allison had expected life with a doctor to mean a high income, status and an end to grinding shifts at work.

She'd become impatient during his residency, and as soon as his income rose slightly, she'd insisted on quitting to have a baby.

Despite misgivings, Will had looked forward to becoming a father, and had hoped motherhood would relieve Allison's perpetual dissatisfaction. Instead, it did the opposite. Twins were a surprise, although a welcome one to him. However, his wife hadn't counted on the extra burden, especially since their tight budget didn't allow for much housekeeping aid.

When the girls entered preschool, she'd returned to work. Will felt guilty about it, but his salary couldn't cover their rising expenses and the loan payments. Although he'd done his best to help around the house, Allison had seemed more irritated by his occasional goofs than pleased by his efforts.

A year later, she'd announced she was leaving him for a wealthy former patient, an older guy who'd promised to maintain her in luxury. She'd flung her infidelity at Will with an air of triumph.

Allison's decision to leave him the girls because her lover didn't want to be tied down had mitigated Will's anger at the betrayal. Determined not to create unnecessary ill will, he'd let his wife go without a fight. He hadn't suggested counseling because by then there didn't appear to be anything worth saving.

She'd sworn she planned to remain involved. Unfortunately, she believed that entitled her to drop in without warning and to criticize every move Will made. She also upset the girls by changing her plans at the last minute to suit her boyfriend's whims.

Will hadn't chosen to move to Tennessee in order to put a gap between his little family and their errant mother. Still, he considered the distance a bonus.

At first, he'd feared Allison would oppose him. She might

have, too, had her lover, Brad, not been openly pleased. He'd taken her on a trip to Paris and Rome to salve her maternal instincts, at least temporarily.

Will tuned back in to her words as she announced, "I called to inform you we're getting married. I want India and Diane to be my flower girls."

"When is this big event?" If she scheduled it near Christmas, he could combine the trip with a holiday visit to his parents.

"A week from Saturday," came the stunning response. "I realize that's short notice, but Brad's so impulsive! He's got a wedding planner working day and night."

She seemed to think she could snap her fingers and disrupt their schedules whenever it suited her. "I can't possibly get away. I just started a new position."

"Put them on a plane. I checked with the airlines and six-year-olds can travel unaccompanied," his ex-wife returned. "The flight attendant will watch them. And before you start arguing, don't forget you're the one who moved out of state."

"These girls are not flying to Texas unaccompanied." The idea of entrusting his kids to total strangers outraged Will. "And they're in school now. They can't just pick up and miss class whenever it suits you."

"First grade!" she scoffed. "They can easily skip a few days."

He tried a different tack. "They'll need supervision while they're in Austin. Are you telling me this child-hating fiancé of yours won't mind you devoting yourself to your daughters during all the festivities?"

"He doesn't hate children! He has two grown kids of his own!" Allison protested. "Listen, it's going to be a huge wedding. His whole family and business associates and a lot of other important people will be there. How will it look if my own daughters aren't part of my big day?"

Will nearly choked. "That's what this is about? You want

to drag India and Diane halfway across the continent for the sake of appearances? Forget it."

"You have no right to refuse!"

"I have every right. You signed away custody," he reminded her. "End of story."

Maybe that wasn't the wisest tactic in the world. Still, he found his ex-wife's arrogance infuriating.

On the other end of the line, Allison sounded as if she were performing breathing exercises. A considerable amount of huffing ensued before she spoke again.

"I didn't put that very well," she said. "I want my daughters to be part of the ceremony, so they'll understand I'm really not abandoning them. How do you think they'd feel if I walked down the aisle and they weren't part of it?"

Despite his resentment over the way his ex-wife had treated him, it was important for India and Diane to have the assurance of their mother's love. Plus, the twins would adore dressing up as flower girls.

"E-mail me the dates," he said. "I'll ask my housekeeper if she's available to travel with them." If Mrs. McNulty agreed, it would solve a lot of problems.

"You don't think missing a few days of first grade will interfere with their future SAT scores?" His ex-wife's teasing had an edge, but Will understood her well enough to recognize an attempt to smooth over their quarrel.

"I'm sure they'll do fine." An insistent beeping distracted him. "It's my pager. I'm on call."

"As usual," she grumbled. He wondered, fleetingly, what she'd expected when she married a doctor. "Well, okay. I'm glad we sorted this out. I hope you're enjoying your new town. What's it called again? Hoedown?"

"Downhome." He suspected she knew that perfectly well. "Allison, I've got to go."

"Ciao," she said and clicked off. She'd been tossing around foreign words since her trip to Europe.

After glancing at his pager, Will phoned the service. "A woman collapsed at the farmers' market on The Green," the dispatcher said.

This could be serious. "Does she have a heart condition?" In emergencies, depending on the severity, either the fire department could transport her to Mill Valley or a helicopter would take her to Vanderbilt University Medical Center in Nashville.

"Not as far as anyone knows." The dispatcher recited the woman's vitals: forty-seven years old, no chronic illnesses, conscious and able to talk. She showed none of the pain, shortness of breath or other symptoms that might be associated with a myocardial infarction. "Frankly, she's trying to pooh-pooh the whole thing, but her son works for the police department and considers it a big deal."

Will got a funny feeling about this. "What's her name?"

"Rosie O'Bannon."

Leah's aunt. "I'm on my way," he said, and hurried outside to tell Mrs. McNulty he was leaving.

THANK GOODNESS he had a parking space at the clinic, Will mused as he strode across Home Boulevard. With vehicles crammed together throughout the downtown area, he'd otherwise have had to double-park.

The usually placid square of greenery bristled with booths and a large crowd of shoppers. Under other circumstances, Will might have taken an interest in the tables of fresh produce and stalls of handicrafts, but today they'd become obstacles in his path.

The dispatcher had said the victim was sitting on a bench near a large dogwood tree. The problem, he reflected as he dodged through the maze, was that the trees didn't wear their showy pink and white blossoms in the fall. Will's farm-honed expertise with trees extended only as far as distinguishing a grapefruit from a pecan.

Amid the hubbub, one face leaped to his attention: Leah's. She sat on a bench, talking worriedly with a plump, middle-aged woman in a pink smock. Behind them paced a young, uniformed officer with the same striking dark hair and vivid blue eyes as his mother and cousin.

Will set a course in their direction, careful not to bowl over a couple of children who raced across his path. As he drew closer, he heard the woman in the smock say, "I have to get back to my clients. My gosh, I left Eunice under the dryer!"

Leah caught sight of Will. "Thank goodness!" To the policeman, she explained, "It's the doctor."

"About time," he grumbled. "I was ready to call the fire department."

Will wasn't offended. "If you considered the situation an emergency, you should have done that."

"It's nothing," said the lady on the bench. "Honestly, I should go back to work."

"I'll tell the salon to let Jolene know what's happened," Karen Lowell said from behind Leah, where Will hadn't noticed her before. "Don't you worry about a thing, Rosie."

Ignoring passersby who gathered to watch as if this were a show, Will began checking the patient. She had a soft, sweet face and a warm smile that made him like her at once. "Mrs. O'Bannon, I'm Dr. Rankin," he said as he finished measuring her pulse. Her heart rate and blood pressure were only slightly elevated. "Can you tell me—"

"Oh, my gosh! Dr. Rankin! I was wondering who you were!" The woman's suddenly shrill voice silenced the onlookers. "Mark, you called the obstetrician! How did you know I was pregnant?"

Mark O'Bannon regarded his mother with full-out astonishment. After several twitches of the jaw, he managed to say, "What?"

Will remembered the dispatcher's having given the patient's age as forty-seven. That was a tricky age for a pregnancy, even considering that she'd obviously had at least one previous child. "How many months along are you, Mrs. O'Bannon?"

"About three," she said faintly.

"Can you tell me what happened?" Despite her alertness, the word *collapsed* could mean anything from a dizzy spell to loss of consciousness.

"It was last May," she blurted. "I volunteered to help Pepe clean up one night at the restaurant after his helper got sick. I guess we drank too much wine, because afterward we went upstairs to his apartment and that's where we did it!"

Although this unexpected confession startled Will, that was nothing compared with Mark's reaction. In a voice that could surely be heard halfway across town, he roared, "Pepe? Pepe got you pregnant?"

Will had to admit to a sneaking sympathy for the fellow who'd inspired this outrage and who might have no idea he was about to become a father. In any case, if he was lurking in the park, he failed to put an appearance.

"I'm a grown woman!" Rosie proclaimed. "I can sleep with whomever I want to!"

"You're too old to be having a baby!" her son snapped. "What were you thinking?"

Attempting to steer things in a more productive course, Will said, "Mrs. O'Bannon, I meant what happened a few minutes ago? Did you black out?"

Leah answered for her. "She was hurrying down the path, going to fetch some lunch during a break, when she turned pale and had to sit down. It's a good thing Karen and I spotted her."

"I've been on my feet too long, that's the problem," the patient said.

"You may be right. It's a hot day," Will said. "Mrs. O'Bannon, have you seen a doctor about your pregnancy?"

She shook her head. "I tried one of those home pregnancy tests you buy at the drugstore."

"I'd like to examine you at the clinic," he told her. "Your son is correct about one thing. At your age, the pregnancy will require careful monitoring."

"I never had any problems with my last one!" she said.

Mark scowled. "That was twenty-eight years ago!"

The two of them didn't speak so much as they shouted, making Will feel as if he were stuck in the middle of a debating contest. "There are a number of problems that can crop up. However, with proper care, you should be fine."

"I'll come with you." Leah took her aunt's hand. "Do you feel well enough to walk?"

"Of course!" Rosie replied.

"Don't get up too fast," Leah warned. "That could make you dizzy again."

Will appreciated the way her calm manner steadied her aunt. Even her cousin subsided.

"I suppose it won't be so bad." Hanging on to her niece, Mrs. O'Bannon got to her feet. "We can be pregnant together!"

Mark blinked as if he couldn't have heard correctly. Karen, who'd returned from calling the salon, dropped her cell phone. Nearby, other people exchanged startled glances.

Well, that let the cat out of the bag, Will thought resignedly.

Realizing she'd revealed a secret, Rosie added, "I'm glad I didn't have artificial insemination the way you did, Leah. You should have done it the fun way!"

Will ducked his head to hide a smile. Although he'd have

preferred to keep both the pregnancy and the invented story under wraps, the woman's manner tickled him.

After smoothing his features, he extended an arm to the patient. "Shall we go?"

She gripped him. "Why not? As long as we're putting on a show, let's have a parade!"

When the crowd parted in front of them, Rosie held her head high. Still, as they marched out of the park, Will heard a hum of conversation rise behind them like a swarm of bees.

Chapter Eight

If she wrote her memoirs years from now, Leah thought, that scene at the farmers' market might sound hilarious. At the moment, however, she only hoped that by then her cheeks would stop flaming and she would no longer feel an urge to sink into the ground.

However unintentionally, her aunt had humiliated her in front of half the town. The other half would hear about it before the weekend was over.

She, Mark and Karen found seats in the waiting room at the otherwise deserted clinic. As soon as Will and Rosie disappeared into the interior, Mark began fuming aloud.

"This is inexcusable. What a blot on the family name!" He scowled. "My middle-aged mother acting like a…like a…"

"Human being?" Karen ventured.

"Never mind," he said. "And you!" He glared at Leah. "What were *you* thinking? Artificial insemination!"

He had a lot of nerve judging her. "Butt out, Mark."

Behind his back, Karen gave her a thumbs-up sign.

"Excuse me?" Mark glared at his usually meek cousin.

"*B-U-T-T* out." Leah derived as much satisfaction from spelling the phrase as any of her students might have done—not that she would encourage them to use such coarse language.

"What's gotten into you?" he demanded.

"You can fuss at your mother all you like, although I suspect her tolerance will be limited," she replied. "But the choices I make are none of your business."

"I happen to be the man of the family!" Perhaps recalling that her father was still alive, Mark added, "In this town, anyway."

Karen made a face at his back. She had zero tolerance for machismo, although the good sense not to intervene in a family argument.

"Then it's lucky that I'm planning to move!" When she saw his jaw working as if about to spew a reprimand, Leah added, "Don't make me repeat the part about butting out, okay?"

"I'm only trying to do what's right," her cousin muttered.

She yielded to a sympathetic impulse. After all, in view of the unexpected circumstances, he could be forgiven a certain amount of bluster. "You know what?" Leah said. "There is something we both need from you."

"What's that?" Mark asked warily.

"Your love and support," she told him. "As you said, you *are* the man of the family around here. That means a lot, especially to Rosie."

Reluctantly, he conceded the point. "I'll do what I can. It really frosts me about Pepe, though. He knocked up my mom and now he's dating Gwen!"

Karen spoke up at last. "Rosie may not have told him she's pregnant."

"Besides, they're all grown-ups," Leah added. "Let them sort it out."

"If you ask me, they're acting more like spoiled brats," Mark retorted.

He broke off as an unfamiliar woman barged through the front door, dressed in a blue nurse's uniform. Before any of them could speak, she addressed them with an air of authority.

"You folks must be the family. Don't you fret now. Dr. Rankin's the best there is," she announced. "I'm Winifred Waters. I always listen to the police scanner when my doctor is on call. When I heard he had a case, I came right over."

Mrs. Waters clearly regarded her work seriously. "We appreciate it," Leah said. "I believe he's examining my aunt as we speak."

"Well, then, I'll go make myself useful." The nurse vanished through the inner door.

"She's efficient," Karen said. Mark nodded his approval.

Silence fell over the room. Although it was welcome after her cousin's storming, it left Leah alone with her thoughts.

She'd admired Will's quiet air of assurance at the park, and how he'd kept his focus on Rosie despite the crowd and the hot tempers flaring around him. The doctor's steady manner had calmed Leah's fears for her aunt almost immediately.

Much as it irked her to admit it, he'd kept a cool head at her house earlier, as well, although his emotions had obviously been strained. He'd adopted a levelheaded approach to the touchy issue of staying involved with his child, except for that ridiculous idea of getting married purely for convenience.

Painfully, she admitted that a part of her wished he'd really meant it. A few times, she'd caught a hint in his expression that perhaps he did, but then, just as quickly, he'd backed off. She didn't understand why sometimes Will reached out to her and other times he pushed her away.

Just like in Austin. Leah sighed. The pattern he'd set that night appeared to extend into the rest of his life, as well. She had no idea what to expect when they went one-on-one tomorrow night at his house.

Mark stood up. "I have to get back to work. Tell Mom I waited as long as I could." Although as a lieutenant he usually supervised others, he filled in on patrol during busy days.

"Okay. I'll stick around in case she needs me." As he stalked out of the room, Leah relaxed a little. At least, things were calming down.

Her relief proved short-lived. No sooner had the clinic's glass door swung shut behind him than Karen demanded, "When were you planning to tell me about your pregnancy? I felt really out of the loop."

Leah studied the pastel stripes on the wallpaper as if she found them fascinating. "I meant to bring it up at lunch today, as a matter of fact." That was true, although time had skimmed by without her finding a way to broach the subject.

"You had artificial insemination while you were out of town interviewing for jobs?" Karen probed. "Why does this strike me as unlikely?"

"Just accept it, okay?" Leah hated not telling her the whole story, but she felt awkward enough already.

Her friend regarded her with keen hazel eyes. "It isn't like you in any way, shape or form. I understood you longed for excitement, but…" The sentence trailed off. "I got it."

"Got what?" Leah held her breath.

"You went to bed with a guy!" Karen challenged. "On your trip. Didn't you?"

No use denying it. She gave a slow nod.

"Does he know about the baby?"

Another nod. Reluctantly.

Her friend poked her. "Don't make me drag this out of you! What's he going to do?"

"He asked me to marry him, but it's a terrible idea," Leah said, "so leave it alone."

No such luck. "Where'd you meet him?" Karen probed. "Who is he? I mean, you couldn't have been acquainted for very long before you…did it. How wild!"

"How stupid," Leah corrected.

"You can't tell me he's a dork!" Karen appeared more upset about that possibility than about the other insane things Leah had done. "You didn't pick just *any* guy?"

"Of course not." She had to bite her tongue, literally, to keep from saying more.

"Who else have you told?" Karen probed. "Jenni?"

Leah's head bobbed.

"Is Dr. Rankin going to treat you?" The other woman was eager for every last detail. Leah didn't blame her. She'd have been equally curious had their roles been reversed.

"I'm sticking with Jenni." Realizing they were entering a danger zone, Leah prayed for Mrs. Waters to come marching in and order her to assist her aunt. Or for Karen to remember some urgent reason to leave.

"Much as I love Jenni, you ought to take advantage of having a specialist," her friend advised. "He really seems wonderful…. No!"

Leah peeked at her. Karen had always been perceptive, but surely she couldn't put two and two together that fast.

"The Wayward Drummer." The name of the Austin bar emerged in a Voice of Doom.

Oh, rats, Leah thought, and buried her face in her hands. She didn't dare argue.

Karen didn't wait for confirmation. "It had to be you and Will!" After a beat to absorb this discovery, she added, "I'll bet he was great, huh? I mean, he's really cute."

"Argh." Leah couldn't find anything else to say.

Her friend wasn't finished—not by a long shot. "Wow! The two of you—I can't even think about it! Yes, I can! Tell me more. I mean, you guys did plan to see each other again, right?"

She might as well get this over with. "When I woke up the next morning, he was gone. No note, no phone number, nothing."

"I can't believe it!"

"Can we drop this now?" Leah asked miserably.

"But you said he asked you to marry him," Karen persisted. "That was decent."

"Damn decent," remarked a masculine voice from the front counter.

Both women peered guiltily. Will studied them with one eyebrow raised. In a white coat, with a stethoscope around his neck, he looked every inch the MD—and thoroughly desirable.

For the second time in less than an hour, Leah felt acutely embarrassed. How much had he overheard?

"Don't blame her," Karen said. "I guessed."

"I assume you understand the reasons we want to keep this private," he said. "Right?"

"Absolutely." Karen stood up. "I'll leave you folks now. Hey, since I'm the one who sort of introduced you by telling Leah about the bar, can I be the baby's godmother?" Without waiting for an answer, she hurried out.

Leah took a deep breath and faced Will. "I'm sorry. She really did figure it out on her own."

He refrained from comment. "Your aunt would like you to be part of our discussion. Why don't you join us in back?"

Despite the humiliation of being caught, Leah was glad he hadn't sent his nurse. She didn't care to consider what the overpowering Nurse Waters might do if she learned her doctor's honor had been compromised.

Will held the inner door. As she walked by him, Leah hesitated. Something about the man drew her, even though she was determined not to yield.

He must have felt the same way, because he slipped his arms around her. "What is it about you?" he murmured. "I can't… Oh, the hell with it." He kissed her.

Pinpricks of fire lit across Leah's skin. The same heat he'd aroused that steamy night in Texas raged again, and, for one delirious moment, she pressed against him. The hint of teeth behind his deepening kiss nearly made her forget where they were.

Will moved away reluctantly. "You do something to me that I don't understand."

It seemed obvious to Leah. "It's sex."

"I've had sex before. It didn't make me lose control in inappropriate circumstances." As if becoming aware of how much risk they ran of discovery, Will added under his voice, "It's better if we don't dwell on it."

"Maybe it'll go away on its own, like a head cold," Leah suggested.

He chuckled. "Something like that."

They cut through the center of the building to his private office, where Rosie was waiting. As they approached, Mrs. Waters's voice carried to them.

"Don't you worry, Mrs. O'Bannon. You've got friends and relatives and you can count on me and the Doc! You're going to do just fine."

Will and Leah exchanged a smile at the nurse's warmhearted assurance. "I hit the jackpot when I hired her," he murmured.

"She's a gem," Leah agreed.

They entered to find Rosie sitting on the couch, hands clutched in her lap like a schoolgirl at the principal's office. After giving them a nod, the nurse departed.

"How's Mark's reaction?" Rosie asked as soon as she saw Leah.

"He went back to work." She eased into the seat beside her aunt. Now that she knew about the older woman's pregnancy, Leah could clearly detect a bulge beneath the pink smock. "Mostly he seems angry at Pepe."

"I can't imagine what we were thinking!" Rosie shook her

head. "Actually, I guess we weren't thinking at all— But it breaks my heart every time I see him and Gwen together."

The fact that the two were dating still struck Leah as odd. Gwen had never shown the slightest interest in Pepe until now. Quite the opposite, they'd been more rivals than friends.

Although born in Downhome, the never-married café owner had worked as an artist's model in Paris before pursuing a career as a chef. Ten years older than Pepe, she'd treated his longing gazes as a mild joke, although Leah supposed the two did have a lot in common. Pepe, who was of Italian descent, had moved to the U.S. from Argentina while in his teens, so the pair shared both international backgrounds and their love of cooking.

Then it came to her. "I'll bet I can guess what happened," Leah said.

"What?" Rosie demanded. Will stood observing the two of them with bemused curiosity.

"Pepe's had a crush on Gwen for years, but she's had a crush on Ethan Forrest." Ethan, a widower a good twenty years Gwen's junior, had returned from Nashville four years ago to become the chief of police. Leah hadn't missed the way Gwen joked with him when he dined at the café. "She must have realized she didn't have a chance, but at least he didn't belong to anyone else. Now he's marrying Jenni. I'll bet she started dating Pepe on the rebound."

Will turned a chair backward and sat down. "If this gets any more complicated, I may have to ask you to draw a diagram."

Rosie sniffed. "You don't suppose she's serious about him, do you?"

"I think she's putting up with Pepe out of loneliness," Leah said. "Once she learns about you and him, she'll toss him on his rump."

"That doesn't mean he'll run back to me." Pulling a tissue

from her purse, Rosie blew her nose. "He's got three grown kids. What will *they* say? He won't want anything to do with me!"

"Mrs. O'Bannon, believe me, a father isn't going to turn his back on his own baby if he's worth his salt," Will added.

Rosie dabbed at her eyes. "I don't know."

Leah decided not to add any assurances, since she had no idea what Pepe might do. "I'm going to drive you home," she said. "We'll have tea and compare our aches and pains, and you'll feel much better."

Rosie sprang to her feet. "I can't! Oh, my gosh, I have to get back to the salon!"

"Whoa!" Will rose quickly. "Mrs. O'Bannon, you're under doctor's orders to rest. You had a dizzy spell today, remember? Pregnancy's hard enough on a woman's body when she's young. I don't want you developing hypertension or any other complications."

"But my clients need me!"

Leah got an inspiration. "You know what I'm going to do? I'm going to call Elsie Ledbetter." The former owner of the Snip 'N' Curl might be in her seventies, but she has remained actively involved with the community center. "I'll bet she'd be tickled at the chance to get back in the saddle."

Rosie hesitated only briefly. "I don't suppose the customers would mind. Some of them still talk about her."

Will signaled his approval. "Mrs. O'Bannon, it's going to be important at least for the next few weeks that you keep off your feet as much as possible. Depending on how you feel, you may be able to work part-time after that, but don't push too hard."

"I won't." Rosie beamed at the doctor. "You are the most wonderful man! Leah, I can't tell you how kind he is, and how he explained every detail of what's happening to me. When I got pregnant with Mark, my doctor hardly told me anything."

"Please don't forget to call on Monday and schedule your

ultrasound," Will told her. "We can shoot a baby picture before you even give birth. I'll bet you didn't have one of those with your first child."

"Oh, thank you!" Rose disposed of the tissue. "It is exciting in a lot of ways. Leah, our babies can play together. That reminds me, I'm sorry I blabbed about your pregnancy. It was a secret, wasn't it?"

"Not anymore," Leah said dryly. "Well, never mind. What's done is done." The reminder of the public's curiosity raised another concern, however. "Rosie, I'd like to have a private word with Dr. Rankin, if you don't mind."

"Of course, dear." Her aunt smiled fondly. "I'll be in the waiting room."

After she left, Will glanced both ways down the hall before closing the door. Leah appreciated his caution.

"Your aunt's a delightful person," he said. "Now, what can I do for you?"

She edged toward the window, deliberately putting space between them. Being near Will tended to distract her. "Maybe it's not a good idea for me to stop by your house tomorrow night. The girls are likely to mention it in class and people might connect the dots the way Karen did."

She wasn't eager to become the subject of even more gossip. Already, she dreaded the wagging tongues she would encounter at school on Monday.

"I did my best to persuade the twins to keep it secret," Will said. "Leah, we *need* to make decisions about the baby. Also, I'd appreciate your opinion on an important matter involving my daughters. I trust your judgment and, frankly, I don't know who else to ask."

When he put it like that, Leah could hardly say no. Besides, regardless of her reservations, they did have to work out certain issues.

She gripped her purse strap. "All right. But we'll keep it strictly business."

"Believe me, with my girls in the next room, I wouldn't have it any other way," he said. "And Leah?"

She caught her breath. "Yes?"

"Hang tough with your aunt," he advised. "She's the kind of person who worries about everyone except herself. She'll listen to you."

"I'll do my best." His concern for Rosie touched Leah.

"Six o'clock," Will added. "I'm counting on you."

"I won't let you down." Her thoughts in a whirl, she scooted out the door and nearly collided with Mrs. Waters.

"You all right, child?" the woman asked. "What did the doctor tell you?"

"He considers you an absolute jewel," Leah said, unable to think of anything else.

The nurse's pleased grin made her feel much better.

Chapter Nine

Taking the girls to church on Sunday morning proved a more daunting experience than Will had anticipated. News of Rosie's and Leah's pregnancies had spread like an epidemic, and he couldn't avoid hearing gossip.

Unlike in Austin, where he knew most of his fellow congregants only by sight, people kept approaching him before the service to say hello. Some were patients or parents of his daughters' classmates, and others were simply townsfolk wanting to welcome him.

Mrs. O'Bannon arrived with her head held high. She was accompanied by her son and an elderly couple, whom she introduced to Will as Elsie and Joe Ledbetter. The former salon owner had evidently come to Rosie's rescue in more ways than one.

As far as Will could tell, there was no sign of Pepe Otero or Gwen Martin. Or of Leah.

He wondered whether she'd been sidelined by morning sickness or by a desire to avoid attention. If that was the case, he regretted it. He hadn't meant to cause her discomfort.

In a situation like this, she ought to let him stand by her, Will reflected as he watched his daughters skipping about the foyer with some of their friends. If he and Leah got married, it would simplify matters, at least socially.

The trouble was, he had to admit that he found relationships mystifying. He still didn't comprehend where he'd gone wrong with Allison, and even sunny Leah had accused him of bringing out her dark side.

Yet the idea of her moving away tore at him. He needed her close by. Why couldn't she stay?

He lost his train of thought as Winifred entered and presented her daughter, Freda, and two toddler grandsons. Several patients approached also—eager for him to meet their husbands and, in a couple of cases, their flirtatious single girlfriends.

Grateful not to have to interject more than a few words here and there, Will listened politely and considered the difference between this experience and his occasional youthful forays to church with his parents. Like the handful of other ranchers present, the Rankins had dressed differently from the townspeople, talked differently and stayed pretty much to themselves. Even his usually rowdy brothers had clammed up in public.

After a while, Will had no longer fit in at the ranch, yet around city folks, he'd needed years to get over pretending to be someone he wasn't. His acute sense of isolation had accompanied him through college and medical school.

Here, people welcomed him freely. All the same, he wished Leah had attended. Just observing her across a room always lifted his spirits.

"Doc!" called a crusty fellow he'd met on his first visit to Downhome. Grocery store owner Beau Johnson served on the City Council, which had approved Will's hiring. "I'd like to hear your opinion on of all these loose women we have around here."

Before he could proceed, Estelle joined them. "Beau, you may not realize it, but your voice carries."

"I don't care who hears me!" the elderly man trumpeted.

"I disapproved when my niece did it, and I think Rosie did wrong. But I want the doctor's opinion about this artificial insemination stuff. You tell me, Doc. Is that immoral?"

The entire foyer and much of the sanctuary, visible through open double doors, fell silent. *Oh, great,* Will thought. "Value judgments aren't part of my profession, Mr. Johnson," he said. "I suggest you ask the minister."

Estelle, whose husband, Ben, filled that role, spoke up. "Since he's about to begin, why don't we go inside."

"Good idea." Gratefully, Will shepherded his daughters into a pew. He chose a spot toward the front, but at the side, in case the girls had to make a potty trip.

India studied him. "Daddy," she said, "is Miss Morris going to have a baby?"

"So I hear." He hadn't considered that people would air such matters around children.

"But she doesn't have a husband," Diane protested, as if it were physically impossible to get pregnant without being married.

Will had no desire to discuss the situation, especially not where other people might hear. "Sometimes these things happen."

"You should marry her," India announced. "Then she'd have a husband."

Will felt heat rising to his face. He prayed silently that neither of his daughters would mention that they expected her for dinner. Mercifully, they didn't.

"Nick's getting a stepmother," Diane added. "We could, too."

A lady sitting to their left favored him with a sympathetic look. "They aren't the first children who've wished Miss Morris would adopt them."

"I'm sure you're right," Will murmured. Thank goodness she didn't read anything particular into the children's comments.

Ben Fellows mounted the pulpit, quieting the audience. The police captain transitioned smoothly into his role as preacher, combining a commanding presence with low-key but unmistakable religious fervor.

Will particularly liked the text of the sermon, which turned out to be "Let he who is without sin among you cast the first stone."

He hoped the worshipers took it to heart.

LEAH LAID OUT three sets of clothes on the bed. After a fierce internal debate, she picked a flowered top and a pair of slacks with an elastic waistband. The girl-next-door style suited her mood.

Her spirits had wavered all day. This morning, she'd been unhappy about missing church. Although she usually enjoyed talking with her friends and found the service uplifting, she hadn't wanted to face the inevitable questions and comments. Particularly not while her stomach was acting up.

Also, she wasn't sure how she would react to Will in public. She wasn't even sure she could handle it in private this evening.

En route to Will's, her car filled with the aroma of the brownies she'd baked earlier. That wasn't the only sort of hunger tantalizing her, Leah conceded. Despite her contrary emotions, she could hardly wait to see him.

She decided to blame her inconsistencies on maternal hormones.

At Will's house, the front door swung open as she approached. "Miss Morris!" a childish voice greeted her.

"Good evening, India," she told the little girl in the pink dress.

The child's eyes widened in astonishment. "How could you tell it was me? I switched colors with Diane!"

"You did what?" Will chided. He opened the door wider. "Hey, no wonder you two have been skulking about where I couldn't find you! What a mean trick!"

Tonight, he wore a black T-shirt and tight-fitting jeans that emphasized his muscular build. *Devastating,* Leah thought.

"I told you she'd figure it out!" Diane, in blue, appeared behind her sister.

"I hope everybody likes brownies." Leah smiled as the two little Rankins scuttled out of her way.

"They'll be perfect with the ice cream I bought." Will closed the door behind her and relieved her of the plate.

The twins caught Leah's hands and tugged her into their room, leaving their father to fend for himself. She did her best to memorize the names of their dolls and stuffed animals, aware of how much such details mattered to children.

A quick survey of the room showed that the shelf of books lacked several of Leah's favorite titles. She made a mental note in case she had a chance to give them presents in the future.

A collage on the wall displayed images of the girls at various ages. There were shots of them riding horseback, playing with Will and enjoying a birthday party. In one photo, a woman with short blond hair frowned as she held her toddler daughters on her lap. How odd that their mother appeared unhappy in the only scene that included her.

When Will joined them, he grinned at the sight of the beds covered with dolls and bears. "They brought out the entire menagerie."

"Miss Morris knows all their names!" Diane told him.

"I have to admit, I only remember a couple," Will conceded.

"But I'll bet you're really helpful with boo-boos," Leah teased.

India agreed. "He bandages them up real good."

"Really well." She corrected the child's grammar out of habit. India repeated the phrasing proudly.

"He put a splint on my teddy," Diane announced.

The image made Leah smile. "You perform first aid on their toys?" she asked Will.

"Stuffed animals get boo-boos, too," he responded, picking up a well-worn bear and, to the girls' squeals of amusement, squinting into its rounded ear. "A clear case of otitis. I recommend de-linting." He plucked out a stray bit of fuzz.

If only her father could have communicated his love so readily, Leah thought with admiration. Why would any woman give up not only her children but also a man so wonderfully suited to parenthood?

"That reminds me. Dinner's almost ready," Will told them. "I wondered if I could get some help setting the table."

"I'll do it!" Diane cried.

"Me, too!" India pelted out on her heels.

The two adults lingered to retrieve a couple of stuffed animals that had tumbled to the floor. "The twins are adorable," Leah said.

"I can't tell you how excited they were about your coming." Will's chest rose and fell visibly beneath the black shirt. "You're like a rock star around here." As she started to pass him, he touched her arm. "By the way, they heard the talk at church about the baby. They didn't know it was possible without a husband."

She hadn't prepared for the gossip to reach the girls so soon. "What did you tell them?"

"I muttered something inane like, 'It happens.'"

Leah resisted the urge to nuzzle the inviting curve of his shoulder. "How did they react? Were they upset?"

"I suspect anything you do would be perfectly fine with them," he confided.

Much as she longed to simply enjoy this moment standing

close to him, Leah needed to find out what else had happened. "What did other people say?"

"Beau Johnson tossed around the term *loose women,* but the sermon about not casting the first stone had a quelling effect." Will led the way into the family room. "Your aunt seemed to bear up all right, but we didn't have a chance to talk. How's she doing?"

Leah dredged up the details of the family powwow they'd held at Rosie's house. "Mark was driving her crazy last night, threatening legal action against Pepe." Through a sliding glass door, she watched the girls setting out paper plates and napkins on the patio table. India worked carefully, while Diane slapped things down and then returned to straighten them, struggling to match her sister's precision. "I persuaded Rosie to write a note to Pepe informing him about the pregnancy and suggesting they meet to discuss the situation."

"Good idea." Ducking into the kitchen, Will added, "What would you like to drink?"

Leah remembered Jenni's advice to consume plenty of calcium. "Milk, if you have it."

"Of course." He emerged a minute later with a tray of glasses. "How did Mark respond to your suggestion?"

"He subsided. That's the best I can say." Leah opened the sliding door for him. When the scent of grilling food wafted in, she discovered she was ravenous.

During dinner, they kept the conversation focused on the girls. India and Diane basked in the attention, displaying good table manners for six-year-olds.

Leah enjoyed the fact that she had her own relationship with the twins, separate from anything between her and their father. Several times, she had to explain to Will about the friends and school events mentioned in his daughters' chatter.

By the time the brownies and ice cream disappeared down

eager throats, the daylight was fading and the girls' yawns overwhelmed their attempts to stay alert. Together, Will and Leah got them ready for bed.

In between brushing their teeth and putting on pajamas, they bestowed so many hugs that it became clear they were struggling to delay the inevitable. Tenderly but firmly, Will kept them on track.

At Leah's suggestion, the two adults shared the reading of a storybook about a pair of lions. He read the boy part and she took the girl part, to the children's delight. A few spontaneous growls and roars from their father sent India and Diane into gales of giggles.

Afterward, Will informed them that he and Miss Morris had important business to discuss. Although Diane thrust out her lower lip, a stern look from her father persuaded her to pull up the covers and pipe down.

"They're very well behaved," Leah said a few minutes later in the kitchen, a comfortable room with oak cabinets. They'd both heard the leftover brownies begging to be eaten and didn't even try to resist the summons.

"I expect that will change when they hit adolescence, but I prefer not to worry about it." Will handed her the serving plate.

"You mentioned asking my advice?" she prompted.

He set out a couple of napkins to accompany their snack. "My ex-wife is getting married next weekend in Austin. She wants the twins to be her flower girls."

After he'd explained his reservations, Leah said, "Missing a few days of school won't harm them. It might even be educational. They can report on the wedding to the class when they come back, and I'll plan a lesson about marriage customs in different cultures." She could weave the theme into a crafts and writing project.

"That sounds wonderfully creative." Will shifted his legs

beneath the table, brushing Leah's ankle. She enjoyed the contact, however slight. "I was wondering about something else, as well. Although Mrs. McNulty can accompany them, perhaps I should be the one to go."

Leah suspected there might be undercurrents motivating the question. "Don't you trust your ex-wife with the girls?"

His forehead furrowed. "She isn't planning to keep them, if that's what you mean. Her sugar daddy—excuse me, her fiancé—doesn't care to have them around. But I don't trust her to supervise them properly when she's so focused on her wedding."

Leah still didn't see the problem. "But you trust your housekeeper and you said she's going." When he didn't immediately respond, she had a flash of insight. "I think the question is, how do *you* feel about Allison getting married again?"

He met her gaze straight on. "It makes me uncomfortable. It's as if I failed her and she's telling the world she found someone better."

Leah decided to risk asking a few more questions. "Who left—you or her?"

"She dumped me." Will's voice held an unmistakable note of bitterness. "It shocked me, Leah. Things weren't perfect, but I never expected her to go out and have an affair."

"Didn't the two of you talk much?" she asked.

"You mean about what was going on inside us? *Never.*" Will spoke the word with finality. "The few times I tried, she acted as if I were finding fault. I'll admit, sometimes I lost patience. Allison always wanted more—more money, more status, more leisure time. I wish I could have done more, but I was working incredible hours and spending my spare time with the kids."

Leah sighed. "I can't pretend to be an expert on marriage." Although she supposed she probably shouldn't ask, she posed one more question. "Do you still love her?"

He gave a start. "No. I doubt I ever did, really. I mistook friendship and emotional need for love. I doubt I'm capable of the kind of romantic feelings poets write about. It doesn't seem to be part of my nature."

"You love your daughters," Leah pointed out.

His eyes half closed. "More than my own life." Then he regarded her assessingly. "But that isn't the same thing."

"No, I guess not."

She became aware of how close they were sitting, at right angles to each other around the table. Even through her slacks and his jeans, she could feel his heat against her thigh.

"To me, love requires becoming completely vulnerable to another person," Leah said. "You lay yourself bare. That's a scary thing, because if they reject you, well, maybe you'd never get over it."

Will drummed his fingers on the table. Instead of inspiring him to open up again, her comments had put him into retreat.

She decided to cut her losses and return to the subject at hand. "If you're asking my opinion, you'd be a wet blanket at your ex-wife's wedding."

"Agreed." He stared down at the last brownie as if wondering where the others had gone. Perhaps observing the crumbs on his plate gave him a clue. "We'd better move on."

Leah dreaded negotiating about the baby, but a postponement would only prolong the agony. "Yes, why don't we."

Will fetched a pad from a drawer. After a hunt around the kitchen, he also located a pen. "As I mentioned, my name has to go on the birth certificate."

In view of the ease with which Karen had guessed the truth, Leah supposed it was futile to fight over the issue. "All right."

Looking pleased, he wrote the point down. "You understand that I won't be able to handle the delivery. I'd like an ob-gyn from Mill Valley to handle it."

"I'm Jenni's patient," she said. "Unless there are complications, I plan to stay with her."

Despite a reflexive click of the tongue, all he said was, "It's your decision. You're the patient."

Tension masked whatever else he might be feeling, but Leah could see what a dilemma this created for him as both a physician and a father-to-be. "Will, this is a strange situation. The thing is, we're not a couple. I have to do what suits me."

"Did you hear me disputing that?" he asked.

"No." Leah wished she could reach beneath this hard surface and reclaim the teddy-bear-cuddling daddy. But that side of Will had temporarily vanished.

"Next point: We need to agree on what to call the baby," he said.

"Right now?" Leah hadn't thought that far ahead.

"Not necessarily. I just want to have an equal say in the choice."

That seemed reasonable. "There goes my plan to name the baby Frodo. Or Froda, if it's a girl." She peeked at him, hoping for a smile.

His mouth quirked. "Good thing I brought it up."

"Okay." She sighed. "What's left on your list?"

"Child support." Will tapped his pen against the paper. "Are you honestly telling me you forgot?"

"It slipped my mind." Leah stifled a yawn. "I get sleepy awfully early these days. I hope I'm not going to be even more exhausted as the months go by or I'll barely be able to drag myself out of bed."

"The morning sickness and fatigue tend to diminish during the second trimester," he assured her.

"What about the third trimester?" she asked.

"Well, the baby gets heavy. That can cause discomfort." After a moment's hesitation, he said, "Since you're tired, let's finish. As far as child support, I'm willing to offer whatever might be standard at my income level. I'll do some research and get back to you."

That suited Leah. "Sure." Another yawn threatened to surface.

"We can adjust it as circumstances change." He studied the paper for a moment before saying, "Now, about custody. We'll share that fifty-fifty."

This bombshell snapped Leah right out of her daze. "Oh, no, we won't!" She glared at him. "I'm moving out of state and my baby moves with me. You can visit, but that's all. I get sole custody."

With a visible effort, Will controlled his annoyance. "Leah, you're not considering the future. This child isn't going to stay a baby forever. He or she will want a relationship with his sisters and me. When he's a teenager, he might even choose to live here."

"Not unless you plant that idea in his head!" Leah retorted. "I am not agreeing to share custody, Will."

"I could fight you in court." He let the threat hang in the air.

She'd realized from the moment she learned she was pregnant that she would do battle for this baby against any and all foes. That included Will if he tried to take control of her child, and she had no doubt that was what would happen if they shared custody.

"I'll sell my house for legal fees if I have to." She braced her hands on the table. "That kind of war can be vicious. It wouldn't be good for the girls, or for anyone."

The anguish on his face squeezed at her heart. Leah ignored it.

"I promise not to shut you out of our child's life," she went on. "But don't forget, it's only by chance that you ran into me again."

She hadn't meant to use his behavior against him. Nevertheless, he'd better learn right now that, if pushed hard enough, she would push back.

Will set the pad aside. "We'd better stop for now, before this turns ugly." He hadn't acquiesced, though.

"If necessary, I will move out of state before I give birth," Leah persisted.

Pain darkened Will's gaze. "What will I say to her someday when she asks why I'm practically a stranger, and why I'm so much closer to the twins? Leah, neither of us wants her to find out the circumstances under which she was conceived, do we?"

"If you have some fantasy about raising this baby, forget it." She refused to get sidetracked. "Sharing custody would force me to stay in Downhome. You are not going to run my life."

"I just…" He broke off. "All right, Leah, you can keep custody. But I insist on staying involved. I'm not going to let some future stepfather push me out of the picture."

The idea nearly made her laugh. "Believe me, marrying someone else is the last thing on my mind!"

"Maybe you think that now, but you're a beautiful woman. You'll have plenty of men after you." Will made it sound like a simple statement, not flattery. "And you're an amazing person. I admire you, Leah."

That surprised her. "After this conversation?"

"Actually, I'm rather impressed with how well we negotiated." He relaxed a bit, despite the fact that he'd conceded a key point. "I thought we'd be at each other's throats."

"Weren't we?" Leah had never opposed anyone with such fervor before.

His mouth curved. "You're a tough opponent. But we didn't sink to insults and accusations. That's quite an accomplishment in my book."

"And you took it well."

He handed her his pad. "If this meets with your approval, I'll go make a couple of photocopies and we can both sign them. It's for our mutual protection. No misunderstandings that way."

Leah read the bold handwriting. The last item said: "Miss Morris to have full custody. Dr. Rankin to be allowed regular visits."

"That looks fine."

After they finished the formalities and she tucked her copy in her purse, they said good-night. As she walked toward her car, Leah glanced back, to see Will silhouetted in the doorway.

He was so solid and protective. She remembered what he'd said about how their child might envy his closeness with the twins.

She hoped they would find a way to balance their baby's needs with their own. And prayed that she'd made the right decision tonight.

Chapter Ten

On Monday, Will spent most of the day in Mill Valley, performing cesarean sections and other surgery. He enjoyed being back in a hospital, using his hard-won skills to promote women's health.

Stopping by the nursery to check on a premature infant he'd delivered, he was pleased to find the baby doing well. A four-pounder, the little girl had a wrinkled red face and impossibly tiny fists. At her relatively large size, she only required intermediate-level care.

She might grow up to be a scientist, a musician, a homemaker—whatever suited her. One of the rewards of working in a small town was that Will might have a chance to watch her as she matured.

He wondered how often he'd see his own child-to-be. The thought of how much he was going to miss made his ribs ache.

For the span of a few hours, as he and Leah had played with the girls and eaten dinner, they'd felt like a family. An idealized family, he supposed, where people laughed together and provided emotional support. He doubted such rapport could last under real-life stresses. It certainly hadn't in his experience.

Besides, Will had a great family right now, just the three of them. Plus Mrs. McNulty, who'd returned from Nashville with a pile of CDs, a cowboy hat and a bag full of gifts. Plus the happy news that her roommate had become a new friend.

Later, he'd planned to cover a hysterectomy for another ob-gyn, but surgery was postponed because the patient had come down with a fever. It was only two o'clock when he arrived back at the Home Boulevard Medical Clinic, earlier than expected despite a downpour that slowed traffic.

Although he still had to dictate reports based on his notes, at least there were no patients scheduled. Amazingly, Will might get to leave early, which would be fair, since he'd stayed late the past two nights.

Estelle, however, had other ideas. Popping into his office, she said, "Since you're free, I'd appreciate if you'd review some of my patients' charts. A couple of them aren't responding to their meds."

The state of Tennessee allowed nurse practitioners to write prescriptions. However, Estelle tended to stick to a handful of tried-and-true drugs, while Will was also familiar with newer medications.

"I'll be glad to help." He'd almost finished dictating into his tape recorder, anyway.

"I'd appreciate it." Estelle gave him one of her strained looks, which meant she had something more to discuss.

"Yes?" he asked.

"That nurse of yours." She rarely referred to Winifred by name. "She has a habit of chatting with patients in the waiting room. She doesn't reveal anything confidential, but her voice disturbs the others. I was hoping you'd speak to her about it."

Guiltily, Will acknowledged that he'd been so pleased to have an efficient, attentive nurse that he hadn't paid attention to how she might affect anyone else at the clinic. She'd kept her word about the pens, spoiling him so badly that he'd felt at a loss today at the hospital when he'd needed to write a prescription and had had to search for a writing implement. "What sorts of things does she discuss?"

"Generally, she gives little speeches about what a great doctor you are." Estelle had the grace to appear embarrassed. "Not that I mind that, of course. But it strikes me as unprofessional."

"I'll ask her to put a lid on it." He had to turn his head to hide his smile.

Estelle returned a few minutes later to deposit a stack of charts on his desk. Will was jotting down suggestions for one of the patients when Dr. Vine entered.

The stern expression on her usually animated face told him she hadn't joined him for a coffee break. He hoped nothing was amiss with her wedding scheduled for Saturday. "What's up?"

After closing the door, Jenni eyed him sternly. "I'm about to plunge right into none-of-my-business territory, except that I have to say something because it concerns one of my patients."

He didn't have to ask which patient she meant. "Leah suggested you speak to me?"

"Leah doesn't know I'm here," Jenni admitted. "Karen spilled the beans last night while she was trying on her bridesmaid dress."

Had he been dealing with a male colleague, Will would have told the guy to stay out of his personal life, and the matter would have ended there. Women were wired differently, however, he'd learned over the years, so he settled back. "Exactly what did Karen tell you?"

Jenni cleared her throat. "That you're the father of Leah's baby."

"And?"

"And you haven't been forthright about it!" she pressed. "Maybe you don't understand how tough people can make life for a woman who transgresses society's norms, even in this day and age. Some Downhome folks are real stick-in-the-muds."

"I certainly got an earful from Beau Johnson on Sunday," Will noted.

She folded her arms. "I doubt he'd apply his double standard to you, though. Men get off easy."

"Jenni," he said, "I am not responsible for society's sexist attitudes."

"You *are* responsible if your behavior reflects badly on the clinic!" she shot back. "For instance, it could hurt our reputation if people found out you went around... No, wait. I didn't mean that."

Too late. "If I went around doing *what?* Dropping my pants every time I met an attractive woman?" he snapped.

Jenni turned red all the way to her blond roots. "Sorry. I was out of line."

He decided to give her a break. "And I'm sorry if what I did might put the clinic in an awkward position. I had no way of knowing that an impulsive action I took halfway across the country would boomerang. But I don't see that it's anyone's business except Leah's and mine."

His colleague appeared at a loss for words. Finally, she said, "The truth is, I charged in here without a clear idea of what I wanted to say. I'm just worried about Leah. She's more vulnerable than you may realize, and she's bent on moving away, which means she's going to be raising this child alone."

"I don't suppose Karen told you that I'd proposed and Leah turned me down, did she?" Will saw from Jenni's face that he'd surprised her.

"No," she said.

"You should talk her into staying so I'd have a chance of protecting her!" He stopped as a glimmer of insight hit him.

Since Sunday, he'd experienced flashes of anger about Leah's refusal to consider joint custody. He hadn't understood why she'd dug her heels in so hard.

Well, he got it now. At some level, he'd hoped that sharing custody might persuade her to remain in Downhome. Or, to be honest, pressure her into it.

He had no right to attempt to control Leah. At least in part, she'd been reacting to his unspoken and unrecognized agenda. Unrecognized by him, at least.

Jenni studied him. "It's too bad the pair of you can't work it out. I've only known Leah for a few months and you for two weeks. I suppose I let Karen's worries influence me unduly."

"You might say that." Will didn't intend to rescue her.

"But one of these days, the truth is going to emerge, and you'd better stiffen your spine, because there's no telling how people will react," she stated.

"With any luck, they'll pay me the respect of keeping their opinions to themselves." Realizing he'd pushed too hard, he added, "That was not a criticism of you. I'm glad you got this out in the open."

"So am I. Thanks for letting me vent." Without further fuss, Jenni went out.

Will respected the devotion with which she'd backed her friend, even though it had been misplaced. Leah didn't need a defender as long as he was around.

Maybe Leah didn't need a defender at all. She seemed quite capable of sticking up for herself.

By TUESDAY, LEAH figured she should be accustomed to the sidelong glances she caught from visiting parents and the conversations that halted abruptly when she entered the teachers' lounge. But she wasn't.

"They'll get over it," Olivia advised as they supervised recess during their lunch break. It had rained the previous day, leaving the grass wet and the trees shining. Despite the inconvenience of muddy shoes, the principal had approved an outdoor session because the kids' pent-up energy was disrupting the classrooms.

Sybill, in particular, had launched into hyperdrive. Since she'd been sick yesterday, Leah wondered at this excess of energy, but the child must have recovered quickly.

"You're not upset with me?" Leah asked Olivia. "I suppose I am setting a poor example."

"We don't stone fallen women anymore," the principal observed dryly. "By the way, I'd appreciate your opinion on a matter."

"Happy to oblige," she said.

"You know the enrichment money from the PTA? I'd scheduled some Irish dancers next week, but they had to cancel," Olivia said. "I'm considering a bluegrass trio called the Fiddle Folks."

"Bluegrass?" Memories stirred inside Leah. Austin. A bar. The first time she met Will.

"They perform folk music and explain the origins of the songs and instruments," Olivia explained. "Several people recommended them. What do you think?"

Earlier programs had featured a mime troupe from Knoxville, a science show and a Nashville ballet company. "It sounds excellent, if they're available on short notice," Leah said. "The kids would enjoy it."

"Good. I'll see if they can make it. Hey, over there! Cut it out!" The principal marched across the yard to separate Sybill from a boy who'd aroused her wrath.

Minnie, who was inspecting another girl's bumped knee, didn't react to her daughter. The problem with having her as a room mom was that, by ignoring Sybill's antics, she encouraged them. Still, Leah had missed Minnie's help yesterday.

When the bell rang, getting the kids cleaned up and settled inside took far too long in Leah's opinion. Every time she looked, Sybill was in the thick of things, and Minnie didn't seem to notice.

Diane got into the action, too, throwing spitballs behind Leah's back, until her sister had had enough. "You stop that!" she rebuked. "I'll tell Dad!"

"Dad doesn't care what we do," Diane shot back. "He's sending us away, isn't he?"

"We're just going for Mom's wedding," India replied in confusion.

"Then why isn't he coming, too? Sybill says he probably wants us to stay there!" Tears trembled in Diane's eyes.

"Whoa." Much as Leah longed to reassure the girls at length, she couldn't take time for a heart-to-heart right now. "I'm sure that isn't the case at all. Let's save this personal discussion for later, okay?"

The twins piped down, but rambunctious behavior kept cropping up, always with Sybill at the center. By the time the last bell had sounded, Leah was exhausted.

Much as she hated to, she had to say something to Minnie. When she approached her after most of the children had left, however, the usually cheery woman avoided her eye.

There must be more to this than she'd suspected. "Minnie, what's wrong?"

The room mom finished putting on her daughter's jacket and sent her to wait in the hall. When she spoke, it was with uncharacteristic petulance. "You should have stopped to think before you chose to have a baby on your own. If there was another first-grade class, my husband would insist on transferring Sybill."

To learn that the town manager held such strong views startled Leah. "I'd rather not expose my students to the consequences of my personal decisions," she said as calmly as she could. "Unfortunately, my physical condition isn't something I can turn on and off during school hours."

"You should have waited until you found a husband!" Minnie insisted. "Or adopted, at least."

Leah decided not to enter into a fruitless debate. The relevant point was the Tuckers' reaction. "Is that why you kept Sybill home yesterday?"

"That's right. We weren't sure we wanted her around you." The woman stuck her chin out pugnaciously.

The antagonism struck Leah like a blow. Although she'd expected criticism, she hadn't been prepared for this kind of hostility.

"I'm sorry you and your husband are taking the situation so hard." Under the circumstances, Leah would have liked to postpone discussing their daughter's misbehavior. However, the girl's conduct was having a bad effect on the other students. "Sybill seemed to be acting out today—"

Minnie cut her off. "My child is just fine!"

"I have to control the classroom for the sake of all my students," Leah told her.

"Then you can do it without me! Find yourself another gofer. Goodbye!" The woman grabbed her purse and stormed out.

Leah stared after her, shaken. Although she'd dealt with hot-tempered parents in the past, she'd never had a room mom quit in a huff. The fact that she'd taught Minnie's other children without problem made the situation even more uncomfortable.

Then she remembered the argument between India and Diane. The way Sybill had planted doubts about her friend's trip to Austin had been cruel. Leah wished she'd had a chance to reassure the twins after school, but they'd left while she was talking with Mrs. Tucker.

Minnie's departure might not be entirely bad, considering the way she subtly encouraged her daughter's problems. Several other mothers had inquired about the room-mom position, although no one had come right out and volunteered. Hopefully, Leah would find someone who knew how to keep order.

Still, she regretted the unpleasantness.

Hoping nothing else had gone amiss today, she decided to drop by the Snip'N'Curl next door. Perhaps Rosie had heard from Pepe about her note informing him of the pregnancy.

At least she and her aunt were in this together, Leah reflected. *What else were families for?*

TUESDAY PROVED to be a busy day for Will. Estelle, who'd finally begun to treat him as a colleague instead of a rival, had referred two maternity patients with high blood pressure. In addition, several women who'd been suffering symptoms of menopause had arrived, on the advice of their friends, to consult him.

About four o'clock, however, his crowded schedule evaporated. A disgruntled Winifred stopped him in the corridor to report that they'd had three patients reschedule. "Mrs. Jones has car trouble. Mrs. Avery's babysitter canceled. Mrs. Halliburton's husband just called to say he's bringing the boss home for dinner, so she has to go to the grocery store." The nurse glowered. "She ought to order from a restaurant and keep her appointment!"

"Three in a row. Well, it happens," Will said.

In his pocket, the cell phone buzzed. After excusing himself, he answered, "Dr. Rankin."

It was Leah. "I'm sorry to bother you. I'm at the salon and Rosie's hyperventilating. She got an e-mail—can you believe that? An e-mail!—from Pepe questioning whether he's the father."

"Is she having difficulty breathing?" He'd learned that people use the term *hyperventilate* rather loosely.

"Not really," Leah admitted. "She's just terribly upset. Being around you seems to calm her. Maybe I should bring her in."

In the background, a man said, "If you're calling that creep Pepe, give me the phone!"

"Oh, simmer down, Mark! It's the doctor," she retorted. Into the cell, she said, "I guess I overreacted. She doesn't really require medical help. I don't know why I bothered you."

"Actually, I'm flattered," he said, and meant it. "If you believe it will be a comfort, I can come there."

"You must be busy." Leah sounded hesitant but hopeful.

"As it happens, I'm free." More than free. And eager to see her.

"That would be wonderful."

The relief in her voice was all the encouragement he needed. "I'm on my way." After hanging up, he told Winifred, "It's Mrs. O'Bannon. She's upset, and I thought I'd go help."

"You're the kindest doctor I've ever met!" the nurse responded loudly enough for the entire waiting room to hear.

Will winced at the undeserved compliment. Besides, he'd promised Estelle to try to reduce the laudatory outbursts, and he'd just contributed to them. "Honestly, it's no big deal."

Before Winifred could argue, he grabbed his medical kit and made his escape. Outside in the fresh air, he cut across Home Boulevard and skirted the edge of The Green.

That he and Leah had argued on Sunday bothered Will, even though they'd resolved their differences. And he missed her. At dinner last night, hearing the girls relate the things Miss Morris had said and done only made him more aware of her absence.

Will strode past the office of the *Gazette*. Barry Lowell had been as good as his word. In the latest edition, delivered to the clinic this morning, he'd portrayed the new doctor objectively and quoted him accurately. That spoke well for the quality of the paper.

Will entered the salon to the hum of hair dryers. On the

front sofa, a woman sat flipping through magazines. Large, heavy drying hoods obscured two other customers, while a couple of employees in pink uniforms worked at their stations.

His attention was riveted on Leah, sitting beside her aunt on a padded bench near the back. She jumped up when she spotted him. "Oh, hi! I'm glad you're here."

So was he. Very glad.

Mark O'Bannon, in uniform with his gun intimidatingly strapped to his hip, stood scowling near Rosie. At least he had the good grace to mutter, "It's decent of you to stop in, Doctor."

With a nod to them both, Will went to sit beside his patient. "How are you feeling, Mrs. O'Bannon?"

"I can't believe Pepe would say such things!" she cried. "I wish I hadn't checked my e-mail until I got home!"

It seemed to Will that every head in the salon inclined in their direction. Although the women pretended to focus on whatever they were doing, he observed one pair of scissors snipping the air and a blow-dryer aimed more at the mirror than the customer.

"My mother called me in tears," Mark told him. "She was sobbing so hard I got worried."

"Well, let's have a look." Will took Rosie's vital signs. Despite her rapid breathing, she showed no alarming physical symptoms, he was pleased to note.

"I don't understand how he can question whether the baby's his!" Mark snapped. "It's as if he's calling my mother a liar. Or worse."

"People react differently to shocking news," Will pointed out. "One of the most common responses is denial. This fellow may simply have trouble accepting that he's going to be a father. He isn't necessarily considering how his statement will affect Mrs. O'Bannon."

Around the salon, heads bobbed in agreement. "Nobody

in his right mind would call Rosie a slut," commented a lady with strange squiggly things in her hair.

Her unfortunate choice of words made Rosie start to wimper. "For Pete's sake!" Mark raged. "Watch what you—" He halted as the exterior door swung open.

In wandered a tall, young woman with her nose in a book. Despite the glasses sliding down her nose and the hair piled messily atop her head, she had an attractive sweetness that Mark obviously didn't miss.

"Amy Arroyo!" Rosie breathed. "I don't believe it. She never gets her hair done here."

"She's Ethan's secretary," Leah told Will.

The young woman glanced around, blinking. "Where am I?" she asked. "Oh, hi, Mark. I was going into the *Gazette* to place an ad for the police auction. I must have made a wrong turn."

"You sure did." Mark, his manner noticeably gentler, went toward her. "Don't worry, Amy. I'll walk you over there."

Since the office of the *Gazette* was next door, Will considered this clear evidence of Mark's interest. Amy, however, merely gazed at him distractedly.

Rosie lurched to her feet. "You're not taking her anywhere! Amy, now that you're here, I'm fixing your hair. It's on the house!"

"What?" The secretary stepped backward. "That's really too generous."

"Let's start at the shampoo bowl." Completely recovered from her attack of vapors, Rosie caught the secretary's elbow and guided her through the salon. "Then I'm giving you a cut. That way, you won't have to staple your hair up there anymore."

"It isn't stapled," the young woman protested weakly as they approached a row of sinks.

After removing Amy's glasses, Mrs. O'Bannon handed them to her son. "Put those somewhere."

"Is that okay with you, Amy?" he queried.

"I guess so." She sounded bewildered.

Will could tell his services were no longer required. Catching Leah's eye, he nodded toward the door. Fortunately, the other occupants were too fascinated by the prospect of Amy's transformation to take notice.

"I can't tell you how much I appreciate your help," Leah said when they reached the sidewalk.

"My pleasure." And what a pleasure it was to stand here in the sunshine on a quiet side street and drink in the sparkle of her eyes.

To be seen together in public was risky, but he didn't want to relinquish her company yet. Besides, they had the perfect excuse: a conversation about her aunt. "Join me for coffee."

No urging was necessary. "Sure. Besides, there's something else I want to discuss with you."

He didn't ask what. Right now, he didn't care.

Will needed all his self-control not to slip an arm around Leah's waist as they walked toward the café on The Green. He knew he ought to be careful. But he was beginning to forget why.

Chapter Eleven

Although tempted to grab the only unoccupied outdoor table, Leah led the way beneath the striped awning and into the Café Montreal. Luckily, she didn't recognize any of the customers. After Minnie's reaction to the news of her pregnancy, she was more eager than ever to keep their relationship private.

Inside, the accustomed scents of coffee, cinnamon and fresh-baked croissants faded beneath the pervasive tang of paint. Arturo's unfinished murals remained veiled during hours of operation, with the drop cloths giving the French-style bistro the air of a house under renovation. The odor discouraged indoor dining, so they had the place almost to themselves.

At a table in a corner, they ordered coffee. After Leah explained about the murals, Will said, "Sounds like they'll be charming. Downhome is full of surprises."

"You might say that."

Their gazes met. He ducked his head in acknowledgment. "I guess I did get a shock, didn't I?"

"Me, too," she admitted. "The first time I saw your photograph I nearly fell over."

"When was that?" He leaned forward, his hands brushing hers on the table.

Leah tried not to show how much she enjoyed the casual touch. "I happened to see Patsy unpacking the stuff for your office."

"You should have called me then," he said. "We could have worked things out in advance."

"Called you? I was hoping to *avoid* you!" Not very realistic, she supposed. "I was too rattled to think straight."

"I'm pleased we can talk about this. There's no reason for us to be at odds. In fact, it might be better if…" His warm tone drew her in and then abruptly shut her out. It happened in the flick of an eye, for no apparent reason. She saw it in the change of muscle tone and the way he straightened, physically pulling back.

Perhaps she should be content, because she didn't want him tempting her to give up her dreams. She knew her weaknesses too well, including her inclination to put other people's well-being ahead of her own.

But she missed the intimacy. Will's guarded quality made his moments of tenderness even more special. Too bad they were so fleeting.

The waitress brought their cups of French roast, along with a tray of condiments that included chocolate sprinkles. Leah set about fixing her drink. "I ought to cut back on coffee, shouldn't I?" she asked reluctantly.

"All types of caffeine," Will agreed. "But a little now and then won't hurt."

She stirred in the cream, sugar and chocolate. "Is Rosie really all right? These episodes worry me."

"As far as I can tell, she's fine." He sipped his coffee black. "Stress is never healthy, though. Do you have any insight into Pepe? Surely he can't expect to get away with denying his paternity."

Leah tried to put herself in the restaurateur's shoes. "He's been smitten with Gwen for years. A short time after he got together with Rosie, Gwen suddenly became available. I guess he couldn't pass up the chance."

"That's tough on your aunt," Will observed.

"Yes. But things might change. I don't believe Gwen really cares that much for…" The topic of their conversation entered from the back with a tray of fresh-baked croissants. In this small restaurant, voices tended to carry, and today there was no chatter to provide cover, so Leah fell silent.

Will dropped the subject. "You had something else on your mind?"

The day's events in the classroom rushed back—the turmoil, Minnie's abdication. That wasn't what she'd meant to broach, however.

"It's about Diane." She related what his daughter had said regarding his motives to send them to Austin.

"Oh, great." In his agitation, Will finger-combed his hair, leaving a tuft sticking up. Leah felt an itch to reach out and smooth it. "Thanks for telling me. It didn't occur to me the girls might worry about the trip."

He'd explained that his ex-wife's boyfriend didn't like having children around, Leah recalled. "How much do they understand about why they don't live with their mother?"

Her question seemed to startle him. "As much as they need to. Or at least, that's what I thought."

"Can you be more specific?" Leah pressed.

Will reflected for a moment. "She told them she wasn't sure where she'd be living, so they were better off with me. I hope they don't feel their mother chose Brad over them."

"Isn't that exactly what she did?" Allison might have made the best choice for all concerned, but those were the facts. "Besides, now that she's getting married, things could change. Is there any chance she might try to claim them?"

Will shook his head. "I'm sure her husband-to-be has no desire to share his life or his wife with a pair of little kids. So any ideas about what I should tell them?"

Leah avoided saying anything negative about the girls' mother. "Reassure them that you love them and that you will never let anyone take them away." Another idea came to her. "Buy them a cell phone with your number programmed into it so they can call. If anything goes wrong, promise you'll fly to Texas and fetch them back."

"I like that. It's concrete, something they can hold on to." Will paused as the waitress refilled their cups, then continued. "Besides, it's good for them to have a phone while they're traveling. There's no telling what might happen."

"How long will they be gone?" She took a sip of coffee and discovered the stuff didn't taste very good. The effect of hormones, she presumed.

"Just a few days. They leave on Thursday," Will said. "The wedding's Saturday and they fly back on Sunday."

He would be alone this weekend. Of course, he'd probably attend Jenni and Ethan's wedding—the same day as Allison's, coincidentally—but otherwise, he'd have time with no children underfoot and no housekeeper.

That didn't mean anything was going to happen between the two of them, Leah told herself firmly. Let the man enjoy lounging around the house in his underwear and sleeping late.

"What are you smiling about?" Will asked.

Caught off-guard, she said, "I pictured you running around in your underwear without the girls home." Her cheeks burned. "Please forget I said that!"

Amusement brightened Will's face. "Is that what you do when you're home alone?"

"No, I'm way too self-conscious."

"Even with no one around?"

"Someone might stop by." Leah clammed up as a couple of new arrivals went by. She was glad when they chose a booth on the far side of the room.

"You didn't seem self-conscious to me," Will noted after they'd passed. "In Austin, that is."

"That was a case of temporary insanity," Leah responded wryly.

They regarded each other assessingly. No use pretending they weren't both keenly aware of each other in every way, and of the reality that as two adults they could do whatever they liked this weekend.

Except, of course, for the emotional repercussions. Leah liked being able to talk to Will. His solid, caring quality made her feel she could rely on him, despite the way he'd acted that night. She mustn't risk ruining this connection by pushing it too far.

Even after she moved away, the two of them would always share concerns for their child. Best to leave well enough alone.

"You're not smiling anymore," he said.

"Let's stay friends. As Robert Frost said, good fences make good neighbors."

"So, we should respect our distance. Very sensible."

If she'd disappointed him, he didn't show it.

Leah glanced at her watch. "I'd better get home."

"Tired?"

"No. I have to do some research on the Internet," she said. "The Rosewell Center still hasn't come through and I'm getting antsy. Some of my college friends live in the Washington, D.C., area. I thought I'd check the possibilities."

"You're awfully eager to leave Downhome," Will said ruefully. "I'm just starting to like the place."

"I don't dislike it." She pushed aside the unpleasant memory of Minnie's outburst. "But I'll never be satisfied if I don't try new things, meet new people and face up to challenges."

"I can understand that. If I'd stayed on the ranch the way my parents expected, I'd have gone crazy. On the other hand, the world didn't exactly welcome me with delight." As if he'd said more than he'd intended, Will averted his gaze. Declining Leah's offer to pay half, he collected the bill and left a generous tip.

"Thanks, Will," she said.

"No problem." He gave a distracted half wave. By unspoken accord, they left the restaurant separately.

Leah liked the idea that they could be friends. All the same, she hadn't lost her intense attraction to the man. Friends could easily become lovers if they weren't careful, she reflected as she walked to her car.

They could also turn back into strangers. Given Will's penchant for withdrawing, that was a painfully strong possibility.

ON FRIDAY, WILL DROVE to the clinic early. Without the girls, the house had a forlorn mood that stole the pleasure from lingering over breakfast.

He'd relayed Leah's comments to Eileen on Tuesday, and together they'd assured India and Diane that their father would never let them go. He'd immediately sensed a drop in his daughters' tension level.

They'd called last night to inform him they'd arrived safely in Austin, regaling him with details of the flight and dinner with their maternal grandparents. Today would be filled with last-minute fittings and the wedding rehearsal.

The only cloud on their horizon, literally, was a hurricane approaching the Gulf of Mexico. Although Austin wasn't on the coast, they faced a possible deluge Sunday or Monday unless the storm veered toward Florida.

"We'll batten down the hatches," Mrs. McNulty had announced when she picked up the phone. "Don't you worry. The girls are having a great time."

"I can tell. I hope you enjoy yourself, too," he'd said and she'd assured him she would.

All appeared to be well, thanks, at least in part, to Leah's suggestions. Will appreciated finding a friend and ally. He didn't want her to move away, especially not with the baby on the way.

Thinking about their child gave Will a bittersweet pang. No matter how he tried to guard his heart, he knew he would love that little one. He just couldn't yet grasp how much.

At the clinic, he parked in his space and went to the back door, only to find it locked. It hadn't occurred to him that no one else would be here nearly an hour before opening. Although he'd borrowed a key last Saturday in case he had to get in, he'd forgotten to make a copy.

Annoyed with himself, Will weighed whether to wait or head back home. He'd hoped to review more of his patients' charts.

Abruptly, the back door swung out. Yvonne's unusual silvery hair contrasted with her youthful face as she regarded him in the morning light. "Oh, Dr. Rankin. I thought I heard someone out here."

"I forgot to make a key. Thanks." He followed her inside. "What are you doing here at this hour?"

"The nurses take turns coming in early so patients can call before school or work," she answered. "Most just need a little advice, but sometimes their symptoms are serious enough to bring them in."

The service must be informal, because Will didn't recall reading about an advice line in the clinic's literature. "Arriving early must be hard on you as a single mom. How old is your little girl?"

"Bethany's fifteen months." Although her earlier antagonism had eased, she remained wary. "My cousin babysits her."

"If you ever need backup, my housekeeper might be able to help. I could ask her when she gets home from Texas." Mrs. McNulty had mentioned feeling at a loss since the twins had started school.

In the doorway to the room, Yvonne paused. "Annette Forrest is my backup—she's the chief's mother—but that's really kind of you."

"I'm sorry we got off on the wrong foot," Will told her. "I didn't mean to make extra work for you."

She shrugged. "That wasn't why I didn't like you."

He decided to make a joke about it. "Must have been my charming personality, then."

"Oh, no. It wasn't personal." Yvonne measured grounds into the coffeemaker. "It's just that male doctors can be real jerks." She stopped, clearly taken aback by what she'd blurted.

"You must have had a bad experience." Before Jenni, the clinic had been staffed by a husband-wife team of physicians in their sixties, who'd retired about a year ago. As far as Will knew, Yvonne had worked here for her entire career, so unless she'd had a terrible experience during her training, that only left one possibility. "You mean old Dr. Allen?"

Her look of revulsion confirmed his guess. It also raised an ugly suspicion. Yvonne tightly guarded the name of her baby's father, and although speculation ran rampant, apparently no one had proposed any likely suspects.

The doctors Allen had retired with little warning, stranding the town for months with only Estelle to provide medical care this side of Mill Valley. Everyone seemed baffled about why the couple hadn't handled the transition in a more orderly fashion. If the female half of the couple had stumbled across information implicating her husband as the father, that could certainly have motivated a rapid departure.

"He took advantage of you," Will said without thinking. Registering the shock on Yvonne's face, he hurried to add, "I don't mean to pry. And I certainly won't mention it to anyone else."

"People around here would consider it my fault," Yvonne said bitterly. "They'd call me names—a lot worse than they're calling Rosie or Leah. After all, Luther was married."

"He didn't offer to help?"

"He and Dorothy closed ranks. They threatened to cost me my job if I told anyone. They could have ruined me in this town, and I've got nowhere else to go." Her hand trembled as she poured water into the coffeemaker. "My mom has Alzheimer's and my dad's overwhelmed just taking care of her. I didn't see any choice but to keep my mouth shut."

"If you plan to pursue your legal rights, I'll be glad to do whatever I can," Will said. "You're entitled to child support."

Yvonne blinked back a sparkle of tears. "Dr. Vine offered to help when I told her, too. But I realize I did wrong getting involved with a married man, and besides, Bethany's better off without the Allens in her life in any way, shape or form."

Will felt relieved to know that Jenni also shared this secret. She'd be in a better position to notice if Yvonne ran into difficulties.

"Just remember, you're not alone," he said. "My offer's not an idle one, either."

"Thanks. I'm sorry I misjudged you." The nurse broke off as the phone rang. "I have to catch that." Off she went.

Will hoped she wouldn't change her mind about him when she found out he'd fathered Leah's baby. Surely she'd stumble on the truth sooner or later, although Jenni hadn't put it in the file. At some point, he meant to disclose the facts to the staff, but first he'd have to secure Leah's permission.

In his office, he put on his white coat and sat down with the files. He was working his way through the stack when Yvonne tapped at the door. To his inquiring glance, she said, "I have Mr. Otero on the phone. He asked if you'd be willing to work him in early. He doesn't want to be spotted at the clinic."

"Is he the husband of a patient?" Will asked, puzzled.

"Not exactly." The nurse cleared up the confusion by noting, "It's Pepe."

"Oh, right." Will hadn't connected the name. "He does realize I can't discuss Rosie's medical condition?"

"I made that point," Yvonne said. "He won't tell me what it's about, just that he has to talk to you."

The possibility that came to mind alarmed Will—that Pepe had an illness or genetic condition that might endanger Rosie or the baby. "Certainly. Tell him to hurry right over. I'm sure Mrs. Waters will be here shortly."

"Don't worry about it. I don't mind helping." When she gave him a smile, Will returned it gladly.

Five minutes later, she ushered in a wiry, dark-haired man. Dressed in an old-fashioned black suit with a bolo tie, he shook hands nervously and took a seat.

"Thank you for accommodating me, Doctor." The restaurateur spoke with a slight accent. "I'm here for a DNA test."

His statement heightened Will's concern about a genetic condition. "What kind of DNA test?"

"The kind that proves I'm not the baby's father," Pepe said as if it should be obvious.

Oh, *that* kind of DNA test. "Mr. Otero, we'd need to compare your DNA with the baby's or with a sample from the amniotic fluid," Will explained. "However, there are health risks associated with conducting an amniocentesis, so we don't perform it purely for the purpose of establishing paternity."

Pepe regarded him blankly.

Will realized he'd better rephrase that. "I'll recommend an amnio because of her age, but it's up to Mrs. O'Bannon."

"I can't wait." Pepe jumped up and paced about the office. "This is ruining my life! Gwen will hardly speak to me. You don't understand what I've sacrificed for her!"

"I'm sorry?" Perhaps Will ought to refer the man to a family counselor, except he hadn't heard of anyone practicing that profession in town.

"Gwen is—how can I put this—" Pepe kissed his fingers "—exquisite! A woman of such sophistication, such spirit!"

"Yes, I find Ms. Martin quite impressive." As a member of the city council, she'd been among the citizens who'd greeted Will during his initial visit to town. He'd enjoyed her keen wit and appreciated her astute questions.

"For years, she scarcely knew I was alive," Pepe went on. "Of course, this proved to my advantage in the business sense."

"I understand you're competitors."

"It isn't that. It's Beau." Pepe clarified by adding, "Beau Johnson. He owns the grocery store."

"Yes, I've met Mr. Johnson." Will wished this conversation came with Instant Replay. Maybe then he could make sense of it.

"Beau's mad at Gwen because she sponsors the farmers' market, so he gives me a discount on supplies for my restaurant," Pepe said. "But since we started dating, no more cut rate!"

"We all have to sacrifice for love," Will said ironically.

His humor failed to stem the tide of heartfelt exclamations. "But at last Gwen is mine! Not entirely mine, but almost! Then this business with Rosie… I can't be the father."

"Why not?" Will recalled hearing that Pepe had grown children.

"I had vivisection."

That threw him for a moment. "You mean that you had a vasectomy?"

"Yes!" Pepe announced triumphantly. "There. I knew you were the right doctor!"

Will hated to deflate the man's balloon, but he had to present the facts. "Mr. Otero, are you aware that vasectomies fail a small percentage of the time?"

"Fail?" Pepe frowned at him. "How can they do that?"

"The body has an amazing ability to repair itself," he said. "Did your doctor perform a follow-up sperm count?"

Slowly, the man shook his head. "He told me to return, but it's a long drive to Mill Valley and I'm a busy man."

"I'd recommend that we conduct one now." The part-time lab technician who visited Downhome a couple of times a week was due today. "If the results are negative, you're off the hook."

The restaurateur unbuttoned his jacket. "Very well. I am not afraid. You can take my blood."

This was the sensitive part. "That's not how we do it." Will proceeded to explain how a man produced a sperm sample.

Panic mingled with disgust in Pepe's expression. "You mean, I have to do *that* in the men's room? Doctor, there's got to be another way!"

Will understood his embarrassment. "If you like, you can bring a specimen from home, as long as it's fresh. I'll ask the nurse to give you a container."

The restaurateur stood up straighter. "I am not afraid. I will do it here and get it over with." He cleared his throat. "Do you think you could give me the container yourself, Doctor?"

It wasn't much to request. "Of course." Will glanced at his watch. "Mr. Li, our tech, should be here about ten o'clock. I'll ask him to run the test as soon as possible."

"Thank you."

This ought to be interesting, Will thought as he went in search of a lidded cup. At least he understood now why Pepe had declared his innocence.

A few hours later, the results came back: the specimen teemed with the wriggly little devils. Will informed Mr. Otero by phone. "Of course, this doesn't prove you're the father, only that you're fertile."

The reaction was a gravelly, "Oh," followed by, "So she's not lying."

"If you'd still like a DNA test…"

"Not necessary, I guess." With that cryptic remark, Pepe hung up.

The rest of the day passed without incident. On call that night, Will encountered only minor problems that could be handled by phone.

In short order, Saturday arrived—a day of two weddings, seven hundred miles apart. A day of new beginnings and romance.

But not for him, Will reflected sternly. After attending his colleague's nuptials, he intended to spend the evening very much alone.

Chapter Twelve

"Ethan's handsome in a tux, don't you agree?" Rosie said wistfully.

She sat between Leah and Mark in a pew, beaming at the groom as last-minute wedding guests trickled into the church. Through stained glass windows, late-afternoon sunshine cast colored shapes across the congregation.

"I'm rather taken with the ring bearer." Leah's student was adorable in his minitux, carefully displaying the ring on a cushion. She'd heard quite a bit from Nick over the past few days about this important role in his father's wedding.

Mark didn't comment. He was too busy twisting around to glare at Pepe, who sat in a far corner by himself. Gwen had stayed at the café to make final preparations for the reception.

Beside Ethan, Mayor Archie Rockwell adjusted his bow tie as he prepared to fulfill the role of best man. She was going to miss these old friends when she moved away, she thought.

Then, across the aisle, she caught sight of the city manager's thin face tightening as he glimpsed her. At his side, Minnie pointedly avoided Leah's gaze. Nor did she attempt to discipline her daughter, who stood facing backward in the pew, clowning for the benefit of some other children. When a woman behind them finally ordered the girl to sit, Sybill flounced down and clacked her heels against the wood.

Leah certainly wasn't going to miss *them*.

Ahead and to her left, rainbow colors from the windows played across a pair of broad shoulders and a dark-blond head. Caught by unexpected emotions, she watched Will slip into place next to his nurse. Then, afraid someone might have noticed her staring, Leah waved to a former student nearby, pretending he had been the object of her attention all along.

She and Will were both adults, for heaven's sake. In any other setting, they'd be free to pursue their friendship—if, of course, they wanted to. Why did this place have to be both so dear and so confining?

Another late arrival found room at the end of their pew. Leah nearly failed to recognize the transformed Amy Arroyo.

The layered haircut that replaced the careless pile atop her head flattered the shape of her face, which used to appear long and thin. In addition, her new makeup brought out full lips and large eyes beneath her glasses. She'd become Cinderella, with a whole salon full of fairy godmothers.

Mercifully, her arrival made Mark forget about Pepe. Welcoming her to the pew, he asked about a book she was carrying. Her animated expression indicated she relished his interest.

The pianist launched into a selection of romantic melodies and Leah sat back to enjoy the music. When the notes shifted into a prologue to the wedding march, Ben Fellows at the pulpit signaled the crowd to hush.

Down the aisle paced bridesmaid Yvonne Johnson, followed at a measured gait by Karen. Peach-colored dresses, peach-and-blue flowers, the faint smell of honeysuckle in the air—Leah found the mixture exhilarating.

Amid the strains of "Here Comes the Bride," Jenni appeared at the head of the aisle, lovely in an off-the-shoulder white gown. She strolled toward the altar on the arm of an older woman Leah had heard was her mentor.

Awaiting her, Ethan radiated happiness. Leah's heart twisted as she recalled that once, not many years ago, Will had waited at the altar for a different bride. How must he feel, knowing that today, perhaps at this very moment, Allison was accepting a ring from her new husband?

She didn't dare peek at him.

Jenni floated toward her groom. Usually down-to-earth, she appeared barely aware of her surroundings.

That could have been me, Leah thought with a pang. If she'd accepted Will's proposal. But it wouldn't have been the same, because what he'd offered had been a marriage of convenience, not love.

Instinctively, she touched her abdomen, which felt large, although she didn't show yet. Both of them loved this baby, even before seeing it. Will had said he wasn't capable of romantic love, yet she'd caught flashes of tenderness in him that took her breath away.

Why was she torturing herself? Will would never stand there as Ethan did, beaming at his bride. And she certainly didn't want to fill a domestic role when she could be jetting off to explore exciting possibilities.

She didn't understand why tears welled in her eyes for things that might have been. Perhaps it was only human to wish for more than any one person had a right to expect.

By the time Leah had collected her thoughts, the groom was saying "I do." Excitedly, Nick presented the ring to his father, who slipped it onto Jenni's finger.

When the couple kissed, a ray of sunlight illuminated their figures, presenting the images of a classic bride and groom. They seemed to Leah to be magically preserved in that moment, apart from the photographer discreetly snapping their pictures.

Then, laughing, they hurried down the aisle. Startled, she remembered that she'd brought soap bubbles, and pulled the plastic vial from her purse.

After a quick "Excuse me" to her aunt, Leah moved along the pew. Amy stood to let her pass.

When she spotted the bubbles, she cried, "Oh! I brought some, too!"

"Let's go get 'em!" Leah said.

The two women scurried down the side aisle while most of the crowd was still getting to its feet. They flew across a foyer still blessedly empty. On the front steps, Leah spotted the couple escaping into a horse-drawn carriage designed to resemble an old-fashioned Hansom cab. From the interior, Nick waved at her.

"Wait!" Amy called to her boss.

"Sorry!" Ethan didn't sound the least bit apologetic as he handed Jenni inside.

"Don't imagine you can't escape that easily!" Leah called. "We're bringing our bubbles to the reception!"

"I'll have Gwen bar the door," Ethan joked, and disappeared after his bride.

The horses clattered off with the carriage. Although the bridal couple had escaped, Leah sent cascades of bubbles floating down the street, and her companion followed suit.

"That was fun," Amy said wistfully, closing her container.

"You're attending the reception, aren't you?" Leah asked.

"Sure," her companion said. "I'm not in the way or anything, am I?"

"Are you kidding? We love having you around. Especially Mark!"

Amy gave a little hop. "Oh, thank you!"

In high school, Amy—three years younger than Leah—had been so shy people had scarcely noticed her. Even after both girls volunteered at the library and got to know each other, Amy had revealed little about herself except that she'd grown up the youngest of six children on a dairy farm.

An idea came to Leah. "Why don't you walk to the café with us." It was only a block and a half away.

The secretary regarded her gratefully. "You don't mind?"

"Not at all." Impulsively, she went on, "I love your new style."

"It's not too fancy?" Amy asked.

"No. You're gorgeous." Leah halted as people began pouring out of the church.

Mark's expression brightened when he saw Amy. With only a bit of encouragement, he soon had a lady on each arm. Leah purposely hung back, giving them space.

A cluster of churchgoers surrounded Will, apparently posing questions. Although he stood in the midst of a crowd, to Leah, he seemed to hold himself a little apart.

Realizing she was gaping at the man again, she caught up with her family. At the reception, a lot of eyes would be observing, and some of them—like Minnie's—would be critical. She needed to be careful.

They and the other guests paraded along Home Boulevard to The Green and arrived at the Café Montreal to find it draped with white bunting. Inside, waiters and waitresses served trays of hors d'oeuvres and champagne.

At Gwen's instructions, two employees began detaching the cloths covering the mural. "Let's do this before the place gets packed!" she told them.

Dramatically, the drapes fell to the floor. Amy clapped her hands in delight, and Leah was tempted to do the same.

On the wall, the artist had created a sidewalk café much like the Montreal, filled with characters drawn from the population of Downhome. Jenni and Ethan, in their bride-and-groom outfits, shared a wedding dinner served by Gwen, wearing a chef's hat, and Nick in his little tux.

Arturo had a keen sense of humor and a taste for irony, Leah thought as she picked out additional faces from the street scene. Grumpy Beau Johnson appeared as a clown, Archie and Olivia as acrobats, and Ben Fellows, in tights and a harlequin jacket, held a hoop for a very athletic Estelle to dive through.

The artist and his girlfriend happily accepted compliments on the painting. It was their wedding gift to the couple and a token of appreciation to the town, Arturo announced. They were leaving shortly for Knoxville, where he'd landed an art scholarship.

"Well, if you won't let me pay you as I intended, then I'll have to give my bride another gift," Ethan said cheerfully. "Dr. Vine, I'm taking you on a tour of France and Italy so you can study how reality compares with Arturo's murals."

Leah sighed. Although she loved the idea of them taking a dream trip, if they departed for a lengthy honeymoon instead of their planned three-day escape, who would she turn to as a physician?

"I've always longed to go!" Jenni cried. "But I don't have a passport."

"Don't worry." He slipped an arm around her waist. "I figured we'd plan this together. We can go next summer if you like."

Leah's tension eased. That left plenty of time for her baby, which was due in April.

So many people had crammed into the restaurant that they left little room to maneuver. Several times in the crush, Leah nearly bumped into Will and had to take extra care to avoid him.

However, she forgot that concern when she heard Minnie raise her voice above the racket. "I certainly didn't mean to give the impression I approve of her behavior, so I quit! If you ask me, a teacher ought to set a good example!"

Heads swiveled. Gazes fixed on Leah, then darted away.

"She was your room mom, wasn't she?" Rosie asked at Leah's side.

Leah nodded. "I don't see why she has to attack me in public. It's not as if I did anything to her personally."

"She should be careful or she's not going to like the haircut she gets next time," her aunt vowed.

The Tuckers hadn't finished, though. Following his wife's example, Alton boomed, "In my opinion, our sweet little girl shouldn't have to be exposed to that kind of thing."

Rosie made a face. "Sweet little girl? She acted like a hooligan in church!" She spoke too softly for the words to carry to the Tuckers, however.

"And she had the nerve to criticize Sybill's behavior!" Minnie chimed in. "She said she was acting out, whatever that means. Miss Morris is the one acting out of turn, *she's* having a baby with no husband!"

A hush had fallen over the room. If anyone had missed the earlier remarks, they couldn't help hearing this last sally.

Leah's dress felt so tight she had to strain to breathe. She saw Will start in her direction, but a couple of ladies blocked his path, apparently determined to engage him in conversation. Unable to make headway without elbowing them aside, he halted.

Archie Rockwell broke the uncomfortable lull. "I want to propose a toast to the bride and groom!"

"A toast!" Olivia raised her glass.

Grateful for the distraction, Leah joined in. As best man, of course, Archie would be expected to salute the happy couple, but she suspected his wife had prompted the timing.

"To the most ornery pair it's ever been my privilege to stand up for!" the mayor declared merrily. "Long may they drive each other crazy!"

Laughter greeted this comment. The toasting wasn't

finished, however. "To a great chief of police," Ben Fellows said. "And to the woman who turned him into a civilized human being."

"To a wonderful colleague," Estelle added.

"Amen to that!" came Will's voice.

The staff poured another round of champagne, with white grape juice for the children and other teetotalers. Before anyone else could speak, Nick seized his chance. Climbing onto a chair, the little boy declared, "To my parents!"

Ethan tapped his glass against his son's. "To a wonderful kid and his beautiful new mom."

"I second that!" Ethan's mother, Annette Forrest, radiated goodwill toward her daughter-in-law. Annette had rented her garage apartment to Jenni over Ethan's initial objections, and done her best to foster the match.

"Hey, Chief, are we finished with the toasts?" Mark called. "I'd like some cake!"

"Are you kidding?" Ethan shot back. "Here's another one. To my mother, who is too terrific for words."

More champagne went down the hatch. Finally, Annette said, "Okay, this isn't a toast. It's an announcement. Actually, it's a request."

"Anything you want!" Jenni declared.

"Not from you, sweetheart. You've done more than enough by taking this big lug off my hands." To Leah's surprise, Mrs. Forrest faced her and Rosie across the room. "Since I'd like to stay as involved as possible in my grandson's life, I'm hoping Miss Morris will accept me as her new room mom, if the position is available."

Although she'd made no mention of Minnie or her uncharitable remarks, the statement clearly carried a rebuke. Annette wasn't just making a point, though. Leah got the impression she really wanted the job. And she'd be perfect—experienced, no-nonsense and, at sixty, still young enough to keep up with the students.

"I can't imagine anyone I'd rather have!" Leah called. "You've got the job!"

She heard a few cheers and some low-key congratulations. Minnie's mouth puckered as if she'd bitten a lemon.

"We'll expect you Monday morning," Olivia told Annette.

"Nick and I will be there with bells on." Mrs. Forrest smiled at her grandson. "Won't we?"

"You bet!"

Although she hadn't consumed any alcohol, Leah discovered that she felt light-headed, and Rosie looked flushed. The two of them found a table, leaving Mark and Amy to circulate.

"God bless Annette," Rosie said.

Leah seconded that sentiment.

A short while later, Ethan and Jenni cut the cake. After the initial few slices, Gwen finished the job for them, and her staff distributed portions.

Karen and Barry stopped by the table, followed by other friends. All had plenty of unpleasant things to say about the Tuckers, but Leah discouraged them.

"Their daughter's still my student." She glanced toward the child, who was leading a childish game of hide-and-seek beneath the tables. "I'd rather stay above the fray if I can."

"You're more charitable than I'd be," Barry responded, "but I admire you for it."

She missed the bride and groom's exit, probably because the two of them purposely slipped away without fanfare. Gradually the crowd thinned, but Rosie had her feet propped up and Leah was in no hurry to walk back to the church, where she'd left her car.

Karen had just departed when voices rose again in what

sounded like an argument. Leah's heart sank. Not the Tuckers, she hoped, and then recognized Mark's angry tone.

"If I hear one more snotty remark about loose morals, whoever's doing the yapping will have me to deal with!" Mark shouted.

Peering through the handful of remaining guests, Leah saw that he was addressing Beau Johnson. "Oh, terrific," she murmured as the older man turned scarlet. "He'll have a heart attack and Mark'll have to give him CPR."

"Beau Johnson doesn't have a heart," Rosie responded heatedly. "If he did, he wouldn't treat his own niece so badly."

The reference to Yvonne reminded Leah that Beau was simply mean to everyone. He also wasn't one to let a whippersnapper get the better of him.

"I'll say whatever I darn well please!" Beau rasped. "What're you going to do—shoot me?"

"Everybody cool down." Gwen held up her hands. "This is a wedding reception, not the gunfight at the OK Corral."

Mark, who'd obviously had too much to drink, transferred his bad temper to her. "I'd like to know why you haven't done more to get that shiftless boyfriend of yours to shape up."

An embarrassed Amy slipped away from where she'd been standing behind Mark. He apparently didn't notice her scooting out of the café.

Leah could have kicked her cousin. The idiot was so caught up in his crusade that he might have lost his chance.

"Whoa!" Gwen said. "I don't tell Pepe how to run his life. Now, why don't you folks finish up this cake? We've got plenty left."

Just when Leah began to hope matters might simmer down, Pepe emerged from the kitchen with a tray of petits fours. Ordinarily, the sight of him helping his competitor might have amused her, but right now she wished he'd stayed out of view.

Mark wheeled on him. "There you are!"

"Not you again!" Spinning on his heel, Pepe attempted to make a getaway. The swinging door smacked into the tray, sending him staggering backward.

"Coward!" The young officer dodged toward him around some tables. "Do you think the whole town isn't aware you abandoned my mother and your own child!"

Regaining his balance, Pepe set the tray on the pastry counter. "This situation is not my fault."

Next to Leah, Rosie buried her face in her hands. Peeking between her fingers, she said, "Someone should stop them. This could turn ugly."

"Mark!" Leah called. "Your mom wants you to cut it out."

He ignored her. Will, who'd finally freed himself from his admirers, glanced between them uncertainly, as if unsure whether to get involved. Too bad both Ethan and Ben, Mark's superiors, had already departed.

While everyone else tried to figure out what to do, the restaurateur and the policeman glared across the counter.

"How can you claim it wasn't your fault?" Mark demanded. "What did she do—drug you and tie you up?"

"She should have taken precautions. I wouldn't expect a forty-seven-year-old woman to get pregnant!" Pepe cried.

Several more onlookers peeled away, probably more afraid of a fight than drawn to the spectacle. Gossip was one thing, violence another.

"You're going to be a father," Mark growled. "You ought to act like one, you creep." In his fury, he gripped the edges of the glass display rack so hard he tilted it.

"You crack that and you'll pay for it!" Gwen interjected.

Too late. The tray of petits fours slid toward Pepe, and his grab went wild, sending the little cakes spewing toward his opponent. One of them hit Mark right in the chest.

Fuming, Leah's cousin stormed around the counter, fists raised. As onlookers stood frozen, Gwen seized a soda nozzle and let both combatants have it, incidentally spraying a few bystanders who didn't get clear fast enough.

"Thank you!" Rosie called to her. To Leah, she added, "We will never live this down! Never!"

Dripping wet, Pepe stared defiantly at his opponent. "This is between Rosie and me! Stay out of it."

"People have been insulting my mother all week, and you're encouraging them, you selfish jerk!" Mark raged. He started forward again, but halted when Gwen raised the soda nozzle.

"Excuse me, gentlemen." Keeping clear of the bottle's range, Will spoke with unmistakable authority. "I have a suggestion."

Both men visibly struggled to hold their tempers. "Okay, Doc," Pepe said. "You explain to this lunkhead how it's not my fault about the baby."

"Of course it's your fault," Mark snapped. "Besides, he's my mother's physician, not yours!"

"If you both don't simmer down," Will warned, "this case will end up in court. Let's make sure at least it's a civil court and not a criminal one."

To Leah's relief, her cousin eased back. "Yeah. Court sounds like a good idea. We'll fry your butt, Pepe."

The restaurateur's hands balled. "Let Dr. Rankin finish."

"Finish what?" Mark asked.

Sternly, Will said, "It's always better to try to arrive at an agreement on your own. You need to choose a neutral negotiator, or maybe a referee would be more accurate. I'd recommend Mr. or Mrs. Rockwell."

"They left," Gwen observed.

"I mean later, after tempers cool."

It seemed to Leah that the two men's stances became less

pugnacious, thanks to Will's calming effect. But neither man was about to relent any time soon.

"While people keep badmouthing my mother?" Mark challenged. "I want to settle this today."

"I agree." Despite his shorter stature, Pepe faced the young officer squarely. "We have our negotiator. I trust you to be fair, Dr. Rankin."

"Me?" Will obviously hadn't expected that.

Mark conceded the point. "I agree. He has my mother's best interests at heart, which is more than I can say for some people around here."

Gwen glanced at Rosie. "You should have the last word."

"Of course I trust the doctor," said Leah's aunt.

Will shot Leah a panicked look. He hadn't meant to inject himself in the middle of a feud, she saw, but if he declined, the situation might deteriorate.

With experience born of breaking up countless playground squabbles, Leah rose to the occasion. "You two guys are dripping wet. Why doesn't everybody go home and dry off and we can all meet later."

Will mouthed a Thank you. The others nodded. "Okay," he said. "Here are the ground rules. We meet again at seven o'clock." It was nearly five now. "That gives you two hours to decide what you can reasonably expect from the other party and what you're willing to concede."

"But, Doc," Pepe protested. "I couldn't help it."

Will chose not to respond. "Second, when we meet, you don't address each other directly. You speak only to me, and you follow my directions. Got that?"

The combatants nodded.

"By the way," Gwen said, "where are we meeting? My restaurant opens for business in an hour."

"At the doctor's house," Mark said.

"Fine by me," Pepe chimed in.

Although Will didn't seem thrilled, he provided his address. "One more ground rule," he added. "Officer, leave your gun at home."

Mark regarded the holster beneath his jacket as if he'd forgotten he was wearing it. "As a peace officer, I'm required to carry it at all times."

"Not in my house," Will responded.

"I suppose I could remove the bullets," he conceded.

"All right, if that's the best you can do."

Leah hadn't even considered that possible threat. She was grateful that her cousin hadn't, either.

As the café emptied, Will stopped by Rosie's table. "Are you feeling all right, Mrs. O'Bannon?"

"Fine. Thanks, Doc," she said. "Thank you for doing this!"

"My pleasure. Leah?" She heard a note of pleading. "Would you mind stopping by around six? I could use a consultant."

"I'd be glad to." She did know the participants better than he, she supposed. And it might be easier to manage them as a team.

"I'm not trained in crisis management." Despite his air of professional detachment for the benefit of onlookers, she sensed genuine concern.

"Neither am I, unless you picture this bunch as overgrown first-graders," Leah joked.

"There are definitely similarities." His mouth curved. "I suppose I ought to prime my garden hose, just in case. Or borrow that seltzer bottle."

"They'll behave," Rosie assured him. "Mark should sober up by then."

"Let's hope so." Will said his farewells and departed.

"What a wonderful man," Rosie said dreamily. "Leah, it's

too bad you went ahead and got yourself pregnant before he showed up. I think he might have been interested in you."

Leah couldn't figure out a sensible answer to make, so she didn't try.

Chapter Thirteen

The first thing Will did when he arrived home was change from his suit to jeans and a black sweater that the girls had given him last Christmas. The second thing he did was to log on to the Internet and track the hurricane's progress.

It was veering toward the Gulf Coast of Florida. While Texas might get some rain, the girls should be spared the brunt of it.

Hoping to hear their little voices, he dialed their cell phone, but found it out of service. Probably they were still attending Brad and Allison's wedding dinner, a much more elaborate affair than Ethan and Jenni's reception. But it no doubt lacked the testosterone-fueled fireworks he'd witnessed.

Hopefully, it also lacked the undercurrent of gossip. As Will arranged chairs in the living room, he fumed about the snide remarks. He'd longed to rush in and tell the Tuckers to mind their own business, but that would only have embarrassed Leah.

He didn't like leaving her to take the heat. Still, as long as she refused to marry him, she might be better off sticking to the artificial insemination story than revealing the truth. At least, she believed so, and it was her call.

Pepe and Mark must be out of their minds to believe Will had any expertise as a counselor. All his instincts seemed to be wrong where women were concerned.

He'd loused up his marriage to Allison, and he'd pretty well ruined things with Leah that first night. He'd failed to make things right by proposing, and she'd gone ballistic when he suggested sharing custody.

For all he knew, he might make things worse between Pepe and Rosie. Thank goodness Leah had agreed to help. She had a sixth sense about people that Will envied.

He wondered why the Tuckers didn't see that they should give serious consideration to whatever advice she offered about their daughter. Sybill had spent one afternoon visiting the twins, after which Mrs. McNulty had declared that they would either meet that child at the park or go to the Tuckers' house in the future. Otherwise, she'd said, they'd have to hire a wrecking crew.

Will stared at the circle he'd created and decided it reminded him too much of a group therapy session. He changed to a more casual arrangement, then went to brew decaf.

When the bell rang, he admitted Leah at once. In the glow of the porch light, a deep-pink turtleneck brought out the bloom in her cheeks. As she slipped by him, the sheen of her dark hair made him long to bury his face in it.

Chalk up another near misstep for Dr. Rankin he thought ruefully, and restricted himself to saying, "Thanks for coming."

"My pleasure. Thanks for helping my family." A flash from her blue eyes threatened to draw him back under her spell.

"What's your opinion?" Will gestured toward the furniture. "I tried a big circle. Didn't like the effect. This still looks kind of formal."

"When kids quarrel, I find the best tactic is to separate them for a while." Leah prowled toward the family room. "Too bad the layout is so open. We ought to split up so each group can decide on key points before we risk a face-to-face."

"That makes sense." At least, it might delay the moment

when the two hotheaded males would turn his house into a boxing ring. "Can you handle one of the groups?"

"Sure, I can deal with my family." He observed as she made a circuit through the kitchen. "My aunt will feel comfortable sitting at the table, so I'll claim this room for my team."

"Suits me." As they returned to the front, he reviewed their strategy. "I'm a little worried. If each side prepares positions, it might simply harden their resolve."

Leah shrugged. "They're like kids. Psychologically, they need to feel that somebody's listening. That actually makes it easier to accept compromise."

Will spread his hands in frustration. "Why can't they just examine the facts and make logical decisions?"

Scooping up a little girl's hair bow that had escaped his notice, she set it on a side table. "Because people aren't logical. They're emotional."

"You see? I'm too impatient for this job." He drummed his fingers on an end table. "They should have chosen you."

"But I can't project authority the way you do." Leah sank into the couch, relaxing against the cushions. "When Pepe and Mark chose you as their negotiator, that was a huge compliment. They've only known you for a few weeks and yet they trust you to help determine their futures."

"I have no idea why."

"Because you have qualities that they recognize and you don't," she said. "You don't truly believe in yourself, Will. Why not?"

How had they traveled from discussing strategy to yanking out his soul for inspection? Still, he answered the question. "Because I screw things up. Like with Allison. Like with you, that night in Austin."

"It has to go further back than that," she said. "Why do you always pull back when I get close?"

"Do I?" He stood behind a chair, gripping the back as if it were a shield. Or a turtle's shell. Obviously, she'd pegged him right. "It isn't just that I make mistakes. It's that after I make them, I still have no idea what I did wrong."

"Can you give me an example?" Her eyes trained on him. Although he hated digging into his guts, he would hate disappointing her even more.

"Okay, I'll give you one." Although it had happened fifteen years ago, the memory still troubled him. "My junior year in college. My adviser urged me to take a summer lab job to help prepare me for medical school. I really wanted it, but my dad had hurt himself on the ranch. Burt—my oldest brother—was in the marines and Mike was busy earning his commercial pilot's license, and my younger brother, Aaron, couldn't handle the work alone. I had to go back and help."

"How did your adviser react?" Leah asked.

"He called it lack of commitment," Will answered bitterly. "He decided to recommend someone else for a scholarship I'd been counting on. When I found out how much medical school was going to cost, I nearly dropped my plans."

"But you didn't," she pointed out.

"I guess I'm stubborn." The truth was that he'd been able to face the prospect of massive student loans better than the death of his dream. "Here's the kicker, Leah. That fall, when I finally broke the news to my family that I intended to be a doctor, they belittled me. I'd kept my plan to myself as long as possible, afraid it wouldn't work out, but when push came to shove—they shoved back, hard."

"Why?" She watched him.

"Because going meant leaving their world behind." Will had understood that much, despite his confusion and hurt. "For some reason it bothered them more than what my brothers chose to do. There were harsh words that came between us for years." He sighed. "I don't know why I'm talking about this. What's the point?"

"I get it," Leah said slowly. "In both cases, you were the one who acted rationally, but people you cared about punished you for it. That made you doubt your own instincts."

He gave her a wry smile. "Are you telling me I was right? Because I figured there was stuff going on that made sense to them that I somehow missed."

"It did make sense to them," Leah told him. "But they were wrong."

Her validation soothed him like balm on a burn. "I always figured that if the rest of the world thinks you're out of step, maybe you are," Will explained.

"Dysfunctional parents can really mess you up, even though they love you." After slipping off her shoes, Leah hugged her knees on the couch. "Take Sybill. She assumes it's okay to misbehave because her parents have convinced her that she's the queen of the world. She doesn't accept the obvious fact that nobody else agrees with them because she's got this self-image firmly entrenched."

"How does that relate to me?" Will asked cautiously.

"You have a self-image that doesn't fit the facts," Leah replied. "You still feel like an outsider, so you protect yourself and stay aloof. Is that true?"

Until now, Will hadn't grasped the extent to which those long-ago incidents and other events had made him doubt himself. "You're good at this," he told Leah.

"It's called being a teacher." She rested her cheek on her knees. "That's why I love the school in Seattle. A lot of the kids bear emotional scars from being square pegs shoved into round holes. The classes are small and the administrator encourages the teachers to get involved. I could do so much good."

A knock at the door dragged him back to the task at hand. "Duty calls," Will said and went to answer it.

LEAH HADN'T EXPECTED the plan to go off without a snag, and she was right. First of all, Gwen called to say she had to stay at work. With rain in the forecast, she had to empty her outdoor dining area. Besides, she said, the issues didn't really involve her. By implication, she was distancing herself from Pepe.

As a result, the restaurateur brought along a different supporter: his elder daughter, Gina. The twenty-two-year-old, who'd recently moved with her husband from Knoxville to Mill Valley, immediately made it plain that, in her view, papa could do no wrong.

Separating the two parties helped, however. After they reassembled, Pepe said that, in view of his high sperm count and his relationship with Rosie, he was willing to concede paternity. Will had also persuaded him to pay at least some child support.

During the kitchen conference, Rosie agreed with Leah's point that she, not Mark, should take charge, and he indicated that was fine with him. His grudging compliance ended, however, the moment Pepe declared that he could only provide a small amount of support because he was helping his two younger kids through college.

"You should have thought of that before you knocked up my mom!" Mark cried.

Rosie cut him off abruptly. "Son," she said, "I love you and I appreciate your support, but for heaven's sake, shut up!"

Her unaccustomed rudeness stopped him dead. Miffed, Mark crossed his arms and sat back, glaring.

"Pepe," Rosie said, "let me tell you what matters a whole lot more than any money. I know you're not interested in me or the baby, but I'd like you to visit her once in a while."

"What's the point?" He bristled with distaste. "I'm too old to start over again."

Will handed Rosie a manila folder. "It's your decision whether you want to show this to him, Mrs. O'Bannon. I picked it up at the clinic on the way home."

When Rosie opened it and gazed down, the light around her seemed to soften. Peeking over, Leah was entranced to see the black-and-white image of a sonogram. "Baby picture," she said.

Gina came to join them. The short, dark-haired woman still slouched a bit, like an adolescent. When Rosie extended the picture, she opened it carefully. "Oh, wow! Papa, you should see this!"

"I don't know." Frowning, Pepe stayed put.

His daughter hurried to him. "It's my little sister! Isn't she cute?" To Rosie, she said, "What are you going to name her?"

"That's her business," Mark grumbled.

Leah ignored him. "Maybe Pepe has a suggestion."

"My mother's name was Maria, but Connie didn't like it. She and Mama didn't get along," Pepe said reluctantly

"Maria's a beautiful name," Rosie responded. "It makes me think of that wonderful song from *West Side Story.*"

"The heroine in *The Sound of Music* is named Maria, too," Gina added brightly.

She was turning out to be their secret weapon. Leah thanked the stars that Pepe had brought her.

"Really? You'd name her Maria?" he asked Rosie.

She beamed. "Of course I would!" Leah suspected she'd have named their daughter Albert if he'd asked.

Pepe inspected the picture his daughter handed him. "Her nose is cute. Like your nose, Gina."

"You'll want to watch her grow up, won't you?" Rosie pressed.

"Sure, I could visit," Pepe said.

"I'm sure Estelle would welcome you at her childbirth-preparation classes, if you're interested," Will ventured.

The father-to-be blinked.

Leah would have bet a month's wages that in short order he'd agree to be Rosie's labor coach. The sonogram and a little encouragement from Gina had done the trick, plus Pepe's own sentiments, of course.

"So you're the new ob-gyn everyone's talking about," Gina said to Will. "When I start a family, I may use you."

"I'd be honored," he responded.

Rosie leveraged herself to her feet. "I'm glad that's settled. Thank you, everybody. Now, if you don't mind, I'm tired."

Gina hurried to open the door. "Be careful. The wind's picking up out there. We don't want you to slip."

She exited right after Rosie. Pepe followed.

Mark paused on the threshold. "I'm glad he's going to pay up, but I don't understand why she's being so nice to him after the way he's treated her. If you ask me, he doesn't deserve to be part of her life."

Leah had no patience left for her judgmental cousin. "Listen, Mark…"

He stopped her. "B-U-T-T out, right?"

"Exactly," she said. "Besides, I hope you realize you embarrassed Amy today at the reception."

"I did?" he asked, startled.

He'd embarrassed a lot of people, but Leah knew which one counted most. "She left when you confronted Pepe. I'll bet she was disappointed you'd forgotten all about her."

"I didn't forget about her!" After a beat, Mark added guiltily, "Well, not exactly. I'd better give her a call." Lost in thought, he said a brief farewell and left into the stormy night.

When Will shut the door, he strained a little against the air pressure. "I'd say that went well."

"Bringing the sonogram was a master stroke." Suddenly aware that they were now alone, Leah got busy collecting coffee cups and crumpled napkins.

Will repositioned a chair. "That reminds me. Has Jenni ordered your ultrasound?"

"Yes. It's scheduled for Tuesday." She hardly dared think about how exciting it would be. "I've arranged to leave school at two. Olivia's going to substitute."

"I usually don't schedule ultrasounds until the second trimester." He continued rearranging the furniture. "You're what—ten, eleven weeks?"

Leah nodded. "Jenni suggested it as a precaution. She won't be back from her honeymoon yet, but the technician's booked for the next few weeks." He'd had a cancellation, and she'd been reluctant to wait any longer than necessary to view her baby.

"It can't hurt." Will paused to listen as a gust of wind hit the house. "Too bad the storm's picking up. I was going to suggest we barbecue some dinner."

Leah, who'd stopped eating at the reception after the quarrel began, had regained her appetite in spades. "You've got food?"

"Hungry?" He didn't wait for a response. "Oh, the heck with the weather. The grill's heavy and it's under a patio cover. I've got hamburgers, salad and baked beans. What do you say?"

"I say, let's live dangerously," Leah joked. Catching sight of a raised eyebrow, she added, "I'm sure we can safely share a meal without arousing…arousing…anything." She blushed at her unfortunate choice of words.

"No problem." He carried some of the cups to the kitchen.

Leah followed with more mugs. Searching for a neutral topic of conversation, she said, "I'm impressed by your matched chinaware. Is this your housekeeper's doing?"

"Allison's, actually." Will began filling the dishwasher. "She wanted all new stuff when she bailed out, so she left this behind."

Leah remembered that his ex-wife might be a sore subject. "I'm sorry. I didn't mean to bring that up, especially today."

He glanced at her. "I'll admit I still have mixed feelings about Allison. I suppose in some way I let her down after she helped me through tough times. She also gave me the girls. But it doesn't tear me up to imagine her sailing down the aisle to that moneybags she ditched me for. They deserve each other."

Despite the disclaimer, she heard the tension behind his words. Enough on that subject, Leah thought. "Okay if I fix the salad?"

"Be my guest."

Working around him, she found a bag of chopped lettuce in the fridge along with dressing, and mixed them in a bowl. After taking the hamburgers outside to cook, Will returned and produced the can of baked beans, which he heated in a casserole.

The scent of approaching rain added a coziness to the kitchen, and after a while Leah relaxed. Will seemed comfortable around her, too. Leah enjoyed sneaking glances at his powerful build beneath the black sweater, and when they bumped each other, he felt solid and warm.

They ate their salads while the meat was cooking. Under the table, their legs tangled and neither seemed eager to pull them apart.

"I wish I'd been able to spend more time with the girls when they were little," Will told her between mouthfuls. "Seeing that picture today really brought it home. I tried to be an involved father, but I was always so rushed I had to steal a moment here and there."

"They're still little. Besides, you've got another one coming." Impulsively, Leah caught his hand and brought it to her abdomen. "You can start spending time with this baby now."

As he gently probed her midsection, the contact heated her.

"It's too early to detect movement, but maybe the baby knows I'm here. I hope so. I want to be a part of this."

Shifting forward, he reached out with his free hand and cupped her midsection, his thumbs stroking her. Sensations rioted through Leah. She almost reminded him to stop, that it wasn't only the baby he was caressing, but she didn't care.

His hands smoothed upward to her breasts, which had grown fuller with pregnancy and become incredibly sensitive. When he chafed the nipples lightly through her sweater, she gasped.

"Is that uncomfortable?" Will murmured.

"Are you kidding?" Afraid he might pull back, Leah placed her hands over his, holding him there. "It's incredible."

"This is only the beginning." He leaned across the edge of the table and kissed her.

Leah's lips parted to welcome him. When he gathered her onto his lap, she noted his hard readiness against her yielding bottom.

She supposed they ought to stop. But why? She wanted him again, wanted all the things she'd experienced in Austin and more. This go-around, she didn't have to worry about where it might lead. They were set on their separate paths, with nothing to lose.

She might never get this chance again.

Will lost himself in stroking her face and hair, as if he'd been longing to do this, stealing little kisses in between. Then he lifted her sweater and bra and, with exquisite care, bent to catch the tips of her breasts between his lips.

Leah relished the tickle of his hair and the movement of his tongue against her bare skin. She pulled off her sweater and tossed them aside.

"You are amazing." Will lifted his head and studied her with heavy-lidded gray eyes. "Just overwhelming."

"You're not even halfway overwhelmed yet," she shot back, tracing the muscular swell of his chest right down to the belt buckle that had given her so much trouble last time. "Let's get rid of this, shall we?"

"With pleasure." Their hands met as if in a familiar ritual, tugging at the metal. He kissed her again, claiming her with his tongue as they pulled the belt free.

Somehow, they managed to remove his pants and her underwear. Leah straddled him on the chair, torn between amusement and desire as they fought for balance, then giving a little cry of joy as he spread her and entered.

Will moaned. "This is heaven."

"Seventh heaven," she said.

They wrapped around each other, connecting at every level. Leah had never felt so daring or so free.

Anchoring herself by his shoulders, she nuzzled the roughness of Will's jaw. She could hardly believe she was allowed to touch him any way she wanted. No hesitation. No worrying about the future. Nothing but pure enjoyment.

He pushed into her from below, holding her hips steady. The delirious pressure made her back arch as he thrust, again and again, losing control without apology. Leah rode him all the way to a surge of sheer ecstasy that she wanted never to end.

At last, they collapsed against each other, holding tight. "Bedroom," Will whispered.

"I can't move," she rejoined.

"Teamwork."

Keeping close together, they staggered to their feet. Laughing, Leah half tugged Will through the house, stopping briefly to hug and kiss him in the hall.

He had a man's bedroom, starkly utilitarian except for a tumbled row of books in the headboard and a queen-size bed that welcomed them both as if it had been waiting. Perhaps it had, and so had she. Subconsciously, Leah had been anticipating this moment since she'd spotted Will across the classroom on the first day of school.

She suspected that this crazy sense of abandon would vanish if they tried to make it last, but she intended to enjoy it while she could. All night, if possible.

EVEN WHEN HE'D met Leah, when Will had poured all his anxieties and longings into making love, he hadn't been seized by such a powerful response. Now no condom reduced his sensations, but it was also because he knew Leah so well and craved her so much.

In bed, she tackled him, rolling deliciously among the sheets. His body needed her again already with the ferocity of a teenager, except that now he had the heart of a man.

When her softness closed around him, Will had to struggle to keep his urges in check. He'd already planted his seed in her. Now he could take things slowly and imprint her with something deeper.

Eagerness claimed him, putting the lie to his intentions. The two of them waged a battle that promised victory for both sides, and won it in a dazzle of radiance. Hardly able to catch his breath, Will felt Leah curl against him, and enfolded her in his arms.

He drew up the comforter and rested his face against her hair. He wanted to lie here on the edge of wakefulness, bathing in their shared glow and in the lingering scent of her perfume. He loved the weight of her in his arms and the knowledge that their baby-to-be lay sheltered between them.

Sleep stole over him without a whisper.

He awoke to the scream of sirens.

Chapter Fourteen

They'd forgotten about the hamburgers. The meat had turned into charred lumps, which might not have been a problem, except that a loose wing of newspaper had blown onto the grill, sending up a column of flame that caught the patio cover.

Although the result consisted of more smoke than flame, the neighbors had summoned the fire department. By the time Leah and Will threw on their clothes and went to see what had happened, the rain had transformed the blaze into wisps of smoke and the firefighters were mopping up.

Aside from some charring to the concrete patio floor and a burned spot in the cover, Leah saw little damage. Physical damage, that was all. Reputations were another matter.

Every one of the volunteer firefighters and neighbors must have seen the two of them rush to the sliding-glass door in a state of disarray. As if that weren't bad enough, the police showed up, too—specifically, Ben Fellows.

Leah shriveled inside as she lingered in the family room, watching the police captain confer with Will. Ben's meaningful look made her keenly aware of her unbrushed hair and the wrinkled state of her skirt. She had to remind herself that she wasn't a misbehaving youngster.

No, just a misbehaving adult, she reflected wryly. How ironic that her and Will's attempts to keep their relationship private had blown up in such a spectacularly embarrassing manner.

The firefighters accepted Will's thanks before departing. Since Ben lingered, they invited him inside for a cup of coffee.

Thinning hair and sun-etched creases gave the captain an air of quiet understanding. Leah respected him not only for his accomplishments, but also because, four years earlier, she'd seen the good grace with which he accepted defeat when the city council had passed over his application for police chief and hired Ethan, instead.

Ben had welcomed the new arrival without rancor, taking it as a sign that God's plan called for him to focus more on the church. He didn't use his pulpit to bully or condescend, either, but to inspire.

"I'm not going to go telling tales to my wife or Mark," Ben remarked as they sat in the living room. "But I can't vouch for the firefighters, and I'm not going to lie if someone asks me a direct question about what I saw."

"We don't expect you to," Will said. "Leah, are you too cold?"

Although cold air had blown into the house, pregnancy boosted her circulation to the boiling point. "Not in the slightest, thanks."

"I'll take the liberty of speaking as your pastor, since you've both attended my church," Ben said. "People can be judgmental around here, as Leah should be aware. Also, Doctor, there's likely to be some unpleasant talk about you getting involved with one of your patients."

"I'm not his patient," Leah said.

"You aren't?"

"She chose to see Jenni." Will reached for Leah's hand.

"Well, I suppose that's different." Ben moved to his next point. "Still, Leah's in a precarious position already, being a schoolteacher and pregnant out of wedlock. Nobody doubts that Olivia will stand by her, but I suppose you've heard the kinds of things the Tuckers are saying."

"The Tuckers should take care of their own problems. Their little girl is a spoiled brat, and no, I didn't hear that from Leah," Will said. "She's friends with one of my daughters."

"That's neither here nor there." Ben regarded them levelly. "I'm just trying to counsel you both on what to expect. It never hurts to be prepared."

Leah agreed. "I appreciate that."

"As for Mark, we can all guess how he's likely to respond if he believes you've been compromised," Ben added. "That young man has a temper."

"Leah gave him a spelling lesson earlier tonight," Will replied with a hint of a smile. "Something to do with minding his own business."

"Good." Ben glanced from one to the other. "But no matter how Hollywood portrays customary behavior, people around here aren't so open-minded."

Will's back straightened. "If you imagine we take this situation casually, Pastor Fellows, you're wrong about that."

"Good." Setting his cup aside, Ben got to his feet. "Leah, I have to tell you, your family's been working me overtime. Last week, I had to change my sermon, and I suppose I should do the same again tomorrow. I wish I could use the let-he-who-is-without-sin text again, but that might be overdoing it."

He was being so kind Leah couldn't keep him in the dark. "Will?" she said, not wanting to proceed without his agreement. "Um…"

"Say whatever you want," he told her.

Ben sat back down. "I gather there's more."

Leah decided to jump in headfirst. "I didn't have artificial insemination," she said. "It's Will's baby. We met in Austin last summer."

Will ducked his head. "Long story."

Except for a slight frown, Ben gave no sign of being shocked. "How many people know?"

"Dr. Vine," Will said.

"Karen," Leah added. "That's all."

"I figured my wife didn't know or she'd have told me. She tries to keep people's confidences at the clinic, but she isn't always as strong as she should be in that regard," the pastor admitted. "Thank you for trusting me. I won't say anything unless you want me to."

"Please don't," Leah said. "We're still…sorting things out."

When it became evident they'd finished the discussion, Ben rose again and shook hands. "I'm sure you'll do the right thing."

To Will's credit, he didn't disclose that he'd proposed and she had said no. She couldn't justify her refusal to Ben or anyone else. But to her, a marriage like most of the ones she saw resembled a prison sentence.

There was a part of Will that didn't belong to her and probably never would. Leah had grown up with a father like him, and he'd broken her heart a thousand times in little ways.

More than that, there was a part of her that she couldn't give away, either. Staying in Downhome meant clipping her wings before she'd had a chance to spread them. If anything, this whole state of affairs reminded her of exactly how confining it was to live here.

"By the way," Ben added, "I hope you'll feel free to attend services tomorrow. Since people will be hearing about this sooner or later, it might be best if they see you together openly. Sunshine has a healing effect."

"Good idea," Will said, and escorted him out.

When they were alone, Leah wasn't sure whether to laugh or cry. Instead, to her embarrassment, she yawned.

"Am I keeping you awake?" Will teased. "Guess you'd better get back under the covers."

She supposed she ought to drive home. But it was still raining, and besides, in one more night, the girls would return.

"Race you," Leah dared him.

She won, barely, and then had the pleasure of warming her cold feet on Will's legs. She held him close, shutting out any thought of what tomorrow might bring.

Just this once, Leah intended to be as happy as she pleased.

ON THE WAY TO CHURCH, they stopped at Leah's house so she could change. Admiring her colorful furnishings once again, Will wished she would transform his dull rental. Or, rather, that they could choose a new home to suit both their tastes.

His mind veered away from such wishful thinking. He had more urgent matters to deal with. Although the rain had stopped, the sight of downed branches reminded him of another weather situation: the hurricane, and whether it might affect his daughters' return today.

"Leah?" he called from her front room. "Can I use your computer? I want to check on the weather."

Her voice floated from the back. "Sure. It's in my study. There's no password. Just turn it on."

Within a few minutes, he'd accessed the Internet and was staring at photos of devastated homes in Florida. Nothing about Texas, thank goodness, but Mrs. McNulty's daughter lived in Tampa.

On his cell, he dialed Eileen's programmed number. Finding it out of service, he left a message.

Will tried the girls' phone next, but they'd either shut it off or forgotten to recharge the battery.

Although he knew he must be the last person his ex-wife wanted to hear from on her honeymoon, he dialed her cell phone next. He had to make sure everything was on track for the twins' flight.

"The party you are trying to reach is not available at this time."

Will swore out loud. He hoped she hadn't already left for her honeymoon—in Hawaii, the girls had mentioned—without making sure Diane and India were safely on board.

"What?" Leah asked, emerging from the bedroom. "You're scowling."

"I can't reach anyone in Texas." It was hardly a dire situation, Will had to admit, but it troubled him. "I just wanted to confirm the girls' arrangements."

"When are they due?"

"They should arrive in Nashville about seven o'clock. I'll leave at five to pick them up." He shut his phone and, for the first time, noticed that she'd donned a silky blue dress that tempted him to run his hands all over her. "You look terrific."

She laid her palm against his chest. "You're gorgeous yourself, Doc." When she stood on tiptoe and curved her mouth onto his, Will forgot everything else.

The uneasiness returned, however, once they reached the car. Finally, Will identified the feeling. Last night, one shoe had hit the floor—metaphorically speaking—when the firefighters' arrival had torn the wraps off their relationship. Now he was waiting for the other shoe to drop.

His apprehension probably resulted from his own frustrated past, nothing more. He certainly hoped so.

LEAH FELT WORSE for Will than for herself. One way or another, she didn't plan to stick around Downhome. But he'd moved here in good faith, intending to settle with the twins, and she'd made a mess for him.

Curious gazes burned into them as Will escorted her to a pew. Of course, if the gossip hadn't spread, their joint appearance at church would quickly accomplish the same thing, yet she knew Ben had been right about getting matters in the open.

A few minutes later, Karen slid in beside them. She'd come alone; her brother hadn't attended church in the nine years since his release from prison. Their minister years ago had been quick to accept Barry's guilt, and the young man had seen almost the entire congregation unite against him.

Despite the passage of time and his return to take over the family newspaper, Barry couldn't forgive or forget. Leah didn't blame him, but she hoped someday he'd manage to make peace with the past.

Karen barely finished exchanging greetings before exclaiming, "I can't believe it! This is the worst news!"

Leah hoped the subject wasn't her and Will. "What news?" she asked cautiously. On her far side, she saw him listening, too.

"Beryl Sanford!" Karen exclaimed.

"Who?"

"The pediatrician from St. Louis! She's withdrawn her application." Karen spoke loudly enough that people ahead of them swiveled in their seats. She didn't seem to notice. "The council's going to decide Tuesday night who to hire."

Tuesday night meant Ethan would be back. He and Olivia would probably support Chris McRay, putting Karen in the minority on the selection committee. Although the council didn't have to abide by their recommendation, it probably would.

"I'm sorry," Leah said.

"Do people really want a perjurer taking care of their kids?" Karen demanded. "Not to mention that Barry thinks he might have killed Norbert Anglin himself!"

Toward the front of the church, Chris's grandmother, Mae Anne, turned in her wheelchair to regard Karen with disapproval. The two women had become good friends, and Leah hoped this issue wasn't going to divide them.

Before she could point that out, Ben entered at the front and the church quieted. Keenly aware of rustlings around her, Leah had to struggle to concentrate on the service. Although Ben's sermon was no doubt excellent, not a single word of it stuck in her mind.

The talk in the foyer centered on the possibilities for a new pediatrician. "I'm glad to see we're not the big deal we thought we were," Will observed in a low tone.

"You spoke too soon." Leah indicated Mark making his way toward them. Rosie followed with Pepe and Amy.

Her cousin glared at them. "You two...I can't believe it! I thought more of you than that, Doctor."

Will went rigid, but kept silent. Before Leah got a chance to reprove, Pepe reached out to shake Will's hand.

"Dr. Rankin, I want to thank you. A picture is worth a thousand words, no?" She gathered he was referring to the ultrasound. "Now that I've seen my beautiful daughter, now that I understand I really am capable of fathering a child, I'm growing excited about the future."

"We've been talking a lot," Rosie confirmed.

"I nearly missed so much." Pepe drew himself up proudly. "We've decided to name her Maria Wilhelmina, after you!"

"I'm flattered." Will unwound a little. "You don't have to do that."

Rosie refused to accept such modesty. "Why not? You deserve it." When her son opened his mouth again, she said, "Mark, shut up."

On the verge of replying, the young man glanced at Amy

and then closed his mouth. His companion shifted a little nearer, and Mark put an arm around her waist.

No one else took much notice of the little group, which made a nice change from what Leah had feared. Instead, a handful of folks clustered around Karen and others around Mae Anne.

While the pediatrician disagreement held center stage, she decided it might be a good time to spill the rest of their news. "There's something I'd like to tell you," she told Rosie. "I hope you won't take it the wrong way."

"You mean that Dr. Rankin's the father of your baby?" her aunt said. "We already heard."

Leah was so startled she could barely respond. "How… who…?"

"Karen let the cat out of the bag before the service," Rosie replied. "Someone was grumbling about the two of you getting caught in bed. She said it was about time you went public, with your baby on the way."

"That's it." Leah spread her hands. "I'm completely out of secrets."

"Good," her cousin said, "because I'm not sure I could take any more."

From across the foyer, she heard Mae Anne declaring that the Lowells had no business slandering her wonderful grandson. "Oh, dear!" Rosie said. "I hate when people split into camps! And I'm going to have to choose sides on Tuesday night."

Since getting elected to the city council, she'd agonized over her responsibilities whenever controversy arose. Leah was searching for a way to reassure her when Pepe beat her to it.

"Guess what?" he said. "This town isn't going to fall apart because of a disagreement about which doctor to hire. Forget them. Let's celebrate our own happy news. Two babies in one family calls for a party!"

"You're welcome to have it at my house," Will offered. "Just don't ask me to barbecue."

Leah grinned and took his hand. Even Mark chuckled a bit, unwillingly.

Gwen stopped nearby. "Did I hear somebody mention a party?"

Rosie glanced at her hesitantly. Pepe averted his gaze. "My house," Will said. "Around two o'clock?" Others nodded, confirming the time.

"I'll bring the wine," she replied. "Pepe, I'm sorry to break it to you, but I only dated you on the rebound. I've had a mad crush on Ethan for years, even though I doubted anything would come of it. Now that he's married, I don't need you anymore. So let's toast the local population boom."

After a crestfallen moment, Pepe recovered quickly. "I knew you weren't in love with me."

"Hearts mend," Gwen told him. "And you've found one worth keeping." She indicated to Rosie.

Just past them, Leah caught sight of Minnie Tucker, grimacing as she regarded the little group. Quickly, the woman moved away, hauling her daughter with her as if Sybill might be contaminated by the contact.

Her attitude drained some of the sparkle from Leah's mood. Then she felt Will's hand on her arm.

For heaven's sake, why waste this precious day worrying about someone else's resentment? "I'll make brownies," she volunteered, and put the Tuckers out of her mind.

By three o'clock, Will's house had taken on a thoroughly festive air. Across the front room hung a large banner, on which Rosie had lettered "Welcome, Maria And Baby Rankin!" Gwen surrounded it with helium balloons left from the wedding that read "Congratulations!" and "Best Wishes!"

Word spread fast. Ben, Estelle and Patsy Fellows showed

up, as did several employees from the beauty salon. At Leah's invitation, Karen and Barry Lowell attended, joined by Annette Forrest. Even Archie and Olivia Rockwell put in an appearance.

The dining room table overflowed with platters of food. Guests helped out in the kitchen and with the serving.

Will strolled through the place, accepting claps on the back and good-natured teasing. He kept wondering if he'd wandered into the wrong house and been mistaken for somebody else.

At Allison's parties, she'd given the impression that she lived in dread of his breaking the china or saying the wrong thing, as if he were a raw kid. Of course, for quite a few years now, he'd commanded respect from his patients and colleagues, but outside of work, Will had found true acceptance only with his girls and Mrs. McNulty.

Now he was hosting a party for a bunch of people who seemed to regard him as their new best friend. It reminded him of a fantasy he used to have as a child, in which he won an entire toy store for Christmas, because this felt just as good. If he wasn't careful, he might fall in love with this town.

At the center of it all glowed Leah. She had an amazing ability to keep track of everyone and everything at once. And people sought her out, eager for her sympathetic company and upbeat comments.

The whole scene was so perfect it worried him. In the back of his mind, Will hadn't quit waiting for the other shoe to drop.

Perhaps it was because he still couldn't reach Eileen or the girls. He hadn't been able to get through to Allison, either. Why didn't they turn on their damn phones?

At least Will had figured out why he kept expecting the worst. On his parents' ranch, disaster had loomed at every turn. Bad weather or a drop in the price of beef could wipe out a year's profit and threaten the family's financial survival. So he'd grown up in more or less permanent crisis mode.

At four o'clock, when another round of phone calls proved fruitless, he confided his apprehension to Leah. "I checked with the airline to see if they made the flight, but no one could tell me," he said. "I may drive to Nashville early and try to buttonhole a clerk at the ticket counter."

For privacy, they'd stepped into the hallway that led to the bedrooms. "Do you really think something might be wrong?"

"I can't imagine what, but it isn't like Eileen not to check in." Despite his concern, he'd been hoping the problem would resolve itself. Now anxiety closed in. "Something must have gone amiss. Maybe I should call my former in-laws." Surely they'd kept tabs on their granddaughters.

A stir from the other room and the cheerful sound of children's shouts yanked him from his thoughts. Hoping the inexplicable had happened, Will strode into the living room.

His heart swelled. There they were, his two little angels.

"Hi, Daddy!" Diane raced across the room and leaped into his arms, followed at a more sedate pace by her sister.

"Hi, sweethearts." Kneeling, Will gathered them close in a rush of love. Then he glanced around for Mrs. McNulty. He didn't see her.

Instead, his ex-wife stood amid the balloons with shock written on her face. She was staring at the banner that contained the words *Baby Rankin*.

At least he wouldn't have to figure out how to break the news, he thought. But what was she doing here?

"Your wedding went okay, I hope?" Will asked. To the puzzled glances of onlookers, he explained, "Everyone, this is the girls' mother."

The others quieted. Several expressed subdued greetings, which Allison ignored.

"It went fine," she stammered. "Mrs. McNulty had to go to Florida to take care of her family. I was supposed to call you, but I thought a surprise might be fun, so we caught an earlier flight."

"Thanks for bringing them home." No point in reproaching her with the fact that he'd spent the entire day worrying. At least she hadn't stuck the twins on a plane and left them to the care of a flight attendant. "I figured you'd be on your honeymoon."

"India has an ear infection. My mother figured she shouldn't fly alone, and besides…" She trailed off as she indicated the decorations. "What is this?"

Before Will could figure out how to answer, Gwen announced, "Everybody out! We've stayed long enough!"

Her brisk statement did the trick. With a minimum of hustle, guests said their farewells and departed.

Allison ignored the hubbub, scarcely acknowledging people's polite goodbyes. Why had he ever believed her to be an expert on good manners?

By contrast, Annette Forrest showed real kindness. "While your housekeeper's away, I'd be happy to take the girls home with Nick and me after school," she told Will. "I'd enjoy it."

"That's very generous," he answered. "I'll have to let you know, if you don't mind."

"That would be fine." Ethan's mother wrote down her address and phone number. "I'm Leah's new room mom, so I'll be in class tomorrow."

"Thank you."

As he escorted her out, Will wished he knew what on earth was running through his ex-wife's mind. From the way she glowered, she seemed ticked about the whole scene, yet he didn't see what any of this had to do with her.

Leah helped India and Diane bring in their suitcases from

the rental car and disappeared with them into the back. Alone with Will, Allison folded her arms and fixed him with an angry stare.

She'd let her once-wispy pale-blond hair grow to shoulder length and dyed it a golden shade. If he wasn't mistaken, she'd smoothed out a few wrinkles in her forehead, too. The tailored suit must be a designer label, since she'd never bought anything else, no matter how tight their budget.

She looked expensive. He much preferred Leah's unstudied beauty.

"Who's that woman in there with the girls?" Allison demanded. "I heard them call her Miss Morris. Is she some kind of maid?"

Will ignored her snobbish tone. "She's their first-grade teacher," he said calmly. "She's also my good friend."

Allison indicated the banner. "You've been busy, unless there's some other guy named Rankin around here who's gifting the world with his offspring."

"Leah and I are having a baby." The simple statement of fact seemed sufficient to him.

"You had no business moving them to Tennessee in the first place. Then you couldn't even wait five minutes to knock up the local talent!" Allison snapped. "Well, I'm glad I brought the twins in person, because when I leave tomorrow, they're going with me. I'm not going to hand my daughters over to a stranger!"

A sharply indrawn breath summoned Will's attention. Leah stood in the hall, watching them uneasily.

This was not a discussion to which she should be subjected. "Honey, I'll give you a call," he told her.

She nodded. His ex-wife averted her face.

"Talk to you later." After casting one last glance toward the girls' room, Leah departed. When the door closed behind her, it felt to Will as if the light had dimmed.

Yesterday, she'd advised him to trust his instincts. He planned to do exactly that, starting now.

When he'd disagreed with his ex-wife before, he'd had to battle the nagging sense that he might be in the wrong. But her behavior since she stepped into his house today had been inexcusably offensive.

If Allison thought she could march in here and act any way she pleased, she was about to find out just how sharp Will's instincts had become.

Chapter Fifteen

Leah could barely concentrate during the short drive home. Outrage at Allison's unfairness warred with concern for Will. If his ex-wife really did manage to take the girls, he'd be devastated.

She hadn't meant to bring this kind of trouble on him. If only she could stay there with him, but of course her presence was likely to intensify Allison's resentment.

At her house, after making herself a cup of herbal tea, Leah went to the computer to surf for baby products. She needed to calm her seesawing emotions.

This entire pregnancy had felt like a roller-coaster ride. Still, she had to smile, remembering the fond teasing she'd undergone at the party. Despite her attempts to deflect questions about exactly how she and Will had met, her friends had grasped the basic idea. Not only had they not held it against her, but some of them had cheered her on.

"You were meant for each other," Rosie had told her. "No matter how you got together."

"If you see what you want, go for it," had been Barry's reaction.

"You won't put this in the paper, will you?" she'd asked, only half joking.

"I'm not running a tabloid," he'd assured her. "The only part I plan to print is the birth announcement."

Returning to the task at hand, Leah skimmed a few Web sites, trying to get some idea of what she might like to purchase for the baby. When the selection of infant clothes, safety equipment and nursery furnishings became a blur, she decided to check her e-mail.

There was the usual glut of spam, along with electronic newsletters from education groups and queries from parents. Several wanted to attend the bluegrass concert scheduled for tomorrow, so she sent them details. As she finished, Leah realized she'd missed a message at the bottom of the queue.

The subject line read simply: "Your application."

Expecting a request for more information or perhaps an ad for an Internet job site, she opened it. And caught her breath.

It was from the director of the Rosewell Center.

For an anguished moment, Leah assumed it must be a rejection. The noncommittal tagline and the opening generalities about budgets and schedules did nothing to reassure her.

The third paragraph began: We would love to have you join our faculty beginning with the January term.

She stopped, stunned. Then she let out a whoop.

They wanted to hire her!

An image popped into Leah's mind of the landscaped campus and the surrounding city with its international markets and bustling coffeehouses. She was reaching excitedly for the phone to call her friend Nell in Seattle, when she stopped.

What on earth was she thinking?

She was due to give birth in April. How could she relocate and handle the demands of a new job? It would mean leaving behind her friends, her aunt, her doctor—and Will.

Just when she needed him most. And when he might need

her emotional support, too, if he had to fight for custody of the twins.

Leah sat back in her chair, torn.

She yearned for the thrill of fresh surroundings and challenges. For the opportunity to learn what kind of person she truly was and what she might be able to accomplish in a larger setting.

But there'd be no one to lean on, no one to hold her. No Will.

Tears prickled in Leah's eyes. If only she knew for sure that he loved her. But even then, would that be enough?

While printing out the e-mail, she decided to postpone her answer. Surely the director didn't expect a response right away.

The phone rang. Wondering who it could be, she answered. "Hello?"

"Hi. It's me." The hint of hoarseness in Will's voice told Leah he'd had a rough time.

"How'd it go?" She retrieved the printout and tucked it in a file.

"I disabused Allison of the notion that she can take the girls anywhere without my permission." He sounded grimly satisfied. "I doubt she's going to fight me, but she seems to feel she has to protect them. From who or what, I'm not entirely sure."

"Why is she acting this way?" Leah asked. "I should think she'd be in a hurry to get back for her honeymoon."

"From what I can gather, her family made her feel guilty at the wedding for not keeping the girls," he said wearily. "She's having what I'd call a knee-jerk attack of motherhood."

Leah remembered that the groom didn't want kids around. "What does her husband make of this?"

"Brad wanted her to stick the kids on a plane and be done with them. I guess the new Mrs. Currier finally figured out that children aren't something you can shuffle off when they inconvenience you." Anger underscored the sarcasm. "I'm just

sorry that you and everyone else at the party had to be subjected to her bad attitude."

"What happens now?" Leah couldn't imagine the well-
dressed Allison camping out on Will's couch, but it seemed
too much to hope that she'd change her mind and leave.

"Mrs. McNulty gave her permission to stay in her house
tonight," Will said.

"And then?"

"She canceled her return flight out of Nashville in the
morning. She's got some cockamamy idea about accompany-
ing the girls to school to make sure they're getting a good education," he said. "I hope she doesn't intend to harass you,
because I won't stand for it."

Leah sighed. As if Minnie Tucker didn't provide enough
hostility! But Minnie wasn't her room mom anymore. "I'll sic
Annette on her," she said. "She can do the whole grand-
mother-knows-best thing."

"Annette's a godsend. She offered to watch the girls after
school, too," Will told her. She pictured him pacing through the
living room, distractedly running his fingers through his hair.

"I'd be happy to take them home with me," Leah replied.
"In fact, I'd love the chance to get to know them better."

"I'd like that, too, but I'm sure your workday doesn't end
when the last bell rings," Will noted. "Plus, you ought to rest
after being on your feet all day."

She had to admit that he was right. "At least let me stay
with them in the evenings when you're on call." Quickly, she
added, "Assuming your ex-wife doesn't plan to stick around
and do it herself."

Regardless of Allison's rudeness, the girls had a bond with
their mother. Leah would never try to interfere with that.

"I doubt she'll last more than a day or two. And I really
appreciate your offer." After a moment, he added, "I never

realized how self-absorbed Allison is. I doubt she gives much, if any, consideration to how her actions affect India and Diane. She never tries to keep her voice down or make sure they aren't listening."

"They're lucky to have a father like you." Recalling how anxious he'd been all day, Leah added, "I'm glad they got home safely."

"Me, too. You know what?" he added more cheerfully. "They told me they missed you while they were gone. They were disappointed you couldn't stick around tonight."

"Well, I'll see them tomorrow." Despite the stresses at work and the pregnancy-induced sleepiness, Leah still loved teaching.

"If Allison disrupts your class, feel free to call me," he said. "I'll haul her out, if necessary."

"We'll handle her." Although the job offer weighed on her mind, Leah held off mentioning it. Not only did Will have his hands full, but she had no idea what she was going to tell him. "I wish we could spend another night together," she said instead. "Oh, Will, this has been so crazy. Nothing about our relationship was normal, right from the start."

"We'll make up for it when things calm down." He sounded comforted by the thought.

She was glad she hadn't mentioned that she might not be around. "Talk to you soon."

"Sleep well, sweetheart."

After she hung up, the endearment lingered in her mind. Leah cherished it more than she ought to, for a woman considering moving to the other side of the continent.

Maybe matters would sort themselves out. But she didn't see how.

ALTHOUGH HE COULDN'T compete with Mrs. McNulty's usual pancake-and-egg bonanzas, Will fixed breakfast for the girls on Monday. He'd heard a few noises that indicated Allison was awake, but she'd hadn't stuck her nose out of the guest-house. She'd never been very interested in cooking, anyway.

It wasn't until he tuned in on the girls' chatter at the table that he realized he'd made an important omission: India and Diane were exchanging theories about how Miss Morris came to be pregnant without a husband.

"Her husband must have died," India said.

"Then she'd be *Mrs*. Morris," Diane pointed out. "Sybill says she did something bad."

"She didn't do anything bad," Will put in, setting down a plate of buttered toast. "Sometimes grown-ups make mistakes, but even so, good things can come of it. And babies are a good thing." He paused, uncertain how to broach the subject of his paternity. Since they were sure to learn of it, he didn't want to delay.

"Was the baby a mistake, Daddy?" India asked with a frown.

"Well, not exactly, but it was unexpected." *Time to face the music, Daddy.* "Girls, Miss Morris isn't married, but the baby does have a father. It's me."

They eyed him uncertainly.

"What do you mean?" Diane ventured.

"Miss Morris's baby will be your little brother or sister," he said. "That doesn't necessarily mean the baby's going to live with us, though."

"Can I hold it?" India asked.

"I expect so." He definitely wanted his girls to feel close to their sibling.

"You mean it's our baby, too?" Diane cried. "Whoopee!"

Will was trying to calm them down and offer further clar-ification when the sliding-glass door opened. "Mommy!" India shouted. "Miss Morris is giving us a sister!"

"Or a brother," Diane noted.

Allison's hard look marred the elegant effect of her pink wool suit and salon-perfect hairdo. "Such interesting break-fast-table conversation."

"They had a right to know," Will retorted. "I figured it was better to hear it from me than from schoolyard gossip."

She poured herself a cup of coffee, ignoring the cereal and fruit he'd set out along with the toast. The woman rarely ate; no wonder she was so touchy. "India, sit up straighter. You look like a country bumpkin. Diane, stop waving your spoon as if you were conducting an orchestra."

Watching her dampen their daughters' high spirits brought back unwanted memories. There'd been good times, too, of course. Allison could be sympathetic and understanding—even playful—when she wasn't having one of her mood swings.

Since she'd been a good friend during their courtship, Will had assumed the fault lay with him. In part, it probably did. However, he believed now that, given her temperament and his restricted finances, there was no way he could have made Allison happy.

"Are you flying home today, Mommy?" Diane asked.

"No, I'm going to school with you," her mother said brightly. "Won't that be fun?"

"Do you mean you're dropping us off?" India asked.

"No, I intend to see the amazing Miss Morris in action." Allison smacked her cup down, sending drops flying across the table. She dabbed at them with a napkin. "I want to be sure you girls have the best of everything."

"You can meet Sybill!" Diane exclaimed. "She's my best friend."

"Nick, too," India added. "He has a cat! And he's diabetic!"

"I'm sure they're charming." Allison regarded Will with an air of triumph, as if by pleasing the girls, she'd scored points at his expense. "Well, then, we'll see you for dinner, won't we?"

Will had never found her duplicitous, but he hadn't forgotten her threat to take the girls back to Austin. "Maybe I'll drop by school, as well."

She waved a hand dismissively. "Don't bother. You have nothing to worry about." In a more serious manner, she added, "Brad won't have them and I'm not into that whole single-mother thing."

Will dropped the subject. Besides, he faced a full day's schedule, with Jenni out of town. "Girls, have a good day. Please don't talk about Miss Morris having your brother or sister. It's private."

From Allison's grimace, he feared for a moment she might make some snide comment, but all she said was, "We'd better get moving."

Will wished he were meeting Leah later today. Just the two of them, not necessarily to make love but to talk. He'd like to find out how Allison behaved in the classroom and hear Leah's observations. And he just liked being around her.

He'd better be careful, he reflected as he got ready for work. If he didn't watch it, he might start depending on her. But Will had learned long ago that the only person he could truly rely on was himself.

That hadn't changed. And it probably never would.

LEAH'S GAIT SLOWED as she walked toward the brick school building. The possibility of leaving made her want to savor the place where she'd worked for nearly a decade.

Glancing at the letters above the portico, she read the full name: Grandpa Johnson Elementary School, after one of the town's founders and the street where it was located. It must seem an odd name to out-of-towners, but having started here as a student when she was five, she took it for granted.

The air smelled of autumn leaves and cinnamon drifting

out of the nearby café. From an early-morning pickup game at the high school came the rubberized thump of basketballs.

Inside, Leah inhaled the familiar scents of sneakers, linoleum and lemon cleanser. Thank heavens the storm had passed, or by now it would have reeked of wet book bags and mold. Kids had a talent for stuffing everything from apple cores to old socks in places the cleaning crew missed.

Leah smiled, thinking how intimately she knew this place. Here she'd suffered a crush on a boy named Ralph, who'd moved away long ago, and here she'd discovered her love of teaching. She'd practiced on Karen, two years her junior, when the sixth grade had started a tutoring program. The result had been a lifelong friendship.

So familiar. So dear. Yet did she really want to stay here another thirty years and grow old walking up these same steps, greeting not only younger siblings of former students but also eventually teaching their children?

The prospect dragged at Leah like an anchor. She longed to soar, the way she had in Austin. Okay, she'd also crashed and burned, but surely it beat dying of boredom.

If only she could have Will and Austin, too! But if he'd stayed there instead of moving to Downhome, she'd never have seen him again, much less come to care about him.

At least now she understood his tendency to retreat after a close encounter. He kept his heart in reserve. It was a factor she had to consider in deciding her future, Leah supposed.

She was setting out materials for the students when the arrival of Allison Rankin—no, her name was Allison Currier now, she recalled—dispelled other reflections. Her smart pink suit and tan pumps completely outshone Leah's flowered shirtwaist and walking shoes. It would be interesting to see how well they held up after six hours with first-graders, though.

After greeting her, Leah said. "I hope you don't mind the seats." They were child-sized.

"Oh." Surveying the room, Allison gazed longingly at Leah's full-sized chair but wisely thought the better of trying to co-opt it.

Annette Forrest breezed in with Nick. "I'm glad to see we have a helper!" she cheered, not batting an eye at encountering the woman who'd broken up yesterday's party. "Just tell us what to do and we'll get to work!"

If their Texas visitor had planned to stay on the sidelines, the room mom gave her no chance. They spent the morning assisting children with craft projects, fixing and cleaning up the snack, and keeping a lid on Sybill, who grew increasingly restive.

By late morning, Allison had tucked her stylish hair behind her ears and given up trying to refresh her bright-pink lipstick. Finally, she kicked off her pumps and padded around in her stockings.

Although her disposition fell short of Annette's cheeriness, Leah awarded the lady points for rising to the occasion and for being a good sport in front of the kids. She'd have hated to see their mother embarrass India and Diane.

Because of the assembly, they ate a quick lunch and skipped recess. That was a blessing, in view of the muddy state of the playground, Leah mused as she shepherded the children into the auditorium.

Allison sank gratefully into an adult-sized folding chair. "My feet are killing me!"

"You should wear something more practical next time," Mrs. Forrest advised, indicating her own jogging shoes.

"Next time?" Allison groaned. When the room mom moved out of earshot, she addressed Leah. "How does she do it? I mean, at her age!"

"I don't think she's more than sixty," Leah said. "That's not old these days." From the corner of her eye, she spotted Sybill sneaking into the midst of the third-grade class. Annoyed, she went to steer the child to her proper seat.

To her relief, the Fiddle Folks bounded on stage right on time, filling the air with toe-tapping music that riveted the kids. The small group of parents who'd attended also appeared to enjoy themselves.

The trio—a woman, her husband and a second male musician—provided a history lesson about the English, Scottish and Irish immigrants who had settled the Appalachians Mountains in the seventeenth century, bringing their musical traditions with them. The isolated communities had remained virtually unchanged until the early twentieth century, they explained.

"Now, you may think this is a violin, but I'm here to tell you it's a fiddle!" exclaimed Joe, the leader of the group. He played an earsplitting series of notes that made the children squeal.

"My instrument is a banjo!" His wife, Nancy, strummed gaily.

To everyone's amusement, the third musician, a tall, shaggy fellow named Clem, tried to speak but instead squawked through a harmonica. He had a knack for clowning, and a little later in the program, he announced a change of pace: magic tricks.

"These aren't exactly from the local mountains, but they're as old as the hills!" He made a show of shading his eyes and peering into the audience. "I need an assistant. Do I have any volunteers?"

Almost every hand went up. Sybill bounced in her chair so hard Leah feared it might collapse.

"Gosh, nobody?" Clem joked. "Oh, wait, I think I see someone."

Sybill stood on the chair and waved.

"Well, I guess I better choose that young lady before she trampolines over your heads and hurts somebody." He waved her up. "What's your name, miss?"

"I'm Sybill!" She beamed.

"Well, Sybill, see if you can pull this scarf out of my sleeve," he told her. The more she pulled, the longer it grew, while Clem urged her on, pretending to be astonished.

The endless-scarf gag convulsed the children. His other tricks, including a live rabbit in a hat, were also familiar stuff but just right for this age group, particularly when accented by Clem's engaging humor.

At the end, Sybill took a bow beside him. When she skipped down the aisle, for once she didn't try to poke anyone.

The other musicians returned for a rousing finale. Leah could have done without the interruption when Allison's cell phone rang, but the trio played louder than ever, and she scampered out of the room.

"That went well, don't you think?" Olivia asked as the children filed out. "Last week, a couple of parents questioned whether this was educational, but I believe it promotes the arts and expands the children's horizons."

"It was perfect." Programs like this one make history come alive.

It occurred to her that, if Leah planned to leave at the end of the semester, she needed to inform Olivia so she could hire a replacement. But Leah hadn't made up her mind.

Allison rejoined the group as they walked toward the classroom. Noting her smile, Leah asked, "Good news?"

"That was Brad," came the response. "He's sorry he gave me such a hard time about the girls. His daughter told him I did the right thing."

"I'm glad to hear it." Hesitantly, Leah asked, "Will he fly here to join you?"

"Brad? Are you kidding?" Allison fluffed out her hair. "He rescheduled our honeymoon and made a reservation for my flight to Austin in the morning. I wasn't sure about leaving the girls so soon, but he promised me a new car. What do you think? Should I get a convertible?"

This man must be incredibly wealthy or recklessly generous, Leah mused. "I'd pick something tamer. I guess I'm the practical type."

"Yes, I can see that." Perhaps realizing that the comment might be taken as a put-down, Allison added, "In a positive way."

"I'm glad you've patched things up." She meant that sincerely.

Allison was leaving. Tomorrow night, Leah decided, she'd find a way to tell Will about the job offer. With his ex-wife decamping and his right to the twins secure, there was no reason not to bring it up.

No reason not to make a decision.

She and Will shared a child-to-be and, she believed, a friendship. She only hoped it would survive her moving to the other side of the country.

Chapter Sixteen

Will worked a long day on Monday, covering acute-care cases for Jenni, along with his own patients. He scarcely gave a thought to the staff's reaction to his personal news, but it didn't matter anyway, since neither Estelle nor Winifred had a problem with it and Yvonne had taken the day off.

That night proved a pleasant surprise. Thrilled with her bridegroom's attentiveness, Allison dropped any hint of antagonism. She even managed to say a few kind things about Leah, especially her ability to stay on her feet all day and put up with the noise level.

Aside from calling his landlord and offering to pay for any fire damage not covered by insurance, Will spent a relaxed evening. Unfortunately, later that night, he got called out on three cases. The upside was that Allison didn't complain about sleeping on the couch so she could be near if the girls needed her.

She showed a trace of reluctance about leaving them Tuesday morning. "They're growing so fast," she said as Will hefted her suitcases into her trunk. "Before you know it, they'll be teenagers."

"Not for seven years," he said. "I hope you'll see them before that."

"Well, of course!" She donned a pair of sunglasses for the drive to Nashville. "I can't bring Brad to visit, though. The only motel I saw around here is a real dump." Will had stayed there when he came for his interview and found it satisfactory, but he doubted he and Brad shared the same standards. "You will bring them to Austin soon, won't you?"

He couldn't very well refuse. Besides, the children should visit both sets of grandparents regularly. "Of course."

They shook hands. "You're a good father," Allison said. "Tell Leah she's a lucky lady."

Will hadn't bothered to correct his ex-wife's notion that he and Leah planned to marry. "I'll do that."

As soon as she drove off, he took the girls to school and went to the clinic. Yvonne had arrived early, and her flash of anger at the sight of him told Will he wasn't out of the woods.

"I guess I'm the bad guy again, huh?" he asked, pouring a cup of coffee in the lunchroom.

"This is between you and Leah," the nurse said stiffly.

"Come on," he prodded. "You're ticked. Talk about it."

"I expected more of you." She plucked some coins from her purse and dropped them into a vending machine.

"I'm not proud of my behavior," Will told her. "But I didn't mean to take advantage of Leah. And I'm sticking by her."

Yvonne pushed a button once, then again. Nothing happened.

Will didn't mean to say more, but the words tumbled out. "In some ways, the woman has more power than you realize in a situation like this. It's up to Leah how much she will allow me into my child's life, or even whether they will stay in Downhome."

"Luther doesn't care about being part of Bethany's life." Yvonne jabbed angrily at the button. "Oh, for Pete's sake!"

Will crossed the room, then smacked the vending machine

with his fist. A granola bar dropped into the tray. "I'm not Luther Allen."

Yvonne pressed her forehead against the glass. "Guys never understand how unfair the system is! Even the darn machine ignores me and gives you what you want!" She straightened. "But you know what? You're not a bad guy, Dr. Rankin. I shouldn't take out my personal disappointments on you."

"Any more dragons you need slain, just let me know," he joked.

"I might do that." She managed a chuckle.

Glad to have ratcheted down the tension level, he spent the next hour catching up on paperwork, after which he tackled a full schedule of patients. At a quarter to two, he was about to go on a late lunch when a frowning Estelle met him in the hallway.

"What's wrong?" Will asked.

"It's Li Lee."

For a moment, the name confused him. Then he placed it. "The tech."

"He called earlier to say he had car trouble, so none of our tests have been run. Well, Patsy just informed me he's not going to make it until three, and he's got an ultrasound in fifteen minutes."

"We'll just have to—" On the point of saying *reschedule*, Will stopped as he made the connection "—that would be Leah."

The nurse practitioner confirmed it. "Normally, Dr. Vine would handle it, but obviously she's not here, and I'm fully booked. We'll have to put her off. I just wanted to check with you before I call her."

Will had intended to slip out for a croissant sandwich. That would have to wait. "I'll handle it. Do you suppose I could talk Patsy into picking up some lunch for me?"

"Of course." Estelle had no qualms about volunteering her

daughter's assistance. "Thanks, Will. I wasn't sure you'd feel comfortable."

Not until she'd marched off did Will stop to think about exactly what he was about to experience. He'd missed observing the twins' ultrasound when he was called into emergency surgery, although of course Allison had brought a sonogram home afterward.

But actually watching the baby move—*his* baby—promised to be an emotional undertaking. To his surprise, Will discovered that his hands were prickling with anticipation.

He didn't know exactly how he was going to react. But, obviously, he was about to find out.

LEAH STUDIED WILL'S FACE as he spread gel on her bare stomach. She'd been glad to learn he was replacing the tech, but he seemed very serious and remote as he moved the sensor paddle.

Dark shapes swirled on the monitor. What if he kept his distance through the whole procedure? Although she understood both his professionalism and his tendency to guard his emotions, it would hurt if he didn't respond to the baby.

"Did Allison get away all right?" she asked, trying to break through to him.

"Hmm?" When he glanced up, she saw a pucker of concentration on his brow. "Oh, yes. Sorry you had to put up with her yesterday."

"We kept her busy." That reminded Leah. "By the way, Annette said she'll bring the girls home after school today."

"Great." He returned his attention to the monitor.

Leah didn't mention that she'd had to separate Diane and Sybill for talking too much during class. The Tucker girl hadn't stopped chattering about her role in yesterday's assembly and it had sounded as if the two might be plotting an escapade. Leah had warned Olivia they might try some magic tricks at recess, and to keep an eye on the second grade's guinea pig in case they attempted to put it in a hat.

She forgot about school as Will made another run across her abdomen with a mouselike device that he'd explained was called a transducer. Seeing his dear dark-blond head bent over her stirred Leah. If only he would give her a smile, or make some joke about the baby! Anything to indicate that he cared.

He showed no signs of breaking his professional reserve, however. "I don't know how much Dr. Vine explained, so I'll go over it again with you," Will said coolly. "This procedure uses sound waves to reflect internal organs. A computer analyzes them and turns them into pictures."

Leah stared at the indistinct black-and-white shapes. "Is that all we can see at this stage?"

"It's not as clear as X-rays or a CAT scan, but when I find the right position, we should be able to spot…there." He pointed to a pulsing point on the screen. "That's the heart."

His voice caught. Leah stared in amazement. Although she'd known intellectually what was going to happen, she hadn't grasped the reality until now. That was her little person there, with its tiny heart throbbing steadily.

"It's just—" She couldn't finish.

"A miracle," Will said breathlessly.

Leah glanced at him in surprise. "But you must have seen this before a zillion times."

He couldn't tear his eyes from the image. "This is different."

The shadowy shape gave a distinct jerk. "He's an active little fellow." Regaining his composure, Will moved the device. "There's the head." At first, she couldn't tell how he made anything out of the blur, and then the baby turned in profile and she made out the tiny nose and chin.

"It's so cute!" The cool pressure on her abdomen reminded

Leah that this activity was taking place inside her as they watched. "I can't believe we can see so much!"

Will swallowed. "Neither can I."

"But you do this all the time!" she pointed out.

He pointed to the screen. "There's an arm."

"I think he's waving at us," Leah teased.

He started to laugh and nearly choked. "I don't know what's wrong with me. My throat clogged up."

Leah grasped what was wrong. Or rather, what was right. She wished she dared reach up and touch Will's cheek as he bent over her, because she yearned for the contact. But that wouldn't be appropriate, she supposed.

"I'm going to shoot a few pictures now." After adjusting the instrument, Will clicked an image and then several more in different positions. "I'll give you one of these to take home."

"Don't you want one, too?" she asked.

He nodded. "Of course I do."

"The girls ought to love it," she prodded.

"I'm the one who's going to love it," he said. "I can't tell you how much." He broke off to stare at the screen. After a long moment, Leah began to fear something might be wrong, and then he said, "I could swear that kid has three legs."

"What?" She nearly sat up in alarm.

"Whoa." He held out a hand, palm down, to stop her. "I'm kidding. I forgot to ask whether you want to know the baby's gender. Of course, it's early to tell."

Now she understood. "You mean you saw *something* sticking out down there. Does that indicate it's a boy?"

"At this stage, we can't be sure." As the baby flopped around, Will peered more closely at the screen. "Darn if he isn't built like a linebacker." He angled the transducer, pressing a little harder to bring the picture into better focus. "I have to get a picture of *that*."

He smiled as he captured the shot, but she could have sworn his eyes had misted over. "Did you want a boy?" Leah asked.

"I didn't expect to care about the gender," he admitted. "After growing up in a house full of boys, I feel really blessed to have girls. But this little guy…" Taking a deep breath, he rested one hand on Leah's stomach. "I'm not giving a very good impression of my bedside manner, am I?"

"It's wonderful." She loved sharing this experience with him.

He shook his head. "I can't imagine what came over me." Before she could comment, he switched subjects. "Have you thought about a name?"

"I was considering Maria Wilhelmina, but it's spoken for," Leah teased, grateful for a chance to lighten the atmosphere.

Will burst out laughing. "Wrong gender, too."

Mrs. Waters appeared in the doorway. "Somebody tell a joke in here?"

"He asked about names," Leah responded. "I hadn't picked one, considering I wasn't aware of the gender until some big-mouth doctor made a crack about a third leg."

"It's a boy?" the nurse chortled. "Well, hallelujah!"

"You'd say that if it was a girl, too," the doctor responded.

"Why not? Either one's a marvel!" She ducked out again.

Reluctantly, he lifted the transducer as if to put it away. Eager to stretch out the session a little longer, Leah returned to the subject of names. "How about Ebenezer?" she ventured.

Will joined in the spirit. "I prefer Elmer Fudd."

"That's two names." She searched her mind for more possibilities, but none materialized. "Sorry, I'm out of ideas."

"There's no hurry." Removing the device, he wiped the sticky stuff from her abdomen. "Well, Miss Morris, Junior seems fine. He's the right size for his age and all systems appear to be go."

"No hereditary problems?" she inquired. "A thick head like his father? Two left feet like his mother?"

"I'm afraid that sort of thing doesn't show up in a sonogram," he responded with mock gravity. "Ready to sit up?"

"I guess so."

He reached for her hand to help her shift positions. When he didn't release her right away, Leah sat on the table drinking in the warmth of his nearness and the open affection on his face.

"I'm glad I got a chance to do this." His voice carried an emotional rasp. "It was incredible."

She wished she dared hug him, but that might wrinkle his white coat, not to mention smearing it with a trace of leftover gel. "Thank you for doing this."

"I'm glad it worked out. For some reason, it hadn't occurred to me to sit in," Will admitted. "It probably would have hit me in the middle of the night, what I'd missed. I'd be kicking myself into the next century."

"You'd need a third leg for that," Leah said tartly.

He ducked his head. "I don't dare comment."

With his help, she slid to the floor. Will steadied her, and they stood inches apart, their breaths mingling in the room's cool air.

"Stay with me, Leah," he murmured, close to her ear. "I don't mean just this minute."

She didn't know what to say. She'd meant to tell him about the offer, but suddenly, she was no longer so sure she wanted it.

Of course she did. But she wanted him, too.

"Excuse me." A tap on the door frame preceded Winifred's entrance. "Doctor, you have a call from Mrs. Forrest."

"It isn't Dr. Vine, is it?" he asked. Leah remembered that Jenni had a new last name. But she would be Dr. Forrest.

"No. It's her mother-in-law," the nurse said.

"I'll be right there."

"Thanks, Doctor." She whisked away.

Will gave Leah a rueful smile. "She probably wants to know what time I'm collecting the girls."

"Go ahead."

He brushed a kiss across her mouth. It sparkled through her. "Did I mention how beautiful you are?"

"You're quite a hunk yourself." One more kiss and she let him go.

If it was this hard to release him now, how would she feel in January? Leah wondered.

She'd hoped the situation would magically resolve itself. Instead, it kept getting more confused.

THE PHONE CALL TURNED OUT to be more problematic than Will had expected. According to Annette, Diane had gone home with Sybill without asking permission.

The girls had already climbed into Mrs. Tucker's car before their volunteer sitter had caught sight of them and registered her objection. "Minnie insisted her daughter was looking forward to playing with her friend, as if that made it all right to take off with someone else's child." Annette's tone dripped disapproval. "She called out the window that she'd bring Diane home for supper."

"She didn't happen to mention what hour that would be, did she?" Will asked tautly.

"I'm afraid not."

He thanked Mrs. Forrest for the information. Perhaps people regarded such matters more casually in a small town than in a city, but short of an emergency, Will would never allow a child in his car without parental approval.

At least he had the Tuckers' phone number. Mrs. McNulty had written it in the kitchen address book when Sybill had visited.

He decided to let the matter pass for now. Later, he would make it clear to Mrs. Tucker that this must never happen again.

Leah was on her way out, so Will didn't mention it to her.

She might volunteer to intercede, and the last thing she needed was a confrontation with that difficult Tucker woman.

So preoccupied with his work that he barely paused to eat the sandwich Patsy brought, Will gave the matter no further thought until he'd retrieved India from Mrs. Forrest's—who firmly declined his offer to pay her—and arrived home. It was close to six o'clock.

India crawled around the kitchen, pretending to be Nick's cat. "Don't I have pretty white paws? That's why my name is Boots!"

"Your paws are going to be filthy," Will returned absent-mindedly. "I don't suppose you have any idea what time they eat supper at the Tuckers' house, do you?"

She meowed at him and crawled away.

Hoping he could keep from snapping at Minnie, he flipped to her number and dialed. She answered with a breathless, "Hello?"

"Mrs. Tucker?" he said. "This is Dr. Rankin. I was wondering when you planned to bring Diane home."

"I can't find them!" the woman wailed.

Will's chest squeezed. "What do you mean?"

"They went outside to play about two hours ago. When I called them to come inside, no one answered. I searched all over the neighborhood, but they're not here!"

He refused to panic. In light of Sybill and Diane's personalities, he wouldn't be surprised if they'd decided to go exploring.

"Where do you live?" Will put together the location—less than a mile from his house—with the fact that Minnie had already driven the entire route to make sure Sybill hadn't decided to accompany her friend home on foot. After ascertaining that the woman had also checked other spots that might have drawn the children, he saw only one option. "I'm calling the police."

"But my husband will be so embarrassed!" Mrs. Tucker cried.

Will lost his last shred of patience. "May I remind you that you removed my child over the objections of my babysitter? Now our daughters are missing and you're worried about embarrassing your husband! You'd better rethink your priorities, Mrs. Tucker. Goodbye."

After clicking off, he dialed 911. The operator agreed that the disappearance of two six-year-old girls was nothing to fool around with and promised to issue a bulletin.

After hanging up, Will glanced out the window and noticed how dark the sky had grown. Every instinct urged him to go hunt for his baby, but then there'd be no one to stay with India.

He reached for the phone again. At a time like this, he needed Leah.

"I CALLED MARK at the station. He hasn't heard any reports of suspicious persons, but he's treating this very seriously," she told Will when she arrived at his house. "He's supervising tonight."

Leah had dropped her preparations for dinner and contacted her cousin on the drive over. Although her common sense told her the girls had probably just wandered off, it hurt to think of Diane lost and frightened. And she couldn't bear for Will to go through this alone.

"Mark's in charge? I'm not sure I find that reassuring," he muttered.

She understood, given her cousin's hot temper when it came to Pepe. However, despite being only twenty-eight, her cousin stood third in command after Ethan and Ben.

"Mark may get emotional about his mom, but he's good at his job. That's why they made him a lieutenant." Leah jammed her hands into her pant pockets. "I was afraid those two might get into trouble, but I never expected anything like this."

"What do you mean?" Will glanced at India, who sat at the table listening. He must have been wondering whether she should hear all this, but to Leah's relief, he didn't send the girl away. Under such circumstances, she believed children were less frightened by the truth than by their imaginations.

She described the previous day's assembly. "Sybill was thrilled about being chosen magician's assistant. The way she and Diane kept whispering together, I got the impression they might be planning some prank. I was afraid they'd borrow a guinea pig and try to pull it out of a hat."

"Is there a petting zoo around here where they might have gone?" Will asked. "Or a magic shop?"

"Not that I know of."

When the doorbell rang, they both jumped. Will went to admit his visitor.

It was Mark. "I've been out searching but I have to talk to you, Doctor. Leah, I'm glad you're here, too." He entered, his manner brisk. "After the bulletin went out, we got a call from a woman who was driving along Jackson Street about five o'clock this afternoon. She saw two little girls walking northbound with a man. The children fit the descriptions."

One glance at Will's face told Leah he shared her shocked reaction. The possibility of an abductor was far worse than a simple case of lost children.

"Did she get a good look at him?" he asked tautly.

"Yes, tell me if he sounds familiar." Mark studied his notes. "Tall and thin, longish hair, mid- to late-thirties."

"Doesn't ring a bell," Will said.

Leah made a connection. "There was a fellow at the school assembly yesterday, a musician who did magic tricks. That description fits him. He chose Sybill as his assistant, so they're acquainted."

"Do you know his name or where he's staying?" Mark lifted his handheld radio.

"He's called Clem, but I don't know his last name. Olivia might. She hired the troupe," Leah said.

Clem's clowning had been so amusing and his goofy demeanor so charming it was hard to imagine him hurting anyone. But that might be precisely why the girls had trusted him.

Mark relayed the information to dispatch, then dialed Olivia on his cell. When he hung up, he said, "The musicians live in a converted bus. Mrs. Rockwell said she recommended an RV camp over on Garden Street. That's not far from where the girls were sighted, although it sounded as if they were walking in the opposite direction."

As he exited, Will grabbed a jacket. "I'm coming with you. I'd go crazy waiting here."

"Dr. Rankin, you should let the professionals take care of this." Mark stopped abruptly. Leah understood why when she heard a woman's footsteps tapping up the sidewalk.

Rosie appeared. "I heard what's going on." That didn't surprise Leah. People in town must be phoning one another since the alert went out over the police radio. "I'll stay with India if that will help. I'd offer to join you, but my feet aren't in such good shape."

Her son accepted the situation at once. "Doc, you can participate if you stay out of the way. Keep a lookout for any sign of your daughter, maybe some possession she dropped that could steer us in the right direction."

"Great," Will said. "I'll follow in my car."

"I'm coming, too." Leah suspected he could use the moral support.

As she hurried down the walkway, it struck her how abruptly everything had changed. Before Will called, she'd been worrying about whether to accept the job offer from Seattle and how to handle her feelings about him.

Now the only thing that mattered was getting Diane and Sybill back safely.

Chapter Seventeen

Will's spirits sank as he parked on the curbless street behind Mark's cruiser. His gut twisted at the image of his little girl wandering through this unlit section of town, which stank of chickens, manure and goats.

Along the way, they'd driven past shabby houses with trash-strewn yards and what appeared to be the remnants of a small farm where goats and cows stared listlessly from inside their pens. He'd spotted a couple of ramshackle huts that Leah identified as chicken coops.

They'd halted in front of a gravel-strewn lot punctuated by a few drooping trees. About a dozen RVs and dilapidated trailers were parked at random angles. Judging by the accumulation of awnings and potted plants, he guessed that the residents lived here long-term.

The exception, he noted as they got out of the car, appeared to be a converted bus whose peeling paint identified it as belonging to the Fiddle Folks. It sat apart from the other vehicles, with a few folding chairs and a small barbecue set up beside it.

To his gratitude, Leah didn't offer meaningless reassurances or speculations. On the trip over, she'd simply sat beside him, lending the comfort of shared concern.

Will supposed he should have insisted she stay with Rosie in the warmth of the house. But he needed her here in a deep, wordless way that he didn't even try to understand.

After signaling them to stay behind, Mark and a patrolman who met them at the scene advanced on the bus. Standing to one side, he rapped on the door.

Gravel crunched behind Will, and a male voice demanded, "What have they found?" He swung around, startled to see the city manager. Thin and of average height, Alton Tucker spoke in an irritable tone. "Are the girls here?"

"We just arrived," Leah said quietly. "The police want us to keep our distance."

Will returned his attention to the scene in front of them. Someone opened the bus door—a woman, drawing a thin shawl against the coolness. Behind her appeared a stout man, definitely not the fellow the witness had described. After a brief conversation, they allowed the officers inside.

It seemed like ages before Mark came out, although it was probably no more than five minutes. "I talked with Joe and Nancy Garrity. They said their harmonica player quit about a month ago and that's when they hired this fellow, Clem Olson. They gave us a photocopy of his driver's license."

"Well, where is he?" Tucker demanded.

"He took off a couple of hours ago. They didn't see him leave, and apparently, he left his stuff in the bus." When his cell phone rang, Mark rapped out, "O'Bannon," and stepped aside to conduct his call in private.

The city manager's gaze swept the area as if seeking a target for his anger. To Will's annoyance, the man fixed on Leah.

"I hope you realize you're the one who set a bad example for the girls," he whined. "Why should they follow the rules when you feel free to live any way you choose?"

"You're letting your emotions run away with you, Mr.

Tucker." She kept her composure a lot better than Will would have. "I recommend not saying anything you might regret."

"I'll say whatever I like," the city manager shot back. "You're a disgrace to this community and I don't care who hears it."

Will's temper snapped. "It's your wife who set the bad example by picking up my daughter without permission," he growled. "As for Sybill, her conduct when she visited Diane was so out of control that my housekeeper refused to invite her back. You and your wife have taught her to defy authority. If you want to assign blame, Mr. Tucker, I suggest you look closer to home."

From the city manager's glare, Will doubted his point had sunk in. He only hoped he hadn't worsened the problem for Leah.

Mark reappeared, his expression stern. "A state trooper picked up our man hitchhiking near the interstate."

"What about the girls?" Leah asked.

"No sign of them. Olson claims they showed up here at the camp and he started to walk them home. He says he got spooked and decided to leave before he got in trouble."

"What spooked him?" Tucker demanded.

When Mark briefly averted his eyes, Will suspected the news was bad. He caught Leah's hand.

"He saw a motorist staring at him and figured it might mean trouble. Our friend Olson was released from prison six months ago," said the lieutenant. "He served a term for strong-arm robbery."

The man hadn't been convicted of a crime involving children. But Olson's attempt to flee twisted Will's gut with suspicion.

Where was his little girl?

AT MARK'S URGING, Leah and Will headed home. There was nothing further they could do tonight, and she agreed with

Mark that their presence at the police station was more likely to interfere with the interrogation than to help.

"I can't believe I let this happen," Will said as he drove slowly along Jackson Street, watching for the children. "I should have realized Mrs. Tucker wouldn't supervise them properly. I should have gone to their house as soon as Annette called."

"You can't watch a six-year-old child every second of the day, Will." A rush of caring for this man swept through her. "You're a wonderful father."

"I don't know what I'm doing," he muttered, more to himself than to her. "I'm winging it, Leah. Raising these kids alone is like juggling too many balls in the air. It's a miracle I haven't dropped one before this."

"That's what it's like for most single parents," she told him. "Believe me, as a teacher, I've seen plenty of families struggling. Oh, Will, if I'd had a father like you, it would have been such heaven."

He made a right turn. "Is he dead?"

"No. He and my stepmother live in Denver, but I don't talk to them more than a few times a year," she admitted. "Dad traveled in his work when I was growing up, and he had affairs while he was on the road. Mom must have suspected it, and I figured it out by the time I reached my teens."

"I'm sorry." When something moved at one side, Will tapped the brake.

To Leah's disappointment, it was only a dog sniffing the bushes.

"He didn't just cheat on Mom. In a sense, he cheated on me, too," she confided. "Even when he was home, he scarcely noticed me. I had this big aching void where my father should have been. Your girls are lucky."

Will pulled into his driveway. In the light from a street lamp, anguish glittered in his eyes.

"I've made so many mistakes," he said raggedly. "I've tried to protect myself from getting hurt. What a damn stupid way to act, as if I could control the universe. Leah, forgive me. What I did to you in Austin was cruel. I love you so much. And my children, all three of them."

She wrapped her arms around him. In the darkness, her cheek registered his tears. "It's going to be all right."

"I'll make it all right," he promised. "Any way I can."

Holding him, Leah realized she didn't want their son to grow up thousands of miles away from his father. And she couldn't bear leaving Will when he needed her so much.

Almost as much as she needed him.

A spill of brightness caught her eye as the door to the house flew open. Rosie waved madly from the porch. "Doc! Your little girl's on the phone!"

Leah could have sworn she heard a sonic boom as Will flew out of the car and raced up the walkway. She followed at a more sedate pace, arriving in time to hear him saying in a choked voice, "Stay right there, angel. I'll come get you. I'm going to put Miss Morris on the line. You talk to her till I get there, okay?"

He handed her the instrument. "She and Sybill are down at the Corner Garage. They got lost heading home. She had the phone in her pocket the whole time but was afraid to call. Silly little thing."

After giving India a kiss, Will ran out the door.

"I'll notify Mark." Rosie took out her cell phone.

Leah settled down to chat with Diane, reassuring her that she wasn't in trouble. According to the child, Clem had told the truth. He'd simply left them walking on Jackson Street.

They'd tried to take a shortcut and lost their way. The little girl sounded tired and very eager to see her daddy.

"He can't wait to see you," Leah told her. "He'll be there any minute."

She didn't feel easy, however, until Diane said, "There he is! There's Daddy!" The connection broke.

When her aunt handed her a tissue, Leah realized she was crying. "Thank goodness that's over," Rosie said. "It's been a tough evening, hasn't it?"

Leah didn't trust herself to speak.

A short while later, Mark called to confirm that the girls were safe and Clem had been released. "He insisted on walking home—didn't want to be spotted in a police car, I guess. I gave him money for dinner at a restaurant. Considering the inconvenience he's been through, it was the least we could do."

They'd been quick to think the worst of Clem, Leah reflected. "I'm glad you did that."

"Also, I called the Garritys and suggested they keep him on," Mark added. "The guy tried to do the right thing by escorting the girls out of that area, and he obviously needs the job. They've agreed."

"Did I ever mention that you're a great cop?" Leah asked.

Her cousin sounded like he was smiling. "Never hurts to hear it. Now make sure Mom goes straight home. If you let her, she'll stay and cook for everyone and probably clean the house, as well."

"Consider it done."

Rosie agreed without argument. "Tell that man of yours that there's a pizza warming in the oven. He had a couple in the freezer," she said as she collected her purse. "He and Diane must be starving."

Leah relished the phrase "that man of yours," yet she didn't quite believe it. Although Will had said he loved her, he couldn't be held responsible for what he blurted out in the heat of the moment, "Thank you so much for coming."

"Are you kidding? I owe Dr. Rankin more than I can ever

repay him." Her aunt patted her shoulder. "And I'm glad Mark showed another side of his character tonight. He's a good man."

"Of course he is! I come from a fantastic family."

Leah saw Rosie out. When she came back, India regarded her worriedly.

"Diane's okay, isn't she?" the little girl asked, clutching a teddy bear.

Ashamed that she hadn't reassured the child earlier, Leah said, "She's fine. She and Sybill just got lost."

India covered her face, then peeked between her fingers. "She told me they were going to see the magic man. I was supposed to keep it secret."

"Oh, dear." Leah didn't want to lay a burden of guilt on a six-year-old. At the same time, India's silence could have been costly. "That was a hard moral choice, sweetheart. What do you think you should have done?"

"I wanted to tell Daddy." The words came out muffled.

"You should have trusted your instincts," Leah told her. "You don't have to keep a secret just because someone asks you to. Not if what they're doing is wrong, or if it could hurt someone."

"Are you mad at me?" India asked tearfully.

Leah reached down and hugged the little girl. "No. But I have to tell your father."

The solemn-faced youngster considered for a moment. "Wait till I'm in bed, okay?" she asked, her face close to Leah's.

It was easy to understand her desire to avoid confrontation. "All right."

The little girl sniffled but gave Leah another hug before letting go. "He won't be so mad by tomorrow."

Another clever strategist in the family, she thought, but was careful to hide her amusement. She didn't want to give India too much encouragement.

Outside, a car pulled into the driveway. Both of them flew to the porch.

Diane, her blond hair tangled and her face dirty, hurried along beside her father. Despite his weariness, he looked tremendously relieved.

"We have pizza," India announced as her twin approached.

"Oh, good! Is it pepperoni?" came the prompt rejoinder.

"You bet!"

The two little girls went inside together, forming a picture in the lamplight that tugged at Leah's heart. Will gazed after them with love shining from his face.

"Daddy to the rescue," she murmured.

"It's good to have you here." One hand lightly touching her back, Will ushered her inside.

Leah helped bathe Diane while India, who'd already prepared for bed, peppered her with questions. Exhausted, both girls were ready for lights out after only a brief storytime.

Leah and Will settled side by side on the couch in the den. "That Sybill is a piece of work." He shook his head. "She tried to order me to let Diane come home with her again tomorrow. Can you believe that?"

"Yes." Leah relaxed against him. "Did her parents get there? I didn't think to call them."

"Mr. Tucker arrived in a police cruiser. He'd been riding around with an officer," Will said. "One of the perks of being city manager, I guess."

"You certainly told him off earlier." She hoped Will hadn't made an enemy.

"I'm glad I did it. He and his wife put my daughter in danger," he said. "First, by teaching Sybill that it's okay to defy authority, and then, by treating Diane as if she were their property. My only consolation is that they're going to have their hands full dealing with their daughter."

"That reminds me." Leah related her discussion with India.

Will studied her tenderly. "You have the most wonderful way with children. You handled that exactly right."

When he drew her close, she melted against him. From his masculine scent to the slight roughness of his jaw, everything about Will appealed to her. But then, he'd had that effect on her from the moment they met.

Still, much as she hated to bring up a difficult subject when they were so comfortable, Leah couldn't go on dodging it. "There's one more thing."

"True confessions?" he queried, his expression hovering between humor and concern.

"Sort of." Leah gathered her nerve. "The school in Seattle offered me the job. They asked me to start second semester. That's in January."

He went completely still. She could feel the tension gathering. "Have you decided what you're going to do?"

Thank goodness she had an answer. "I'm going to turn it down."

Silence invaded the room. Leah heard the distant rustle of the wind and, in the bedroom, the creak of springs as one of the girls turned over.

Maybe she'd assumed too much. Will might be drawing away again. If he did, she thought she might punch him.

"Are you sure?" His tone revealed nothing.

When she tried to speak, her voice caught. She had to clear it before she said, "Yes."

"Leah, if you're not certain…"

"I am," she told him. "Are you trying to get rid of me?"

"Never." Cupping her face with his hands, he kissed her.

Neither of them bothered talking after that.

As BADLY AS WILL ached to make love to Leah, he stopped short. If the girls awoke, it would be too awkward.

All the same, he relished her kisses and the impact of their bodies curling against each other. He was tempted to ask her right now to marry him, but some occasions deserved special treatment. Like a proposal.

"Will you have dinner with me tomorrow night?" he asked. "I'll hire a babysitter and we can go somewhere private. Preferably outside town, where we aren't likely to be interrupted."

"I'd like that." She ran her hands along his arms. If she kept doing that, he might forget his resolve. "There's a seafood restaurant on the highway called the Landlocked Mariner that's pretty good."

The name was familiar. He remembered seeing it by the motel where he'd stayed once. "I'll make a reservation. Pick you up at seven?"

"Perfect." Leah smiled at him.

Yet as he walked her to the car and kissed her one more time, he thought he saw a trace of sadness in her expression. What was that about? Will wondered.

Unfortunately, he had a pretty good idea. She'd assured him that she didn't mind refusing the job offer, but that catch in her voice and her reaction now said otherwise.

Will didn't know what to make of it. After tonight, he couldn't imagine life without Leah any more than he could imagine it without his children. When her taillights turned the corner, she left a void in the night.

Lingering outside, he remembered how it felt to be held back. That autumn during his senior year in college, when he'd realized what a crushing financial burden he faced if he went to medical school, he'd nearly given up his dream.

He'd considered a compromise. Earning a master's degree

in biology, perhaps, or becoming a paramedic. But accepting any other career would have felt like amputating an arm.

He didn't want Leah to make that kind of sacrifice for him.

Will had never truly been close to another person, not even Allison when they first married. He'd never opened his heart so completely or needed anyone as much as he'd needed her tonight.

Lost in contemplation, he went into the house and locked up for the night. Drawn to the girls' bedroom, he said a prayer of thanks for Diane's safe return. If only he could protect them always.

And Leah, too. But he didn't know how to do that. How to let her go, or whether he should.

It wasn't his decision to make, he supposed. But he'd better prepare himself. A good night's sleep and a day to reflect might put matters into a different perspective for her.

Tomorrow night, he intended to propose. If by then Leah's need to spread her wings overcame her love for him, he was going to have to accept it.

But he wasn't sure he could.

Chapter Eighteen

Before school on Wednesday morning, Leah ran into Olivia in the teachers' lounge. "I'm glad everything turned out okay with the girls," the principal told her as they snacked on pastries the sixth-grade teacher had brought. "We heard about it at the council session."

In the turmoil of Diane's disappearance, Leah had forgotten about the city council meeting. The most important agenda item had been the hiring of a new pediatrician.

"Oh, that's right! I should have called Karen!" Judging from the fact that her friend hadn't called her, she guessed what had happened, but she couldn't be sure. "Did they pick—"

"Chris McRay," Olivia confirmed. "I'm afraid the Lowells are taking it hard, but he has a wonderful résumé and great recommendations. And no real competition."

"His grandmother abstained from voting, I guess." Leah could imagine what a tense scene that must have been. "I hope this won't come between her and Karen."

Mae Anne resided at the Tulip Tree Nursing Home. Since Karen had taken over as director five years earlier, the two women had become fast friends and often went on outings together. She hoped that wasn't going to change.

"I expect they'll get past it eventually." Olivia sighed. "I never expected to run into this kind of controversy when I helped set up the physician-search committee. In any case, he can't start for a few months. Perhaps things will die down."

"We'll see." Privately, Leah doubted that the passage of years would be long enough to calm Barry's obsession with proving his innocence and exposing the man he believed had lied about him on the witness stand.

The two parted, and Leah went to her classroom. No one else had arrived, so she mulled the posters and drawings on the wall, trying to figure out what to put up next. Her usual method was to replace them during the fall semester with drawings and samples of the children's first printing, along with celebrations of various holidays. Although she tried to inject fresh ideas each year, she'd fallen into a routine.

Her thoughts flew to the Rosewell Center. There'd been a palpable air of excitement, and several teachers had eagerly discussed their experiences. They'd said each group of kids offered unpredictable challenges, with a payoff that came when an unresponsive or out-of-control youngster began to connect to the world. Sometimes the transformations were little short of miraculous.

She itched to get started. To meet kids who required the full range of her intuition and skills. To give direction to lives that might otherwise be wasted.

"Leah?"

Dragged back to reality, she swung toward the entrance. Minnie Tucker stood there clutching her purse, her round face suffused with color.

Leah braced herself for a verbal attack. Nevertheless, common courtesy, as well as genuine concern, prompted her to ask, "How's Sybill?"

"She's fine. I let her play outside so we could talk." The former room mom fidgeted. "Alton got awfully mad. It didn't help his temper that he had to hurry off to the city council meeting and sit there and stew."

"About what?" She was in no mood to listen to ranting about what a bad influence she'd been.

"About what Dr. Rankin said," Minnie answered.

"You can hardly blame Will," Leah said. "He had good reason to be upset."

"Oh, no! That isn't what I meant!" Her visitor regarded her in surprise. "I mean what he said about the way Sybill acted when she visited Diane's house. Apparently, she was so out of control his housekeeper refused to allow her back."

Footsteps sounded in the corridor. Minnie glanced nervously in that direction, but they passed by.

"You mean he was angry at Sybill?" Perhaps this conversation wasn't headed in the direction she'd feared, Leah thought.

Minnie nodded. "And at me. Sybill made it worse when we picked her up, pouting and talking back. I thought Alton was going to blow a fuse, but he was in too big a hurry to get to the meeting."

"It's never a good idea to let anger build," Leah agreed. Still, she understood that the city manager's attendance was an important part of his job.

"When he got home, well, he was furious about my taking Diane without permission. Also, he said I've been spoiling her rotten." Minnie's lower lip quivered.

"And he's played no part in this?" she prompted gently.

Her visitor twisted her hands together. "At least he conceded that he was partly to blame, too. We both dismissed what you said about Sybill acting out. We should have listened."

The Tuckers must have gone through the same agony last night that she and Will had, Leah reminded herself. "I'm just glad both girls are safe."

Minnie took a deep breath. "Yes, but Sybill thinks she runs

the world, and when I punish her, she throws tantrums. Neither of our boys ever acted like this. I don't know what to do."

"Are you asking my advice?" Perhaps the comment had been meant rhetorically.

"I guess I am," Mrs. Tucker conceded. "Your getting pregnant without being married didn't seem right, but I shouldn't have made a federal case out of it. Alton and I aren't exactly flawless ourselves. Besides, you're the teacher. We hired you to educate our children, not serve as the community saint."

What a relief! The Tuckers' open criticism had bothered Leah not only as a personal disagreement but also because it might influence others.

"Well, I'll admit that, not being a parent, I've still got a lot to learn," she said. "But the first step is for you and your husband to decide on reasonable, firm rules and on the consequences for breaking them."

"That sounds good in theory, but Sybill doesn't know the meaning of the word *obey*," Minnie moaned.

"You'll have to be consistent and strict. And you're right, she'll fight you every step of the way." Leah had seen it happen in other families—with positive outcomes so long as the parents held their ground. "Don't let your husband duck his share of responsibility. Sybill needs to realize you're united on this."

"I know he'll try, but he thinks the children are my responsibility," she answered.

Other children were starting to arrive, and more would pour in shortly when the bell rang. Leah needed to hurry. "You should both consider taking a parenting class at the community center. Mr. Tucker might have to swallow his pride at first, but it's in Sybill's best interest. The instructor can help you develop a discipline plan. Tell him to consider it an education in management techniques."

For the first time today, her visitor smiled. "He'll like that. It might work." She seemed on the verge of turning away when she added, "Also, I want to apologize for how I acted. I was so proud of being your room mom that when you slipped, it seemed like it reflected on me. My pride got hurt, but that's not your fault."

Leah had no desire to nurse a grudge. "Let's put it behind us."

"Thank you!" Minnie glanced over as Annette came through the door. "I'm sorry I quit in a huff. Maybe I can help out at class parties."

"That would be great," Leah told her.

The rest of the day passed smoothly. Sybill seemed subdued, and Diane stuck close to India and Nick. Rosie called at noon to invite Leah to a party that ran all afternoon, in honor of Helen's last day at the salon.

Grateful for a way to pass the time before her dinner date, Leah strolled to the Snip'N'Curl after school. Balloons floated from the hairdressers' stations and a large banner across the back read Hasta La Vista, Helen. The scent of chocolate-chip cookies proved irresistible.

The manicurist, seven months pregnant and beaming, greeted Leah by the cookie plate. After they compared notes about their pregnancies, Leah said, "It must be difficult moving at this point. Finding a new doctor and a new place to live so close to your due date can't be easy."

The manicurist shrugged. "It'll feel strange at first, but as long as Arturo and I are together, that's what matters. He needs to grow as an artist. Besides, other people do it all the time."

"I guess so." Leah had hoped to find some encouragement in the conversation, but instead, it left her unsettled.

Helen moved away to serve a client. Elsie Ledbetter, a woman in her late seventies who'd once owned the salon, gestured Leah over.

"I've got a few minutes to chat," she said. "It's so much fun being back at work! I'm sorry I ever left."

"Rosie hasn't taken as much time off as I'd expected," Leah told her. "I'm a little surprised there are enough customers to go around."

"My old clients haven't forgotten me, so business has picked up a little," the hairdresser replied happily. "Besides, Rosie's busy catching up on paperwork. There are so many regulations these days!"

"Your feet must hurt." It was a problem Leah could relate to.

"Oh, I only work three or four hours a day." Tall, with regally upswept hair, Elsie had a remarkably unlined face. "This has been good for me. Rattling around the house while Joe works on his stamp collection doesn't suit. And with all these babies coming, it's almost like being a grandmother." Elsie's only son had died in military action before Leah was born.

"Watch out," she warned. "Rosie's likely to ask you to babysit."

"I've already volunteered!" Elsie answered.

Rosie came by with a fresh plate of cookies. Peanut butter—Leah's second favorite after chocolate chip. Although she was trying to watch her diet, she couldn't resist.

Elsie excused herself to check on a color job. Rosie seized the occasion to invite Leah into her office, a small room in back. Hair products lined the shelves and a couple of spare uniforms hung on pegs. From a small radio played a country-flavored waltz.

When Rosie closed the door, her niece saw that she was hopping with excitement. "I didn't want to say anything that would steal the limelight from Helen's big day, but Pepe and I are getting married!"

Leah swept her into an impromptu dance. "I'm so glad for you!"

"You will be my maid of honor, won't you?" her aunt demanded as the song ended.

"I'd be thrilled!" This was great news. "Have you set a date?"

"Around the middle of October. It depends on when his kids can make it." Rosie's eyes twinkled. "We're not planning anything fancy, mind you. A church ceremony and of course we'll have the reception at his restaurant."

They discussed the details for a while, agreeing on a deep-rose dress for the bride and light-pink for Leah. Rosie spilled over with tidbits about how Pepe had decided that as parents-to-be, they ought to get married. He'd become increasingly cheerful about the idea, sending her flowers.

"He's lived alone for quite a while. I expect he'll have to be domesticated," her aunt explained matter-of-factly. "At least he can cook!"

Even in a small town, people changed and events moved forward, Leah mused as she departed. It seemed to be enough for many people.

Yet Helen's words rang in her mind: *Arturo needs to grow as an artist.*

So, in a sense, did Leah. But she would have to find a way to do her growing here.

THE SPEED WITH WHICH word spread about what had happened to Diane amazed Will. Her disappearance and safe recovery evoked concerned comments from the entire staff and a number of patients on Wednesday.

The hiring of a new pediatrician also stirred plenty of debate. On top of everything, Jenni's return from her honeymoon stimulated a wave of visits, many without appointments, from patients who'd held off consulting a physician during her absence.

At noon, she set up a slide show of honeymoon pictures

on her office computer. The images of Graceland and other Memphis attractions featured her and Ethan in the foreground, to the hip-gyrating strains of an Elvis Presley CD.

Will had a very busy day. With tomorrow devoted to performing surgeries in Mill Valley, Patsy had fit in as many patients as possible today.

To complicate matters, Estelle had twisted her ankle playing tag with her youngest two children. Although she could treat clients, she had a hard time hobbling back and forth to the waiting room, and by afternoon she was fading fast.

"You're looking mighty pinched, Estelle," Winifred said when the two of them crossed paths in the hallway. "Why don't I fetch the charts and weigh the ladies for you?"

The nurse practitioner hesitated. "That's awfully kind, but I wouldn't want to put you out."

"It's no trouble. I'm so thrilled about little Diane being safe I feel like I've grown wings!"

Will, who was reading a chart before going in to see a patient, tried to hide his amusement at the image of his substantial nurse sprouting angelic appendages. Apparently, he didn't succeed, because Winifred fixed him with a mock glare.

"Now, don't you go laughing at me, Dr. Rankin!" she boomed, loud enough for the entire office to hear. "I'm only half in love with you, and the other half don't take nonsense from nobody!"

"Yes, ma'am," he responded crisply.

"Now, I got work to do!" she announced, and marched off.

"I'm starting to like that woman," Estelle commented dryly.

"With good reason." Will considered Winifred among the best nurses he'd ever worked with.

As the hours flew by, he realized how much at home he felt in the clinic after only a month. He'd never worked in such an intimate setting before, and it required much closer inter-action with staff members. He liked it.

He liked the clients, too. Several mothers-to-be mentioned their delight at learning that a pediatrician was going to be available soon, talking to Will as if he were an old acquaintance.

It was exactly the kind of environment he'd sought when he moved to Downhome. Despite last night's scare, he could see how well the girls were settling in, also.

But none of it meant anything without Leah.

He didn't understand why he kept worrying about her giving up the West Coast job. She'd said she didn't mind.

But he hadn't missed her hesitation. Maybe the fact that he'd once been in a similar position made him sensitive.

At dinner tonight, he wanted everything to go perfectly. Will wished he were smoother with women. He'd never been the type of charmer that ladies flocked to, which was why he'd been so surprised by Leah's response in Austin.

Tonight, he'd better figure out the right thing to say.

She'd advised him to rely on his instincts. He just hoped they would be up to the task.

Chapter Nineteen

Located a few miles outside town on the road to Mill Valley, the Landlocked Mariner featured a large aquarium in the center that cast magical blue light across the room. Mounted fish and fishing tackle decorated the pine-paneled walls, and secluded booths kept the noise level to a hush.

Leah eased into a seat across from Will. Cuddling next to him would have been more fun, but he seemed a little nervous, so she gave him space.

It was going to be fine, she told herself. Just fine.

On the drive over, she'd explained about Rosie and Pepe's engagement. Having finished discussing the good news, they fell into unaccustomed silence.

"Is something bothering you?" she asked after she finished studying her menu.

"What?" Will glanced up.

"You're so quiet."

"Am I?" He dropped his menu and made a quick grab to rescue it.

She definitely should have sat next to him. Had the waitress not appeared at that moment to take their orders, Leah might have shifted positions.

Tempted by the aromas wafting through the air, she ordered

stuffed trout. Will chose the salmon. The woman ran through a list of preferences for side dishes before departing.

"Who's watching the girls?" Leah asked.

Will jumped on the topic. "Patsy Fellows. Her mother mentioned she moonlights as a babysitter."

"That's good to know. I might need her services later."

When another lull descended, the uneasiness that had dogged Leah all day came into focus. Will didn't look like a man in love. He looked as if he might bolt for the exit.

For heaven's sake, she wasn't trying to trap him! "Just spit it out!" she said.

"Spit what out?" His gray eyes met Leah's. "I'm sorry. Since last night, I've been thinking a lot."

Now they appeared to be getting to the point. "About what?"

"You." He rested his elbows on the table. "You and Seattle. The job. Your dream. Leah, that means a lot to you."

"Other things mean more." She couldn't be specific without making unwarranted assumptions about their relationship.

"I love you." His jaw worked. "But I don't have the right to hold you back."

Her spirits plunged. "Don't have the right or don't want to?"

He blinked. "I'm not making myself clear."

"Maybe you are." Leah understood him better now. "You withdraw when people get close."

"Sure, at times, but I'm not doing that now!" Astonishment colored his words. "That wasn't the point."

The waitress stopped by with their salads. Leah could scarcely breathe until she left.

"Will, if you want to call the whole thing off, just say so," she told him. And awaited his answer with nerves stretched near the breaking point.

"No! I just can't figure out how we're going to handle..." He brightened as if hit by inspiration. "That's it!"

She could hardly bear another moment's delay. "What is?"

"I can't believe I didn't see this before." From inside his sports coat, Will pulled out a prescription pad, then patted his pockets. Giving up, he said with a hint of embarrassment, "Would you lend me a pen?"

If only he'd speak up and clear the air! But obviously, he intended to do things his own way.

Rather than waste time arguing, Leah retrieved a ballpoint pen from her bag. "I'll be lucky if I ever see it again, right?"

His crooked grin made her heart leap. "Right." On the paper, he scribbled rapidly.

She wished she could read upside down. What was it?

Will tore off the small sheet and handed it across the table. "I'm sorry I'm not better at making speeches, but I'm afraid I gave you the wrong impression. I hope this helps."

Leah could barely breathe. Angling the paper to catch the light of a wall sconce, Leah read what he'd jotted.

The top line said, Prescription for happiness. A list followed:

1) Ask Seattle to hold the job until next fall.

2) Marry me.

3) Have baby in April.

4) Move—we'll all go.

5) Live happily ever after.

She reread no. 2 and no. 4—"Marry me" and "Move—we'll all go"—until moisture blurred her vision. She couldn't believe the man who'd fled intimacy was offering to shape his life to hers.

A lump in her throat made it hard to speak. But she had to make sure he'd considered the full impact of his proposal. "You wanted to bring up the girls in a small town. And you're enjoying your job. What about that?"

"Living in Downhome wasn't my life's dream," Will answered. "It won't kill me to give it up."

Still, he might look back later and feel that he'd sacrificed too much. Hesitantly, Leah ventured, "We could wait till the children are older."

Will leaned toward her across the table. "You need to spread your wings," he said. "You can't do it here. If we stay, assuming you'd have me, there'd always be regret for what might have been. I didn't accept that for myself and I can't accept it for you."

Just like that, she had Will on her side. They'd become a team.

It was the best feeling she'd ever known.

Leah couldn't bear the distance between them any longer. Moving around the booth, she slid in beside him.

"You," she said, "are now officially the most wonderful man in the world."

The next thing she knew, they were kissing and hugging like two people who'd been apart for months. Only by great good luck did they avoid dumping his salad and glass of water on their laps, and she wouldn't have cared if they did.

"I hope this means yes," Will murmured.

Clinging to him, Leah started to tremble.

"Are you laughing? Crying?" His mouth grazed her hair as he spoke.

"I don't know." When she raised her head, moisture cooled her cheeks. "Both."

The waitress halted beside the table with a bottle of sparkling grape juice they'd ordered and took in the changed seating arrangement. "I'll just move this around," she said, switching Leah's salad to the place in front of her.

"I'm not sure she's staying," Will noted. "She hasn't told me yet whether she'll marry me."

"Are we taking bets?" the waitress asked. "Because I'm going with yes."

"Me, too," Leah said.

"I guess I'd be a fool to bet against you, then," Will told the server earnestly. As soon as she left, he said, "I'm holding you to that. We're engaged."

Leah released a long breath. "I can't believe it. Will, I love you."

"That reminds me!" He produced a jewel box. "I understand women like to make their own choices when it comes to rings. But I couldn't resist bringing a little something."

After drying her eyes, Leah opened the velvet container. Inside, a solitaire diamond sparkled from a pendant looped around a gold chain.

"It's beautiful," she breathed.

"Leah, you've brought magic into my life," Will said. "I hope I'll always make you happy."

"I can't imagine being any happier than this." With his help, she fastened the gift around her neck. It felt almost weightless, yet Leah knew it would endure for a lifetime. "Oh, Will, can I really keep you forever? And have the adventure I've dreamed about, too?"

"That, plus the baby." He brushed a kiss across her hair.

"Our little boy," she said blissfully. "And our two little girls."

They were snuggling when the waitress returned with their plates. "Still working on that salad, I see," she observed as she made room on the table. "How's the proposal going?"

"I wore her down," Will said. "She agreed to marry me."

"Congratulations!" The woman beamed as she went about her duties.

Leah glanced again at the list Will had written before tucking it away to save. *Marry me…have baby…live happily ever after.*

She wondered if anyone had ever framed a prescription. If not, she intended to be the first.

IN THE MIDDLE OF OCTOBER, Leah walked down the aisle at Rosie's wedding, through a congregation filled with smiles. Pepe only fidgeted a little inside his tuxedo, standing next to his twenty-year-old son, Paolo.

A few weeks later, it was Leah's turn. Will's brother Mike, the pilot, flew in to serve as his best man, and Karen put her bridesmaid's dress from Jenni's wedding to good purpose.

The twins made adorable flower girls, although Diane pelted the congregation with petals a bit too enthusiastically. Sybill, whose parents had initiated a strict but loving regimen, managed to keep her seat.

To Leah's delight, her father and stepmother arrived from Denver. Her dad, whom she hadn't expected to take much notice of her marriage, walked her down the aisle with tears in his eyes.

Most precious of all, Will stood at the altar glowing with love. Once he'd accepted Leah into the inner circle of his heart, there'd been no more room for hesitation.

After a reception at Pepe's diner, they left India and Diane with Mrs. McNulty for a long weekend. Despite the temptation to go away together for a few weeks, they'd decided it was more important not to make the girls feel abandoned.

There would be enough changes with the baby due in April and the big move in August. The Rosewell Center's director had graciously agreed to hold Leah's position, and Will had applied to join a medical group in the Seattle suburb of Bellevue. Mrs. McNulty planned to stay on in Downhome until she packed them off, at which point her daughter had urged her to move to Florida.

Anticipating busy months ahead, Leah treasured the charming isolation of the cabin they'd reserved outside the Smoky Mountains resort town of Gatlinburg. The pine-scented air had a wintry tang when they arrived after a two-hour drive.

They unpacked and, in the living room hearth, Will built a crackling fire. Leah's weariness from the drive vanished as her new husband turned out the overhead light and settled beside her on the thick rug, with their backs against the sofa. The only illumination came from the flames.

"Dr. Rankin." She brushed a wisp of blond hair from his temple. "Firelight becomes you."

"Mrs. Rankin." Mischief glinted in his smile as he began unzipping her dress. "I think it's going to become you even better without all these pesky clothes."

A sense of enchantment enveloped Leah as she shed her dress and helped him remove his ski sweater. For once, they had the leisure to study each other, to touch and caress for as long as they liked.

Dumb luck as much as instinct might have guided her to the right man that first night, Leah knew. But now the closeness they shared had grown so profound it intensified every whisper and every touch.

They lay beside each other on the rug, kissing and entwining until she climbed atop Will and took him inside her. He gazed up at her figure, highlighted by the flickering glow, and said, "This has to be the most glorious moment of my life."

Leah moaned her agreement. His hands guided her hips before smoothing upward to cup her breasts.

Without warning, he rolled, capturing her beneath him. They matched each other in a fierce, loving battle that brought them both to a climax so wild that Leah thought she might rocket into space.

But her husband was holding her. Keeping her safe.

"I don't think I've mentioned lately that I love you," she

teased as they rested against each other. "Not for at least half an hour."

"I love you so much I'd write a poem about it—if I could find a pen," he joked.

Bathed in warmth, Leah was dozing when she felt an unfamiliar wiggling in her abdomen. Embarrassed, she wondered if her stomach was playing tricks, and then the truth hit her.

"Will!" She touched her bulge. "The baby's moving!"

"He moves a lot. You saw him on the sonogram," he reminded her lazily.

"Don't be such a doctor! This is your son!" She felt a slight squirming against one palm. "I think he's celebrating."

"Let's see." Will pressed his ear to her midsection. "You're right! I just heard him say, 'Encore!'"

She swatted his shoulder. "Don't be silly! He won't be able to speak French until he's old enough for kindergarten. Or at least preschool." Scooting into a sitting position, she felt the little guy intensify his gyrations. "His name! He just told me his name!"

"If it has more than three syllables, I object." Will murmured from where he lay. "He'll get tired of spelling it for reporters when he wins his Nobel Prize."

"It has two syllables," she said. "Liam. He wants to be named after both his parents."

"Liam," Will repeated. "I like that." He reached up and pulled her gently down beside him. "But I'm absolutely certain I heard him say, 'Encore.'"

"It can't hurt to humor him in case you're right," Leah agreed. "Whatever we were doing a few minutes ago, I guess we'd better do it again."

So they did.

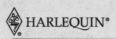

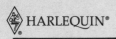

Signature Select™

A good start to a new day…or a new life!

National bestselling author

ROZ *Denny* FOX

Coffee in the Morning

A heartwarming volume of two classic stories
with the miniseries characters you love! A
wagon train journey along the Santa Fe Trail
is a catalyst for romance as Emily Benton and
Sherry Campbell each find love.

On sale March.

The story continues in April 2006 with
Roz Denny Fox's brand-new story,
Hot Chocolate on a Cold Day.

SMCITM

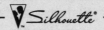

SPECIAL EDITION™

Stronger Than Ever

THE IRRESISTIBLE BRAVO MEN ARE BACK IN *USA TODAY* BESTSELLING AUTHOR

CHRISTINE RIMMER's

THE BRAVO FAMILY WAY

March 2006

The last thing Cleo Bliss needed was a brash CEO in her life. So when casino owner Fletcher Bravo made her a business proposition, Cleo knew it spelled trouble—until seeing Fletcher's soft spot for his adorable daughter melted Cleo's heart.

THE FORTUNES OF TEXAS™: Reunion

Coming in March...
a brand-new Fortunes story
by *USA TODAY* bestselling author

Marie Ferrarella...

MILITARY MAN

A dangerous predator escapes from prison
near Red Rock, Texas—and Collin Jamison,
CIA Special Operations, is the only person who
can get inside the murderer's mind. Med student
Lucy Gatling thinks she has a lead. The police
aren't biting, but Collin is—even if it is only
to get closer to Lucy!

The Fortunes of Texas: Reunion
The price of privilege. The power of family.

Silhouette®
Where love comes alive™

Visit Silhouette Books at www.eHarlequin.com   FOTRMM

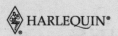

HARLEQUIN®

American ROMANCE®

Fatherhood

Fatherhood: what really defines a man.

It's the one thing all women admire in a man—a
willingness to be responsible for a child and to care
for that child with tenderness and love.

SUGARTOWN
by
Leandra Logan
March 2006

When Tina Mills learns that her biological mother
isn't the woman who raised her but someone her late
father had an affair with, she heads to her birthplace
of Sugartown, Connecticut, in search of some answers.
But after meeting police chief Colby Evans and his
young son, Tina realizes she might find more than her
mother in Sugartown. She might find her future....

Available wherever Harlequin books are sold.

www.eHarlequin.com HARLLMAR